W9-BME-355

"ZERO," LT. COMMANDER KEVIN RILEY SAID AT LAST.

Full thrusters helm, Admiral Kirk thought to himself as he watched the launch from the roof of the Admiralty. For a moment, Kirk's hand closed, as if he were grasping the arm of a chair.

The command section of the *Enterprise* lifted vertically and ever so slowly from the ground. Its landing legs retracted smoothly into the shell, shaking the dust of Earth from their pads. The saucer continued rising.

And for the first time in half a year, the *Enterprise* was under way, once again a creature that lived in the sky.

Look for STAR TREK Fiction from Pocket Books

STAR TREK: The Original Series

STAR TREK: The Next Generation

Most Pocket Books are available at special quantity discounts for bulk purchases for sales promotions, premiums or fund raising. Special books or book excerpts can also be created to fit specific needs.

For details write the office of the Vice President of Special Markets, Pocket Books, 1230 Avenue of the Americas, New York, New York 10020.

STAR TREK®
A FLAG FULL OF STARS

BRAD FERGUSON

POCKET BOOKS

New York   London   Toronto   Sydney   Tokyo   Singapore

This book is a work of fiction. Names, characters, places and incidents are either the product of the author's imagination or are used fictitiously. Any resemblance to actual events or locales or persons, living or dead, is entirely coincidental.

The plot and background details of *A Flag Full of Stars* are solely the author's interpretation of the universe of STAR TREK® and vary in some respects from the universe as created by Gene Roddenberry.

An *Original* Publication of POCKET BOOKS

POCKET BOOKS, a division of Simon & Schuster
1230 Avenue of the Americas, New York, NY 10020

Copyright © 1991 by Paramount Pictures. All Rights Reserved.

STAR TREK is a Registered Trademark of
® Paramount Pictures.

This book is published by Pocket Books, a division of
Simon & Schuster, under exclusive license from
Paramount Pictures.

All rights reserved, including the right to reproduce
this book or portions thereof in any form whatsoever.
For information address Pocket Books, 1230 Avenue
of the Americas, New York, NY 10020

ISBN: 0-671-73918-2

First Pocket Books printing April 1991

10 9 8 7 6 5 4 3 2 1

POCKET and colophon are registered trademarks of
Simon & Schuster.

Printed in the U.S.A.

Historian's Note

This adventure takes place shortly before the events chronicled in *Star Trek: The Motion Picture.*

A FLAG FULL OF STARS

Chapter One

ADMIRAL JAMES T. KIRK stopped in mid-pace, hands clasped behind his back, and gazed through the transparent north wall of his Starfleet office at the Golden Gate and the magnificent old bridge that spanned it. Had he been less impatient at that particular moment, he might have appreciated the unobstructed view of the big bridge, its sharp angles softened by a hastily scheduled shower. Obscured by the rain, the view took on the subtlety of a painting done in oils, and Kirk had a certain taste for that sort of thing. The bridge's spare beauty was once again uncluttered, as he preferred: the Fourth of July weekend was over and the holiday bunting had been taken down from the towers, though the decorations would be back up for the coming Apollo Day festivities. The display of the old U.S. flag had evoked the usual protests against narrowminded nationalism, but Kirk saw the banner's symbolism as prophetic: the stars were intended to represent states, but Kirk thought of them as actual stars, as if the flag's designers had anticipated the United Federation of Planets and its own star-dotted flag.

He was tempted to curse the weather, but restrained

himself; the emergency rain was needed, and had in fact been scheduled—hastily, at the last minute, just in time to delay the countdown for the *Enterprise*'s launch.

Kirk abruptly turned his back on the view, strode to his desk, and thumbed the direct-connect on his companel. The image of the Navy Yard Chief, a red-bearded Scottish giant, swam onto the screen. The giant was dressed in one of the new Starfleet uniforms —the white-bibbed "penguin grays," as they had quickly come to be known.

"Good morning again, Chief."

"Aye, Admiral, an' a wet one it still is, too," Alec MacPherson answered, his tone as gloomy as the weather. "We're all just lookin' at the rain an' gettin' a good case o' th' fidgets. The hold's now at one hour an' fifty-three minutes." The big Scotsman snorted in disgust.

"Status?"

"Ready an' waitin', Admiral. Everythin' is go. No problems from th' nasty weather, either; I've got environmental shields up, an' th' saucer is locked tight as Grandma's purse in any case. I wouldna mind settin' th' new launch time for as soon as practicable, though, sir. All o' this is wearin' me a wee bit thin."

Kirk smiled faintly at the Chief, who'd put as much of his soul into the *Enterprise*'s refit as Kirk had himself. Now, MacPherson looked as nervous and proud as an expectant father. "That makes two of us. Let's go with what we discussed earlier. I make it just under fourteen minutes until the rain's scheduled to end. Let's send her up five minutes after; the sky over the city will have cleared enough. Keep in mind there are a few tractor-pressor gangs topside who've got a good case of the fidgets, too."

"I can well believe it. I'll be sending 'em a tick at

T-minus eighteen." His voice warmed suddenly. "Admiral, are ye sure ye won't change your mind about comin' over for the launch? Still plenty of time for ye to beam across town and stand wi' us here."

Kirk hesitated. As badly as he wanted to accept MacPherson's offer—to see the *Enterprise* off in person, with those who had worked with him these many months on her refit—she was Will Decker's ship now, and it was time to let her go. Kirk had decided long before to watch the launch from his office, to remind himself of the fact. His response sounded deceptively casual. "Thanks, Mac, but you don't need me getting in your way. I'll stay here."

MacPherson nodded gravely, as if he understood. "As you wish, sir. Well, here's hopin' the gods are smilin' on us."

"Aye to that. Kirk out."

"G'bye, sir." MacPherson's image faded as Kirk pressed another toggle.

Uhura's dark, elegant features filled the screen. "Communications, *Enterprise.*" Her tone, serene and steady, belied the anticipation Kirk knew she must be feeling. At the sight of her former captain, she grinned hugely. "Admiral, hello. Looks like she's finally going to be under way again, sir. If the rain ever lets up."

Kirk repressed a pang of envy and returned the smile. "It'll let up, Commander. If I have anything to say about it."

"This new bridge is fantastic. I wish you could be here to see it, sir," Uhura blurted, then hesitated as if worried she had just said something insensitive.

But Kirk's amused expression never wavered. "I know it is. I've seen it," he said easily. "Let me talk to Captain Decker, please."

"Aye, sir. Right away."

* * *

"Captain?" Uhura called.

Moving with deliberate calm to conceal the restlessness he was feeling, Willard Decker swiveled in his chair to glance at his communications officer. He felt fortunate to have a veteran like Uhura on the bridge. Her confident demeanor had a steadying effect on the less experienced crew members—including her new captain. When the countdown had begun, Decker had been pleased at his ability to remain inwardly relaxed. That was before the rain, and the hold.

"Admiral Kirk calling, sir. On six."

"Thanks." Grateful for the distraction, Decker touched a button on the console arm. Kirk's features appeared instantly on the main viewer. "Any news, Admiral?"

Before Kirk responded, Decker quickly studied the admiral's face for signs of envy—what Decker would be feeling were their positions reversed. He recalled a moment when, almost nine months earlier, he'd learned that Kirk had recommended him to oversee the *Enterprise*'s refit as her new captain. Decker had called the admiral at HQ to thank him, but at the time, Kirk's response had taken him aback:

Quite frankly, Will, I envy you. If I were still a captain, I'd do whatever was necessary to get command of my ship back.

Now, sitting in the command chair on the bridge of the *Enterprise,* Decker understood Jim Kirk's words perfectly. The way Will felt today, nothing short of an anti-matter explosion could have pried him away from this ship, this bridge, this crew . . .

The admiral's expression was good-humored, and his voice carried a hint, not of jealousy, but of the anticipation Decker himself felt.

"Get ready to take a time tick from MacPherson, Will. The rain is supposed to stop in about fourteen minutes. You'll lift off five minutes after that."

"Understood, Admiral," Decker said, relieved that the delay was not longer. "We're raring to go, sir."

Kirk grinned. "Well, just be sure you put all the little pieces in the right places. It'd be embarrassing to have anything left over when you're finished."

"Scotty says he knows where all the parts go," Decker replied, grinning back. "Thanks for the advice, though, Admiral."

For an instant, the two men locked gazes. Kirk's eyes reflected the same emotion Will knew shone in his own: the deep pride and admiration only a captain can feel for a first command. And then Kirk said abruptly: "Smooth sailing, Captain. Kirk out." The screen blanked.

Decker released the comm line and directed his attention forward, to the pilot station. At the helm was Lt. Commander Sulu, who was in charge of the upgrade to helm systems.

Former navigator Pavel Chekov had left ship's company to attend the Starfleet security school at Annapolis. Decker looked forward to having Chekov back shortly as the ship's security chief when he had completed the program.

Since Chekov's permanent replacement as navigator had not yet been assigned, Chief Suzanne DiFalco —Montgomery Scott's number-two for navigation systems—was pinch-hitting as navigator for this short flight.

"Chief," Decker said, "I trust you're ready to receive the time tick?"

"Aye, Captain," DiFalco answered evenly, though her eyes were unusually bright. She paused for a moment and then added, "Got it, sir. The clock is now running." DiFalco's fingers flew across a series of buttons on her board. "Our projected course to Spacedock Four has been corrected for the new time of departure."

"Amended course laid in, sir," added Sulu.

"Very good."

It was quiet now on the bridge; everything that could be done had already been done, and then checked and rechecked. Decker looked around him. Most of the people on the bridge were new to the *Enterprise*, having been assigned aboard only during the six months that the saucer had been sitting in the Navy Yard. The green bridge crew had found its identity quickly, though, forming itself around the few veterans still aboard—which was exactly what Admiral Kirk and Decker had hoped would happen. Much the same thing had occurred in Engineering, where Scotty had seeded a number of old hands among the new personnel who'd been trained in the latest methods of ship design, construction and maintenance.

Decker slowly released a silent sigh. He had been preparing more than eight months for this launch— but these last few minutes seemed the longest part of the entire wait. "Well, it seems there's nothing left to do but cool our heels. Lieutenant Commander Uhura, patch into the local relay for WorldNews and put it on the main viewer. Let's see what they're saying about us."

"And now there's just a little more than twelve minutes to go until the scheduled end of the rain," newscaster Nan Davis said, smiling into the trivision scanners. Outwardly, her manner was one of total ease, as if it were a perfectly natural, ordinary thing for her to address an audience that numbered in the billions. As natural as breathing, which she had forgotten to do at the moment. As she paused between sentences, she reminded herself to take a nice, slow, even breath.

Inwardly, she was frantic. After several uneventful —and unnoticed, Nan had thought—months at WorldNews, she'd finally been given a huge break: the chance to cover the *Enterprise* launch. If the producers liked what they saw, her one-year probationary hire at WorldNews could turn into a permanent position. And if they didn't . . . time to update the résumé.

Which, the way things were going this morning, she might be doing a lot sooner than expected. For the past two torturous hours, she'd been trying to fill air time with information she'd repeated several times in as many different ways. Her first worldwide feed, and it was going down the chute.

Damn the weather.

"The weather might be terrible outside," Nan continued brightly, her professional smile intact, "but we're nice and dry here in our San Francisco studios —and with us this morning are our special guests, Admiral Timothea Rogers of Starfleet Command Public Information, and retired Starfleet captain Robert April, the very first commander of the starship *Enterprise*."

Both guests nodded to the scanners as their names were mentioned. April was a tall, distinguished looking man of about eighty with a handsome shock of white hair; he was casually but neatly dressed in civilian attire.

Rogers was in Starfleet dress uniform and wore a severe, intimidating expression. Her straight salt-and-pepper hair framed a long face that seemed unused to smiling. Earlier that morning, when Nan had met the admiral, she'd felt a sudden chilly gust from one of the studio's air vents—or had it simply been her imagination, looking into Roger's cold, forbidding features? She'd been prepared for Rogers to be reserved—

Nogura calls her his Vulcan, the aide scheduling the interview had confided—but Vulcan-like reserve was one thing, and Rogers' demeanor was quite another. The woman radiated all the personality and warmth of an ice sculpture. And Nan had known, with heart-sinking certainty as she shook the admiral's hand, that Rogers was going to be perfectly *awful* on 3V.

So far, the interview had proven her right. Admiral Rogers had been adequately responsive throughout the feed, but with her habit of citing statistic after dull statistic in that flat, uninflected voice, she was about as endearing as a Rigellian fever sore.

"For those of you just joining us," Nan said, "the countdown for the liftoff of the renovated command section—the 'saucer'—of the *Enterprise* has been put on hold due to a two-hour rain ordered early this morning by California Governor Sarah Meier. The shower was needed to help extinguish a small forest fire that started around dawn near the city of Mill Valley, just north of San Francisco. We're told the fire is out and damage to local property is minimal."

Nan, Rogers and April were seated on a small studio set that had been put together overnight by the WorldNews studio crew. The animated backdrop consisted of a moving starfield dominated by an artist's conception of the way *Enterprise* would look once her renovation had been completed. The setting looked good, better than the credit-pinching WorldNews art director usually managed to provide. Nan had been quite pleased with the set when she'd first seen it that morning, and had taken its presence as a good omen.

But that had been before she'd met Rogers.

So much for omens.

"Starfleet has delayed the launch until just after the rain," Nan told her audience, "for fear that turbulence from the command section's powerful impulse engines could turn the weather stormier than Weather Control intended."

The prompt bug in her ear buzzed. "We've just been informed by Starfleet that the command section of the *Enterprise* will lift off five minutes after the scheduled end of the rain—fifteen minutes from now." She could not quite hide her relief from the scanners.

Buoyed, she turned slightly in her seat to face April. In striking contrast to Rogers, Captain April was an interviewer's dream—animated, warm, relaxed, and most of all, *interesting.* If, without being too obvious, she could focus the remaining time on him . . . "Captain, it seems we're on our way again. Tell me, as the first skipper of the *Enterprise,* how do you feel about seeing her reborn?"

April grinned, showing a flash of white teeth against suntanned skin. "Quite proud, Miss Davis, quite proud indeed. I still feel as if I'm a part of that ship; I spent quite a while aboard her, you know. Though the changes in technology since the *Enterprise* was launched have been considerable."

Nan sincerely returned the smile, then, careful to hide her reluctance, turned to Rogers. "Admiral, can you tell us something about those technological changes? For example, the new warp engines. Is it true they're so powerful they would have torn the old *Enterprise* apart?"

Rogers pursed her thin, pale lips as if in distaste. "Well, yes, I suppose so," she answered dryly, "if you care to put the matter in those terms. The new warp drivers generate six times more power than the old ones, and such a strain would have been a problem for the old *Enterprise.* However, the re-design—"

"That brings up something else, Captain April," Nan said quickly, before Rogers could continue. The admiral closed her mouth and fixed a fishy stare on

Nan. "Why renovate the *Enterprise* instead of building an entirely new cruiser from scratch?"

"Well, Miss Davis," April began, "my understanding is that the new design incorporates so much fresh technology, it can't even be finalized for more than—"

"The decision was made by Starfleet for two reasons," Rogers snapped. Careful to tilt her face away from the invisible audience, Nan looked daggers at her.

Rogers pretended not to notice. "Money and time. *Enterprise*'s renovation will cost only sixty-two point six percent of the price of constructing an entirely new cruiser, and work will be completed a year sooner. The time factor was also shortened by giving the job to our Starfleet Operations people. Since things have gone so well with the *Enterprise* refit, Operations will be handling all of Starfleet's ship renovation projects from now on."

"Fascinating," Nan said feebly. If Rogers was going to bring up the subject, she may as well follow through with questions and try to kill some of those fifteen minutes. "Who's responsible for the change?"

"Admiral James Kirk was put in charge of Starfleet Operations eight months ago. The renovation plan is his."

"But aren't starship repairs and so forth usually done in orbit, in special docks?" Nan asked. "The entire starship is usually left in one piece, isn't it? Why was the command section detached and flown down for renovation?"

Rogers gave a single curt nod. "Before now, Starfleet has always done this kind of work in the microgravitational environment freely available in orbit. However, Admiral Kirk determined some of the renovation work could be done much more efficiently in a gravitational field. He found a substantial savings in time and budget could be realized if we did most of the work on the command section on the ground."

"Isn't working in a gravity field inconvenient?"

"Not when you're painting, running wiring or laying carpet, among any number of other jobs. Admiral Kirk knew that the *Enterprise*'s main gravity generators would not be up and running until rather late in the renovation process; in fact, they came on line only last week. We gained a great deal of time by not waiting for the engineering section to be made ready before beginning substantive work on the saucer. While the command section has its own, smaller gravity generators, they are not intended for months of continuous operation. So we took advantage of the biggest gravity generator in the immediate neighborhood—Earth itself."

"That construction technique is being called revolutionary. Is that a fair assessment?" Nan asked.

"It is . . . unprecedented," Rogers replied coolly.

Nan nodded. "I see. So what's scheduled to happen next?"

"Work on the command section is nearly complete," Rogers answered. "As I've mentioned, Starfleet felt that the larger part of the work on the saucer . . ."

The control room called up a computer-generated graphic of the *Enterprise* and put it on the air. Blinking arrows indicated the saucer-shaped command section.

". . . could be done faster, easier and more cheaply on the ground. The engineering section, on the other hand . . ."

The arrows moved quickly from the command to the engineering section.

". . . needed to be worked on in orbit. For one thing, the engineering section can't be landed. In a procedure we call 'saucer separation' the command section detaches from the rest of the ship and, under its own impulse power, can rendezvous with a rescue craft or make a surface landing."

In 3V displays everywhere, sparks appeared around the neck of the *Enterprise,* and the ship seemed to be decapitated by an unseen headsman. The command section flew toward a bluish-green planet.

"Your viewers will recall that the *Enterprise* returned from its historic five-year mission early last year," Rogers droned on. "Six months ago, a skeleton crew separated the saucer and flew it down to the San Francisco Navy Yard. That's where it's been ever since, straddling four repair bays."

The control room switched to a live shot of the Navy Yard, the eastern part of which was dominated by the *Enterprise*'s command section. The remote 3V scanners caught the diminishing rain pattering on the shields that protected the saucer from the weather. The mist in the air had condensed on the normally invisible shields. They overlapped repeatedly, looking like exquisitely thin plates of clear crystal piled in shinglelike fashion above the saucer, protecting it.

"When do you think the whole job will be finished, Admiral?" Nan asked.

"Another year. After a shakedown cruise, the *Enterprise* will return to active service, to continue its peaceful mission of exploration and discovery."

Nan nodded. "Getting back to the business at hand, will it be difficult to rejoin the two sections of the ship?"

"No, not particularly," answered Rogers, "but it *is* a job that calls for the utmost precision. The saucer will go into orbit, make rendezvous with Spacedock Four, and then be brought into precise position by tractor-pressor crews. Correctly mating the saucer with the engineering section will take careful handling —but our people are very good at that sort of thing.

We're beginning to think about designs for ships that will permit easier saucer recovery, but that's still to come."

Only a few minutes left now. Just two or three more questions, and the torment would be over . . . but Nan found herself suddenly at a loss. *Were* there any questions left that she hadn't asked a dozen times already? A half second before the pause would have turned awkward, one she hadn't thought of finally came to her—one that should take more than a sentence to answer.

Grateful for the inspiration, she asked, "Will Admiral Kirk be working on similar renovation projects in the future, Admiral Rogers?"

Which would be answered affirmatively, most likely, leading into *which* projects, and, with any luck, the end of the interview.

"I have no idea." Roger's tone grew cold as Plutonian winter. After her burst of talkativeness, she fell stonily silent.

The unexpected reaction threw Nan into a well-concealed panic. This was it, the interviewer's worst nightmare: at a total loss for a question, *any* question, even a shred of innocuous small talk. Nan blinked and looked to her other guest for help, but even the usually ebullient Captain April appeared cowed.

After another stretch of dismal silence, Nan surrendered and turned to face the nearest scanner. Hoping the control room would manage to cue up something in time, she said, "We'll be right back after these important messages."

If I still have a job, that is.

Across the continent, a slightly degraded 3V image flickered in the corner of a secondary school classroom in the endlessly rebuilt Chelsea section of New York.

Joey Brickner leaned, elbow on desk, cheek scrunched against fist, and looked away from the screen at the gray, rain-softened sky. The *Enterprise* launch sparked no interest in him, not even for the practical reason that the teacher thought it important and might put some of the information on the exam, or assign reports on the subject.

Joey didn't care much about school these days. In fact, he didn't care much about anything, except daydreaming. Most of all, he wanted things to be the way they'd been before Jase had gotten sick.

Nothing was the way it should have been.

It was early July, and he should have been somewhere other than a classroom, three weeks into another school year after only two weeks off from the last one. Who ever heard of starting school in June? Oh, it was an honor to be allowed in the experimental class, his mom kept telling him. A real honor, especially at his age. All the other parents were desperate to get their kids enrolled, because the class got results.

Yeah. A real honor. Big deal. Only he should have been on vacation. Should have been outside, playing in the rain with Jase. For a moment he indulged his imagination: He and his kid brother were outside, playing Klingons and Feds with water phasers. Getting soaked by the rain and each other's potshots.

Jase laughing, carrot-colored hair turned dark auburn and plastered to his scalp by the rain. Joey closed his eyes and let the corners of his mouth turn up slightly as he tried to satisfy his imagination by getting the image perfect. Jase would have been six months' older now, six months taller, coming maybe to big brother's chin. Yeah, to the chin. Joey almost smiled.

Hey, Joey! Jase was outside the classroom window, waving the toy phaser, the skin beneath his freckles— so many freckles, more than Joey'd ever seen on any one person, including himself—flushed bright pink as

14

he laughed convulsively at some private joke, almost doubled over. *Hey, Joey, hey—*

"Brickner," Ira Stoller hissed from the desk behind Joey's. "Hey, Brickner!" Stoller jammed a knee against the back of Joey's desk and started jiggling hard, in the precise area of Joey's right kidney.

Joey swiveled his head and eyes in Stoller's direction, watching with his peripheral vision to be sure the teacher hadn't noticed. When Stoller got that certain tone, you could be sure he was about to say something that would land them both in trouble. But the teacher—a real, live person, not an artificial intelligence program—was still staring distantly at the trivision. He had a thoughtful expression on his brown-skinned face, even though the news program had been replaced by an antacid commercial. The other students were beginning to turn in their chairs to whisper to a neighbor. Even the two teacher's pets, Ricia Greene and Carlos Siegel, had ducked their heads together and were speaking in low, serious voices. Probably talking, of all things, about the launch.

Stoller was grinning wickedly. He was tall—a full two heads taller than Joey—and skinny, all knees and elbows. At sixteen, he was also the oldest member of the class. Stoller had a sparkly, crazy edge to him— sometimes a little *too* crazy; he respected nothing and no one, including the teacher. But after the first few weeks of class, Joey was grateful for any attention; most of the students were fifteen, and wanted nothing to do with a thirteen-year-old. Especially a thirteen-year-old who was *short,* even for his age.

"Hey, Brickner! If Tarzan and Jane were pigfaces, what would Cheetah be?"

Joey rolled his eyes. "Pigface" was Stoller's term for Tellarites; Stoller knew more insulting names for aliens than Joey had ever imagined existed. Turning his head just enough to glance at Ira, Joey whispered, out of the corner of his mouth, "This'd better be good."

"The other woman," Stoller said, one knee still jiggling, and ignored Joey's pained grimace. "If Tarzan and Jane were jackrabbits"—i.e., Vulcans—"what would Cheetah be?"

"Bored," Joey offered.

"An outworlder. With a Master's degree."

Joey gave his head a slight shake. "Not funny."

"If they were turtleheads . . . " Stoller began, his eyes narrowing with malicious delight.

Stricken by guilt, Joey glanced nervously over at the teacher, who had looked away from the 3V and was now gazing absently out the window, apparently oblivious to the growing noise in the classroom.

"If they were turtleheads," Stoller seemed to relish repeating the term and watching Joey's dismayed reaction, "what would Cheetah be?"

"I give up," Joey whispered.

"A gifted child." Stoller leaned back, pleased with himself.

Joey squeezed his eyes shut and tried, really *tried,* not to laugh, but despite the pale freckled hand he clamped over his mouth, a high-pitched giggle escaped.

It seemed to summon the teacher from his reverie. Doctor G'dath looked up, frowned—though really, with the protuberant bony ridge that ran from just above his eyebrows to the crown of his head, it was hard to be sure—and said, in a low, rumbling voice:

"The prelaunch activities will best be appreciated in silence."

All motion, all sound—except for that of the 3V—ceased. Like every other student in the class, Joey faced forward, folded his hands atop his desk, locked

16

his gaze on the screen and devoted—well, pre*ten*ded to devote—his full attention to the commercial. Stoller stopped jiggling his knee.

The teacher, Doctor G'dath, did not repeat himself, nor did he threaten. He did not have to.

He was a full-blooded Klingon—a turtlehead, to use Ira Stoller's terminology—and Joey and every other one of his students were scared to death of him.

Across town, in shabby, ill-maintained living quarters at the Klingon Embassy, another Klingon—a Klingon whose bloodline was tainted by human ancestry—watched G'dath and his class watching the trivision feed. Though officially part of the Embassy staff, Keth, and his subordinate, Klor, had only one responsibility: to observe the Klingon physicist, G'dath. They performed their duty with almost no contact with Earth's human population and very little direct contact with the ambassador or the rest of his staff—to ensure that the ambassador could deny responsibility for any of Klor's actions that might be deemed "questionable" by the humans or by Klingon command.

After weeks of surveilling G'dath, Klor had difficulty believing the charge. How could a secondary schoolteacher prove dangerous to the Empire? Especially a teacher of human children? A ridiculous concept, a Klingon teaching humans. But dangerous? Even G'dath's private research—what little they had been able to learn of it—meant little to Klor. Nevertheless, the Empire had ordered the surveillance, which Klor faithfully carried out. He had always been eager to prove himself to his people, largely because his mother was the result of a mating between a Klingon warrior and a human prisoner from one of the frontier worlds. Everyone said his grandsire, old K'Marrh, was crazed to fall in love with his captive and take her as his consort—even more crazed to raise his daughter, Klor's mother, as legitimate and a member of the warrior class. Yet she had made a good match with another warrior and produced Klor.

And Klor had spent most of his short life trying to show his Empire that he was a loyal Klingon, indeed a warrior, willing to spill his blood. He had worked hard to show himself to be the best, the fastest, the brightest of all.

But the Imperial Fleet remained steadfastly unimpressed, and Klor was denied promotion after promotion, sheltered from battle, given less desirable positions—such as this one. It did not befit one of the warrior class to sit the day through watching others' routine activities. It befitted a warrior to act, not react.

Klor's dark bronze lips thinned at the thought; he shifted in his uncomfortable chair as his muscles rebelled at their disuse. With the hope of alleviating his boredom, he reached out and pressed a toggle underneath G'dath's console screen. The picture changed immediately to what the class was watching: the WorldNews coverage of the *Enterprise* launch. Normally, Klor did not mind—in fact, secretly enjoyed—watching the class. His own education had been somewhat curtailed by the fact of his parentage, and he found G'dath to be an interesting lecturer. Klor found himself learning things—things that were probably untrue, since G'dath was purported to be a crackpot. But it made interesting listening, nonetheless, and he found himself spending more time studying this particular screen at the expense of the others.

Footsteps behind him. Klor swiveled in his chair

and straightened to attention. At his back stood his superior, Keth, a tall, hawk-faced male with oddly piercing eyes. Klor prided himself on never shrinking from that gaze.

"Anything to report?" Keth snapped. His manner was curt, almost sullen, but Klor did not take offense. He knew the reason for his elder's disgruntlement did not come from working with the blue-eyed grandson of a human—most remarkably, Keth had never made mention of the fact. Rather, Klor knew, Keth's foul mood was due to a recent encounter with political disfavor. Keth had spent many honorable years at the helm of a small fighter, but had recently been disgraced by a kinsman who had dared speak out politically, suggesting a more bona fide effort be made to reach real peace with the Federation.

Klor felt a tie with his superior: both he and Keth had been assigned this unenviable duty due to the misdeeds of family.

"Nothing, Superior."

Keth craned his neck to glare at the screen beside Klor's right elbow. "And why are you watching trivision news at the Empire's expense?"

Klor started guiltily at that, but managed to recover in time, even to think of a plausible lie. "The exile G'dath's class was watching this particular broadcast, Superior. I wished to view it carefully to understand why it was of such particular interest to him."

Keth grunted in acceptance. "Any further news on the chip assembly he has ordered?"

"No, Superior."

"Hmm." Keth put a hand to his sharp chin and stroked it. "The billing records were vague, you said, as to the chip's function?"

"Yes, Superior. But they did indicate it was of custom design."

"Anything else of note?"

Klor took advantage of the opportunity to show his worth. "The chip assembly must be rather intricate. According to the itemized bill, it took several weeks for Custom Electronics to construct. The bill itself came to a considerable sum."

Keth tilted his head in Klor's direction and raised a heavy brow in interest. "Really? More than G'dath could afford?"

Klor shook his head. "No, but the amount nearly depleted his savings. It was equivalent to several months' salary."

For a moment, no more, Keth's eyes brightened with the light of a brilliant strategist's mind at work. "Be sure to notify me when he receives it. Our orders are very clear: if he constructs anything of value with it, we are to seize it at once."

"And G'dath as well?" Klor asked out of idle interest, his eyes darting for a moment from Keth's taut, dark face to the console screen. A Starfleet admiral was talking, a woman whose tone was as drab as the weather outside the claustrophobic apartment. The two Klingons listened for several seconds, then Klor switched the screen back to the classroom, and augmented the sound.

Keth drew his attention from the screen at last. "Of course." The light in his eyes dimmed abruptly, as if he had just realized that whatever private hope he had entertained was unobtainable. Most uncharacteristically, he gave a small, weary sigh. Then without another word, Keth turned and went back into the other small room that served as his private quarters.

Klor interpreted the sigh as homesickness, something he was well familiar with: Keth had left a wife and children, and the current assignment did not allow for direct communication with family. Still, they were both warriors; Klor could not permit himself the luxury of self-pity. The time would come when he could prove himself to the Empire, and at last gain recognition for his efforts rather than his ancestry.

He turned his attention back to G'dath's classroom and, without hearing it, released his own soft sigh.

Chapter Two

VICE ADMIRAL LORI CIANA sat in her office at the Admiralty watching Starfleet's closed-circuit video of the flight. She hadn't been able to bring herself to watch WorldNews coverage; while she genuinely liked Bob April and considered him a friend, she could not stand listening to Timothea Rogers. It was bad enough that, as part of Nogura's inner staff, she had to do business with Timothea. She'd be damned if she'd listen to her on 3V as well. She was mystified as to why Nogura, the most skillful strategist she knew, would allow Rogers to represent Starfleet on trivision. Especially for such an important occasion.

Ciana muted the sound on the feed and for a few seconds hesitantly fingered the control on her companel. Indecision was something new for her, something she had learned over the past eight months.

Months before, Jim Kirk and Ciana were working together as diplomatic troubleshooters. It was an ideal situation: Jim saw enough action to negate any accusations that he'd become a paper pusher—and Lori had promised him that, in a year or two, if he helped her get what she wanted, she would recommend he get the

Enterprise back. In the meantime, she learned from him. Learned when to trust her instincts, when not. Learned diplomacy. Enough diplomacy, she had felt, to earn her Nogura's recommendation for the position she craved—that of Starfleet's diplomatic liaison to the Federation.

But Nogura disagreed. After eight months, he promoted Kirk to Chief of Operations and gave him the *Enterprise* to refit. A brilliant move: the chance to work near his beloved starship again totally absorbed Jim. But had it really occurred to him that after all his months of hard work, he would have to surrender the *Enterprise* to another?

Which was no doubt why Nogura had now put Operations in charge of refitting ships. If Kirk had to lose the *Enterprise* again—well, give him another substitute. The *Endeavor,* say. After all, Lori wasn't much of a substitute these days . . .

She stopped the thought. It was true, she *was* deeply bitter at Nogura. He had given Kirk the *Enterprise,* but he had given her nothing—no recommendation for the diplomatic post, which meant little chance of ever achieving her ultimate dream: an ambassadorship. The diplomatic troubleshooter position evaporated, and though Nogura never offered an explanation, Ciana knew why: he simply did not trust her judgment. Not without Kirk's help. Over the months, she had come to realize that she'd achieved all she would ever achieve, that for the rest of her life she would be working for the head of Starfleet Command. Jim had scarcely noticed her growing disappointment; he was far too involved with his precious ship.

She was used to getting what she wanted from life. She did not know how to deal with this situation.

She lifted her hand from the companel. As a dutiful spouse, she should have called Jim to offer moral support—but then, she'd never been particularly dutiful. She'd withdrawn, and Jim hadn't even noticed. If she called him now, it would only startle him, and the resulting conversation would be awkward.

Her hesitance to call her own husband was a bad sign, and Lori knew it. Jim Kirk didn't need her anymore. In a way, they had both disappointed each other: he had no ship, she no diplomatic post. She looked at Jim now and saw her own failure.

The way he looked at her had changed as well; his expression was a little grimmer, a little more distant, more preoccupied. Older. Did he see in her his failure to get his old command back?

Maybe she could learn to deal with her own disappointment, but she could not sit idly and watch it happen to Jim, too.

Not another day. You used to be able to make decisions, right? Time to make one now. The hell with timing.

She jabbed a button on her companel and called, not Jim, but Heihachiro Nogura's office. The aide must have been out of the office, Lori thought, because Nogura answered himself, on the first signal.

"Lori," he said pleasantly, almost paternally, like the white-haired great-grandfather that he was.

Like we're all just one big happy family here, Ciana thought ironically. *Well, Heihachiro, that's about to change.*

Certainly, from her expression he must have sensed her agitation. It was hopeless to try to hide her feelings from Nogura. He had always read her easily, too easily. He read everyone easily, knew how they felt before they knew it themselves.

Yet if he had sensed her distress, he did not let on. His round, delicately boned face remained composed in a benign expression of goodwill. Nogura read others, but no one read Nogura. "Lori, how are things going? Have you spoken to Jim lately?" Spoken in an easy, warm manner, but Lori sensed a reproach lurking there.

She did not smile in greeting. "No. No, I haven't spoken to him all morning. But I need to talk to you, Admiral."

His thin silver brows lifted a millimeter; not in surprise—Ciana could not recall ever seeing the Fleet Admiral looking surprised—but in a question.

Ciana answered it before he could ask. "You remember the conversation we had a few weeks ago—how I should consider a visit to some of the more farflung 'new human' settlements—Well, I've considered it. I want to do the full tour, however long it takes."

Months, at least. Both of them knew it.

There was a long pause as Nogura scanned her face and interpreted what was hidden beneath her composed, slightly defiant expression. "I see," he answered softly. Ciana did not doubt that he did. "Does Jim know?"

"Not yet. I'm telling him tonight." Not: *I was thinking about telling him tonight.* No. No backing down. She gazed steadily into Nogura's dark, ancient eyes and waited for him to try to talk her out of it.

"And when do you intend to leave?"

"As soon as possible," Ciana said. "Tonight, if I can arrange it. Either way, I'm out of the apartment as of tonight."

Nogura looked away, gave a single, thoughtful nod, then met Ciana's gaze again. "Lori, I think you should know I'm giving Jim a new assignment—public relations liaison with the press. I was planning on telling him this afternoon after the launch. He'll replace Timmie Rogers."

"Why are you telling me this now?"

"Could it wait, Lori? Your . . . telling Jim?" His tone was gentle, almost pleading.

Ciana flushed, angry heat on her throat and cheeks. *Scared, Heihachiro? Worried I'm going to mess things up for you? That Jim might come to his senses and see how you've been manipulating him all along?* In a flash, she saw: Nogura had used her as unwitting bait to lure Kirk to the Admiralty, away from the *Enterprise.*

"You used us both," she whispered, scarcely aware she was voicing her thoughts aloud. "Threw the two of us together, counted on us stumbling into each other's arms." Worst of all, she was just as guilty as Nogura— she had used Jim, too, to try for the diplomatic post—but she had been up front about it. She glared hotly at Nogura.

A flicker of dark emotion crossed the old man's features and was gone. Impossible; Ciana convinced herself she had imagined it until she heard the faint trace of hurt in the admiral's calm, even tone.

He gazed unblinkingly at her. "I have known you since you were a child, Lori. I knew your parents very well. I thought you understood the degree of fondness —and respect—I have for you. And I had hoped you had forgiven me by now for not giving you that diplomatic assignment." His voice rose, very slightly —it was still steady, but the hurt was unmistakable now. "Is it so hard for you to believe that I have always had your best interests—yours and Jim's—at heart? I thought the two of you were happy—"

Her throat tightened dangerously at his words; she cut him off before she lost her resolve. "We're not. My telling Jim can't wait, Admiral. I'm leaving. I think we both know it would be better if I got away from this office for a while." *From you, too.*

"I see," Nogura said again. He hesitated, and for

the briefest instant Ciana got the impression he was at a loss. He glanced down at his folded hands. When he looked up, he said: "Very well, Lori. Make whatever arrangements you need to."

"Thank you, sir," she answered flatly, not even trying to sound like she meant it. She was about to terminate the link when Nogura spoke again suddenly, surprisingly.

"Lori . . . I'm sorry. I truly am."

She did not know whether he was sympathizing with her, or apologizing for the way he had used her and Jim. Perhaps both; at any rate, the concern on his face seemed so genuine that Ciana believed him.

"So am I," she whispered, and closed the channel.

Kirk watched through his window as the rain shower came to a gentle, gradual halt. The bridge stood out in sharp detail now, and pedestrians and bicyclists were once again beginning to cross it.

There was a knock at Kirk's door. "Come," he said.

The door slid open and Lieutenant Commander Riley stuck his head inside the room. At twenty-nine, Kevin Riley looked far older than the young man Kirk had hired as his chief of staff, due in part to the close-trimmed golden brown beard that hid a baby face. But the change was deeper than just appearance. Over the past year, Riley had matured into a competent officer, and Kirk was glad to have chosen him.

Yet during the past week, Riley had grown increasingly preoccupied, distracted, uncharacteristically prone to forgetting details. Kirk suspected a personal problem, perhaps even a recurrence of the one that had brought Riley close to resigning his first week on the job. Riley volunteered no information about his private life, and Kirk did not pry—merely resigned himself to being patient.

Nor did he mention his own difficulties with Lori—

though Riley had no doubt noticed that Vice Admiral Ciana no longer stopped by Kirk's office, and rarely called. Kirk liked and respected Riley, but they were not friends. The only two people Kirk trusted enough to confide in were worlds away.

Though I trust Lori, of course, Kirk thought with a twinge of guilt. Certainly, he was close enough to her to confide in her. Or at least, had been.

"Admiral?" Riley asked, his tone unusually subdued. There were faint beginnings of dark half moons beneath his eyes. "With your permission, I'm going up to the rec area to eyeball the launch. Thought you might want to come along, sir. Can't beat the view."

Kirk swiveled around and looked at Riley, considering it. Once the saucer left the ground, the ship would officially belong to Will Decker. At that point, Kirk's direct responsibility for the *Enterprise* would be completely ended at long, long last. He'd been planning to stay in his office and watch the launch by himself on trivision, but . . . dammit, he should see her off with his own eyes. It was only right that he do so. After all, she had once been his best girl.

"Fine," Kirk said. "We'd better hurry; there's not much time left."

"Agreed, sir. I'm having a lift held."

"Be right with you." Kirk rummaged quickly through a desk drawer and drew out an old clamshell-model communicator, on the chance that Decker or MacPherson might need to talk to him at the last moment. It had been quite a while since Kirk had last used the gadget, and in the intervening time Starfleet had changed over to a more compact and efficient wrist model. The clamshells were compatible, however. He'd had this particular one with him at the end of the five-year mission and had kept it afterward as a souvenir. Kirk attached the communicator to his belt near the small of his back, under the jacket of his penguin grays.

Kirk walked over to the bookshelf on which he kept Old Yeller, the stuffed armadillo he kept as a mascot and memento, and rapped Yeller's shell three times for luck. "Hello, Jimmy," the armadillo said in a deep, gentle voice that sounded like Texas.

"All right," Kirk said. "Let's go, Mr. Riley."

He and Riley left the office and strode down the corridor to the lifttube bank, where they entered their waiting lift.

"Roof," Kirk ordered. The door sighed shut and, with a very slight jolt, they were on their way.

Riley swayed as he caught his balance. "I sometimes wonder what would happen if I was in one of these things and the inertial dampeners failed."

"Riley-flavored toothpaste," Kirk said shortly, without meeting Riley's eyes. He was in no mood for idle conversation. The full impact of the *Enterprise*'s loss had finally struck him . . . and for some odd reason, he'd been reminded of Lori, as if she, too, was receding from him, slipping from his grasp.

Riley raised an eyebrow and looked away.

Kirk sighed, instantly regretful. "I suppose I'm off my feed today. Sorry."

"No need, Admiral," Riley said quietly. "I'm going to miss her, too. We both spent a lot of time on board."

Kirk idly watched the floor indicator count off the two hundredth story of the building and hurry on past it. "That we did, Commander," he said softly. "That we did."

"Roof," announced the tube, and its door eased open onto the recreation area. The Admiralty was huge—huge enough for the tall, tapered building to have a large, flat summit that housed tennis and basketball courts, a jogging and running track, a swimming pool, and other athletic facilities. The whole area was covered by a transparent aluminum dome that protected the rec area from the howling winds and allowed its use in all sorts of weather. The rec area would not have gotten the least bit wet from that morning's rain even without the dome, however, since the summit of the Admiralty was well above that day's cloud cover.

This morning, the major activity on the roof was not sports, but sightseeing. Kirk and Riley walked quickly to the southernmost part of the rec area, joining the small crowd of Starfleet personnel already gathered there.

Kirk noticed that the clouds immediately above the city had dispersed already and he let his gaze wander southeast toward the Navy Yard. From this great height, on a perfectly clear day, Kirk would have been able to see more than three hundred kilometers in any direction. Because of the low clouds hanging over the area, though, Kirk's view was limited to most of a San Francisco that had apparently not changed very much since the late nineteen hundreds, even though the Greater Quake in the middle of the twenty-first century had leveled the old city and most of the surrounding area.

While many of the towns and smaller cities around San Francisco had been lost and forgotten, the city itself had been painfully reconstructed over the course of the next twenty years. What growth San Francisco had experienced since the rebuilding had been kept largely underground. Sub-San-Fran, the subterranean city, ran more than twenty levels down in some areas, and the city was forever digging wider and more deeply.

"Good morning, gentlemen," came a deceptively soft voice.

Kirk and Riley turned as one. Standing near the edge of the dome and looking out over the city was a short, slight, very old man: Starfleet Commanding Admiral Heihachiro Nogura.

"Going to give me another ship today, Jim?" Nogura's placid features brightened in a smile.

Kirk returned it. "Yes, sir. A big piece of one, anyway. The rest of her will be ready soon."

"I look forward to that day. You know, Jim, when your proposal for the renovation of *Enterprise* hit my desk, I was a bit doubtful. It's been quite a long time since we've done any significant portion of starship construction on Earth instead of in orbit."

"I know, sir."

Nogura nodded. "I honestly didn't think it could be done—at least, not within the cost and time limits you suggested."

Kirk shrugged, inwardly impatient. The occasion was for him a solemn one, and Nogura's flattery seemed curiously inappropriate, like a joke at a funeral. He wanted to wait silently for the *Enterprise,* wanted to prepare himself to say good-bye to her. "It's working."

"You've made it work," Nogura said. "You're bringing the job in on time and under budget. I've had more than a few fences to mend with the Construction Authority people; they didn't like my taking the *Enterprise* away from them. But you've delivered handsomely, and no one argues with results—at least, they dare not argue them with *me.* I'll make it more formal later but for now, accept my sincerest congratulations. Well done." He held out his hand.

Kirk took it. "Thank you, Admiral. I'll take those congratulations not just for myself, but also for the topside and ground crews who've been busting their—I mean to say, have been working very hard to meet the schedule."

31

"Of course." Nogura glanced expectantly at the sky. "Kevin, do you wear a chrono?"

"Yes, sir. Um, it's coming up to the T-minus-thirty-seconds mark."

"Then, gentlemen, let's watch the show."

The southeast sky over the city was now clear. Kirk could see all the way across town to the Navy Yard, and he plainly saw the large saucer shape within it. Crowds clustered here and there in cleared areas of the city. Once the weather improved, people had come swarming outside. Even greater crowds now gathered along the waterline across the bay and east of the city.

"Count down from ten, please, Mr. Riley," Kirk said.

"Yes, Admiral. We are at T minus thirteen seconds." Riley paused and then began counting.

At T minus five seconds, a shimmer of heat appeared at the aft end of the command section, where the impulse engine outlets were located. Dust flew around the saucer as its mighty belly thrusters cleared their throats. Kirk closed his eyes for a second and imagined the bridge as it must be now, seeing in his mind's eye the quiet tension and professional calm.

"Zero," Riley said at last. *Full thrusters, helm,* Kirk thought. His hand closed, as if he were grasping the arm of a chair.

The command section lifted vertically and ever so slowly. Its landing legs retraced smoothly into the shell, shaking the dust of Earth from their pads. The saucer continued rising.

For the first time in half a year, the *Enterprise* was under way, once again a creature that lived in the sky.

"Holding steady, Captain," Sulu reported. "Altitude now fifty meters. Climbing slowly, as per program."

"Start bringing her around to starboard," Decker ordered.

"Aye, Captain," Sulu said, and he played a rapid tattoo on his thruster command pad. Their course was going to take them the long way around San Francisco. The Navy Yard was located in the southeastern corner of the city. The saucer would head right out over the bay at first and then make its way north along the eastern edge of the city's waterline, past China Basin and North Beach. It would then turn to the west over Fisherman's Wharf and sail the skies just off the Marina and the old Presidio, where the Admiralty was located. After that, the saucer would pass through the Golden Gate and head farther west to position itself for its leap into orbit.

"Captain, we are at three hundred meters," Sulu reported. "Level-one altitude, condition nominal. Awaiting go for level two."

"Rig shields for aerodynamics, helm," Decker said. "Impulse power, one tenth. Continue gaining altitude to level two. Ease off thrusters." One-tenth of full impulse power was all Decker would order until the saucer was clear of the city. Any more than that would rattle windows and bother several million sets of eardrums below.

Sulu smoothly cut in the impulse engines and swung the saucer out over San Francisco Bay. He headed it north by northwest and, as per orders, allowed the saucer to climb gradually.

"Let's have a look down, helmsman," Decker said.

"On the screen now, Captain," he answered. "This view is below and to port. Magnification two."

Decker could see people gathered all along the east side of San Francisco. They were waving hands, arms, flags, jackets and even bedsheets. Every other person seemed to be using a camera to record the launch. The crowd seemed to be enjoying itself quite a bit. *Well, so am I,* Decker thought, struggling to keep from grinning.

Seeing all those cameras in use reminded Decker of something. The sun was high in a bright sky now; the bottom of the saucer would be obscured by shade. "Give me full navigation lights, Chief," he told DiFalco. "Let's let 'em see who we are."

"Navigation lights on full, Captain," DiFalco said, pressing a button.

The sudden appearance of the powerful lights drew an instant, enthusiastic response from the crowds below as the proud name and number of the *Enterprise* leaped out at them. Decker could no longer hide a grin. *Jim Kirk was right about the launch,* he thought happily. *There is nothing like this. Nothing!*

"This is the view below and to starboard, Captain," Sulu said. The scene on the screen changed and zoomed in to scan equally happy throngs standing at the edges of the thick woods in the New Oakland area. *They're even cheering us over in Berkeley,* noted Decker. *I thought all those "new human" kids absolutely hated Starfleet! Fan-tas-tic!*

"View angle ahead and below, please," Decker requested, and Sulu complied. The screen now showed the wild redwood growth of southern Marin County and, farther north, a thick white carpet of nearly unbroken cloud that stretched to the limits of his vision. Decker looked in vain for the blackened patch of woods left by that morning's fire. Mill Valley was only ten kilometers or so north of the Golden Gate, but the area was hidden under lingering low clouds. However, Decker thought he could make out tiny motes—flitters—swarming above what must have been the burn zone.

The saucer sailed between the towers of the great, gray Bay Bridge east of Rincon Hill and swung westward, still gaining altitude. It then passed directly over the resort on Alcatraz Island. Looking down into the exercise yard, Decker saw several hundred people in prison stripes waving replica firearms at the saucer. Judging from all the bodies sprawled on the ground, there seemed to be yet another recreational riot in progress. Decker had never understood the attraction of Alcatraz as a vacation spot—he preferred the surfing reservations down the coast, around Big Sur—but the people down below seemed to be having a good time.

The saucer was approaching the Presidio now. "Admiralty to port," DiFalco said.

"Mr. Sulu," Decker said, "let's gain some more altitude. I want us to come level with the roof. Chief, make ready to circle the building." Working together, Sulu and DiFalco smoothly brought the command section level with the summit of the Admiralty tower. They began to circle.

"Dead slow," Decker continued. "Sulu, let's have a look at the rec area—tracking view, please. Let's see if we recognize anybody."

"Yes, sir," Sulu said. "Tracking view, magnification three."

Magnification three was sufficient to make the features of the people in the rec area plainly visible. The command section was approaching the northern face of the Admiralty, but the crowd at that end of the roof was relatively sparse, and Decker saw no one he knew.

As the saucer passed the southern end, the much larger crowd there came into view. *Admiral Nogura,* Decker thought with pleasure. *And standing right next to him, Jim Kirk. We're getting quite a sendoff.*

"Helm, slow us a touch as we pass Admiral Kirk," Decker said. "Navigator, as we do so, blink your lights in a captain's salute."

DiFalco did, and the captain watched as Nogura,

Kirk and some of the others in the crowd returned the salute in the ancient manner: fingertips to eyebrow, longest way up and quickest way down. It seemed to Decker that Kirk held his salute the longest, if only by a fraction of a second. A hand salute in Starfleet, very rarely given, was intended to be quite a compliment.

After a moment or two, DiFalco reported, "Captain, we've passed the Golden Gate and are now approaching Point Bonita."

"Fine, Chief," Decker said. He leaned back in his chair. "Mr. Sulu, let's stop wasting time. Get us to our departure point. Impulse engines, full."

"Full impulse power," Sulu acknowledged. "Aye, aye, sir."

The crowd of spectators was breaking up, but Kirk continued to watch as the saucer began its long sprint out over the Pacific. Nogura watched Kirk. The two men remained there, quietly, even after the saucer had disappeared into the clean cobalt vastness of the western sky.

"A nice departure, Jim," Nogura said at last. "Very impressive."

Kirk's eyes remained on the horizon. "Yes, sir. It surely was."

"Miss her?"

The abruptness of Nogura's question took Kirk aback at first, but he turned and forced himself to gaze steadily into the old admiral's eyes as he answered. "I've got a good job, Admiral," he said. "I have no complaints. In fact, I've got to get going on the renovation of the *Endeavor*. Everything's ready, of course, but I've learned a great deal from the *Enterprise* project. I think I can cut the time factor even further."

"Mm," Nogura said, and the look he gave Kirk said that he had noted the fact that Kirk had not answered the question, but was not going to press. "As a matter of fact, Jim, we need to talk about that. In my office. Do you have a minute?"

It did not sound like a direct order, but Jim knew Nogura better. Knew him well enough to guess from his tone that the fleet admiral really wanted to discuss something other than the *Endeavor*. "Certainly, sir."

As he followed Nogura and Riley, Kirk felt oddly light on his feet, as if—like the *Enterprise*—all ties to Earth had been severed, and there was nothing left to hold him here.

Chapter Three

To ECONOMIZE ON FUEL and to minimize wear and tear on its impulse engines, the *Enterprise*'s command section would take three leisurely, rising orbits to catch up with Spacedock Four. G'dath did not plan to have the class sit in place for nearly four and a half hours while the saucer made the trip. As soon as WorldNews confirmed the saucer had reached its departure point safely and was on its way up, G'dath rose and ordered the trivision set to turn itself off.

"I trust you have all learned something from this feed," G'dath said. Most of the students nodded their quick agreement with that statement, but some failed to respond—most notably Joseph Brickner, who was absently staring out the window at the now sunny day.

G'dath was disappointed. He had hoped that his conversation with Mrs. Brickner had been relayed to her son, and that it would spark a change in Joseph's attitude. A Klingon student in similar circumstances would have known to prepare to be challenged by the instructor at the earliest opportunity—and G'dath had observed, in his years of teaching on Earth, that human students were not so very different. Perhaps, he told himself, Joseph was staring out the window in order to collect his thoughts, to reflect on what he had learned. At any rate, G'dath determined to find out.

"Mr. Brickner," the teacher said, pointing to his victim, "please rise and tell us what you learned from watching the event." He was careful to use what he considered a very quiet tone. Even had he not been Klingon, the commanding sound of his voice would have intimidated anyone. Deep and resonant, it filled the room and left no space for another ego. English was not G'dath's second language; it was his eleventh, and he spoke it flawlessly, with a North American accent. Upon his arrival here, he had learned of the Terran belief that all Klingons had rasping harsh voices. He therefore took care to train his so that he now sounded like an actor who'd learned projection and diction during an extended tour with the American branch of the Royal Shakespeare Company.

It became immediately clear that the boy's reflections had nothing to do with the *Enterprise* launch. The hapless Brickner stood, nervously shifting his weight from one foot to the other, and his pale, freckled face flushed dark red. For a moment he gaped, wide-eyed and helpless, at G'dath. When he found his voice, he asked timidly:

"Um, could you please repeat the question, Dr. G'dath?"

At the beginning of the semester, one or two students might have giggled; but now, the room was deathly silent. Any student who dared make fun of another would find his or her own preparedness tested.

"No, I cannot," G'dath said. Brickner's failure to respond to the warning meant that there was something seriously wrong, either with Joseph's personal situation or with his attitude. G'dath made a mental note to confront the boy about it later. In the meantime, he noticed Carlos Siegel nodding his head with an intent, thoughtful expression. In terms of his ability to make deductions and to abstract, Siegel was the strongest student in the class. "Please sit down, Mr. Brickner. Mr. Siegel, how about you?"

Joseph Brickner slumped down into his desk in a huddle of defeat and Siegel, a dark-haired, olive-skinned young man of fifteen, stood. For all his brilliance, Siegel was undeniably shy and hated speaking in front of the class, though G'dath could see he worked hard to conceal his nervousness. "It seems like Starfleet is in an awful rush to get the thing finished," he said, in a voice so quiet everyone had to strain to hear. "That lady talked about saving all kinds of time and money on the project."

Somebody in the class tittered, and G'dath cast an icy glare in the direction of the sound—Ira Stoller's direction, naturally. "You might think that what Mr. Siegel has just said is funny, but he has hit upon the *only* important thing that was mentioned in that entire feed. Very good, Mr. Siegel. Please be seated."

G'dath's chair scraped against the floor as he rose from his desk. He began pacing slowly back and forth at the front of the room. "Let us consider the motives for rushing a starship to completion. What do you think that means? Mr. Stoller?"

Stoller gulped audibly and twitched in his desk; his long, thin face colored pink, and G'dath pitied him for his pale, all-too-revealing flesh. "I'm not sure—"

"Please stand when you address the class, Mr. Stoller." The education board had recommended against letting Stoller in the class, on the basis that he had a history of being a disciplinary problem, but G'dath had insisted. He was not afraid of disciplinary problems—and Stoller had a good, inventive mind.

He simply needed to learn the discipline to apply it in a given direction long enough to achieve results. It did not take long for G'dath to learn the real objection the board hadn't had the nerve to voice: that Stoller hated Klingons.

G'dath chose to see the fact as an opportunity.

Stoller rose on his long, thin legs. "I'm sorry, sir. Uh, I think that if Starfleet is in a rush, it needs the ship back on duty pretty quickly."

"No doubt. And why might that be?"

Stoller hesitated.

"Come, come, Mr. Stoller," G'dath prompted. "Why might that be?"

"Well," Stoller said, with a glint of defiance, "since you asked, Dr. G'dath, the Federation is worried about the Klingons."

"Indeed? What makes you think so?"

Stoller's face twisted with the effort to repress a hateful smirk. "Well, we almost had a war with you a few years ago. In case you've forgotten."

"'You,' Mr. Stoller? I think you mean 'them,' do you not? For my part, I have never engaged in combat with the Federation. In the future, please attempt not to paint your targets with so broad a brush." Stoller's expression turned sullen, and G'dath smiled. It was not, he knew, a pretty sight, and he let it fade quickly.

"That point aside, though, you're quite right," G'dath continued. "Some six years ago, the Federation and the Empire almost went to war. The fighting ended shortly after the outbreak of hostilities due to the Organian Intervention, and the truce declared at that time was soon formalized into the Organian Peace Treaty. That treaty is still operative. Simply put, it states that the Empire cannot attack the Federation, or vice-versa, without inviting an Organian response. Be seated, Mr. Stoller. You suddenly look tired."

A hand went up in the back of the class. This time, G'dath forced himself not to smile. Of all his students, he personally liked Ricia Greene the best, for the simple fact that she was not afraid of him. Even Stoller, for all his arrogance, was clearly terrified of the fact that G'dath was a Klingon; but Ricia feared no one, perhaps because she possessed the ability to see beyond the superficial, at what lay beneath the surface. Her light brown forehead was puckered in thought, though G'dath could not see how that was possible, with her wiry dark hair pulled back so tightly at the nape of her neck. Miss Greene belonged to the ethnic Terran group called black, though her skin was several shades lighter than G'dath's own.

"Miss Greene?"

"Dr. G'dath, the thing Mr. Stoller mentioned about the Federation being scared of the Klingons: Why should we be scared of them, if the Organians are preventing a war between us? Yet, everybody seems to be paranoid about Klingons."

"Paranoid about *all* Klingons, Miss Greene?" G'dath's face, hard for humans to read in any case, was expressionless.

The girl's frown deepened. "With all respect, Dr. G'dath, you can't bait me. I mean the warrior class— the ultraconservative influence that dominates the Empire."

G'dath finally smiled, this time quite warmly. He liked it when his students fought back, although most of them did not seem to realize it. "Very well. Stretch your mind, Miss Greene. Think about what you've said. Tell me why people are afraid of Klingons, as you put it, if the Organians are preventing them from starting a war with us."

Her answer came quickly. "I don't think people trust the Organians, either."

"Hah!" G'dath cried, slapping his hands together in glee. Ricia Greene jerked in her seat and blinked, startled. "Yes! You've pinned it, Miss Greene," G'dath said happily. "Excellent!"

G'dath stopped pacing and faced the class, standing tall, his feet planted widely, arms akimbo; it was his accustomed posture of dominance, and now he truly dominated. "The Federation does not trust the Organians to keep the peace," he said. "The Klingon Empire does not, either. Interestingly, the reasons for this feeling of mistrust are exactly the same on both sides of our common border. Does anyone care to venture a guess as to what they might be? Mr. Sherman?"

Sherman, plump, short and straw-haired, rose. "I'd have no reason to trust the Organians. I mean, there's no guarantee they'll continue to keep the peace." Sherman sank back into his seat with a sigh.

G'dath nodded. "Exactly so. Neither we nor the Klingon Empire can be sure the Organians will keep their part of the agreement, because neither side is quite sure why the Organians got themselves involved with us in the first place. Great minds—pardon my sarcasm—on both sides of the border have considered all the possibilities, and they have time and again seized upon the worst of them."

G'dath reseated himself at his desk. "Therefore, both sides feel they must act as if the Organians will not be there tomorrow. Starfleet states that its primary purpose is exploration and discovery, and its record of accomplishment in these areas is unarguable. However, Starfleet also has a role to play in maintaining the security of the Federation, and so the fleet is periodically augmented. One of Starfleet's cruiser-class starships, the *Enterprise,* is being rushed back into service after extensive renovation, and other aging cruisers will be presumably updated in the near future. These ships will be used primarily for exploration and discovery, certainly, but they also carry weapons—and the Klingon Empire knows it.

"At the same time, the Klingon Empire has developed an entirely new type of warship, the *K't'inga*-class heavy cruiser, and it is building them as well. Those running the Empire do not even bother to claim that the Imperial Fleet is intended to serve any purpose other than conquest and consolidation. It is also an interesting fact that the Organians have done nothing to stop the buildup on either side, despite the risk to peace the buildup itself entails. Why they have done nothing about it is yet another question without an answer."

G'dath raised a finger. "And so, the following is what was to be learned from watching the trivision today. Despite the Organian Peace Treaty, the threat of hostilities between the Federation and the Empire continues, and this is due to policies that are guided not by reasoned thinking but by fear, apprehension and suspicion. Mr. Siegel also mentioned the budgetary savings realized in the renovation of the *Enterprise*. I suggest to you that credits not expended on one ship can be spent on others."

He glanced at his chrono. "We will discuss the pros and cons of a Federation presence in space next week. It still lacks a few minutes of fifteen, but I think we will end our session now. It is a very pleasant day, and we should go out and enjoy what is left of it."

As the members of the class gathered their things and prepared to leave, he cleared his throat.

"Extra assignments first," G'dath announced, and there was a low groan. Despite all precedent, some of the students had begun to hope that the teacher had forgotten.

"Mr. Brickner," G'dath said, "I desire from you a paper of two thousand words with your thoughts on the subjects we've just discussed. Include an outline— and, this time, please do the outline *before* you write the paper, and not after."

Brickner's face fell.

"Mr. Stoller, a paper discussing the role of the warrior class in Klingon society, three thousand words, if you please. Mr. Rico, the paper you submitted to me this morning on the mechanization of infantry during the second millennium was quite unsatisfactory. I want the paper rewritten—and you may add another thousand words to its length. The deadline for all papers is Monday, as this is Friday.

"One last announcement: As I mentioned earlier this week, a trivision crew will be here to film the class in progress. I therefore suggest that all of you be prepared to answer questions about the assigned reading." He ignored the eyes that widened at this. "Enjoy your weekend, everyone."

The students began making good their escape; Joseph Brickner sat in the aisle farthest from the door, and was one of the last to leave. As he and Stoller went shuffling past, G'dath said in a low voice, so that the others in the hall would not overhear, "A word with you first, Mr. Brickner."

Brickner paled and his blue eyes widened as they glanced from his friend to the teacher. Ira Stoller nudged the boy with an elbow and said, his eyes downcast but glancing sidewise at G'dath: "Meet you outside."

Once the room had emptied, G'dath motioned for Joseph to sit in the chair beside the teacher's desk, then took his own seat. The boy sat stiffly on the edge of the chair.

"Mr. Brickner," the Klingon began in what he hoped was a gentle but firm tone, "did your mother tell you of the conversation we had yesterday?"

"Yes, sir." Joseph's gaze dropped to his shoes.

"Mr. Brickner, it would be easier for me to be certain we are communicating if we maintained eye contact."

Joseph flushed but raised his face and met G'dath's gaze with eyes that were defiant and—yes, definitely—tinged with anger. An improvement over apathy, at least.

"Then why," G'dath continued, "have you made no effort to improve?"

The red in Joseph's cheeks darkened to the color of human blood. He seemed unable to speak and—for one instant—on the verge of tears, which unsettled G'dath. Any self-respecting Klingon old enough to walk would have preferred death rather than shed tears in front of a superior. But G'dath had to remind himself that to judge Joseph Brickner an emotional weakling because his, G'dath's, Klingon standards of appropriate behavior were different would have been wrong. As wrong as the joke about Klingons he had overheard Ira Stoller tell during the trivision commercial.

Finally, Brickner got control of himself and found his voice. "I'm making an effort, Doctor G'dath. I mean, you only told my mom yesterday that I'd be put on probation if I didn't start preparing my assignments. So I did, I prepared last night." His tone grew stronger, almost defensive. "I read the material about the *Enterprise* launch. But when the commercial came on, I got bored and looked out the window, so I didn't hear the question."

"Joseph," G'dath said quietly, "the launch coverage resumed and continued for several minutes afterward, then I asked the question."

Joseph looked down, at a loss. Apparently, he hadn't realized how lost he had been in his own daydreams.

"That is why I am concerned," G'dath continued. "Not by your failure to hear a single question, but by your consistent inability to pay attention in class or do an adequate job on any of your assignments. Your past academic record and aptitude scores imply you are well able to handle the material. Yet your performance is worse than average. Can you explain to me why the discrepancy exists? Or tell me how I might help you find a solution to this problem?"

He watched Joseph's defenses go up, watched the muscles in the boy's face and body tense, watched Joseph's eyes harden, and knew that he had failed to reach his student.

"No. It's nothing you can help," Brickner said woodenly, looking at G'dath without really meeting his eyes. "And I'll pay attention in class from now on. Is there anything else, Dr. G'dath?"

G'dath sighed. "No. No, Mr. Brickner. You may go. Have a good weekend."

As he watched Joseph leave, he felt a resounding sense of failure. Unable to procure the research positions for which he was qualified, G'dath had continued with this teaching job—and would probably continue with it until his temporary visa expired in one year. In his more optimistic moments, he felt he was doing both the Klingon Empire and the Federation some good by training young minds to think, to realize the vast universe that existed outside their own narrow culture—at the very least, helping a few young humans overcome their fear of Klingons.

But today he felt discouraged, for as Joseph Brickner left the classroom, G'dath saw the hatred smoldering in his eyes.

* * *

As he stumbled, unseeing, into students heading across the schoolyard, Joey's thoughts condensed into a single, furious phrase:

Dirty rotten filthy turtlehead, *dirty filthy rotten* stupid *turtlehead.*

The rational part of him knew, of course, that the last thing Dr. G'dath was was stupid. But still, it felt good to think, even if he was too upset at the moment to say it aloud.

Stupid turtlehead, stupid stinking turtlehead.

It wasn't fair. Most times when G'dath called on him, Joey forgot what he was going to say. Answering a Klingon was enough reason to be nervous, and Joey was shy about talking in front of groups, anyway. Now it was getting worse.

It wasn't bad enough that Dr. G'dath had embarrassed him in front of the entire class today, then hadn't even given him a chance to show what he'd studied. No, he had to go and upset Joey's mom, too. As if, with Jase gone and Dad moved out, things weren't bad enough. As if Mom needed that dirty, stinking turtlehead to give her *another* reason to cry.

And then for G'dath to give him the extra assignment, and make him stay after class, and ask him *why.*

What was he supposed to say? Tell the truth—confide in a *turtlehead,* and ask for pity? *Gee, Dr. G'dath, ever since my little brother died, my parents haven't gotten along, so I really don't give a damn about the honor of being in your lousy class.*

He stopped—he hadn't really been aware that he'd been going full tilt across the schoolyard, bumping blindly into other kids, not bothering to murmur an apology—and fought to hold back angry tears. The weather had turned clear and sunny. The only reminders of the earlier rain were the fat droplets sparkling on the grass. Students continued to move past him and the yard was becoming rapidly deserted. It was, after all, the beginning of the weekend, and by the time Joey managed to have full control of himself, the yard was almost deserted. Stoller was supposed to have been waiting for him—but he was relieved Ira wasn't there. He wasn't in the mood to talk to anyone now, least of all to have to pretend with Stoller that the talk with Dr. G'dath hadn't upset him.

He began to move, more slowly, toward the schoolyard exit where the autobus would be waiting—but he was in no hurry. If he missed the bus and had to wait for another one, fine. He'd just as soon walk the twenty miles home.

But as he passed through the yard's far end, a sound—a familiar voice, crying out with uncharacteristic agitation—brought him to a halt.

"Stop it! *Stop* it, leave him alone!"

Ricia Greene's voice, high-pitched, indignant. Joey turned in its direction. In a corner of the schoolyard half secluded by tall trees, Ira Stoller was trying to wrest something from Carlos Siegel's grasp while Ricia struggled to get between them.

Joey wavered for several perilous seconds, and almost—*almost*—kept walking. He was too upset to get involved in any of this; he had his own problems.

But there was something a little frightening about the light in Stoller's eyes, something that made Joey hesitate. And then Stoller let go of whatever he was fighting over. Siegel staggered a little, trying to regain his balance, and Stoller moved in and struck him, full in the face.

"Hey!" Joey yelled, and broke into a run before he realized he was moving. "Stoller, what do you think you're *doing?* Stop it!"

By the time he got there, Siegel was sitting on the ground, hands cupped around his bleeding nose, and

Stoller was holding his treasure aloft. Ricia Greene was kneeling beside Siegel, trying to get him to move his hands so she could inspect the damage.

Joey gasped, trying to get his breath. "Stoller, what are you, crazy? What *is* that?"

Stoller was grinning—sort of, but his expression was contorted, as if he were angry at the same time. He turned and registered Joey's presence for the first time, but before he could answer, Ricia Greene looked up, eyes flashing, and said, in a voice that shook:

"Library tapes. Carlos's library tapes. He needs them for a project . . ."

Stoller's voice was uneven, half angry, half laughing; he looked at Joey with wild eyes. "For an extra credit report, Brickner, can you believe it? *Extra* credit. As if these two turtlehead's pets need extra credit—"

"Don't you call him a turtlehead!" Ricia cried hotly.

"Turtlehead, turtlehead," Stoller chanted in singsong. He dropped the tape onto a nearby rock and gently positioned the heel of his boot atop it.

"Hey!" Carlos Siegel's shout was muffled by the hands still cradling his injured nose. "Don't hurt that! That belongs to the library, not me!"

Ricia Greene scrambled to her feet, but Joey held her back and faced Ira. "Look, Stoller," he said reasonably, "give them the tape back." He held out his hand.

Stoller looked as if he'd just been betrayed. "So when did you join the turtle lovers camp, Brickner?"

"I *haven't*," Joey replied vehemently, remembering his anger at G'dath. "But picking on them—" he angled his head back at Greene and Siegel—"isn't going to make things any better. It's not going to hurt G'dath. It's only going to get you in trouble. C'mon, Stoller." He gestured with his hand.

Stoller's face hardened; he eased his boot down on the tape.

"Stoller . . ." Joey pleaded. He really couldn't believe Ira was this crazy after all.

"Turtlehead put me on probation, did you know that?" Stoller's voice rose. "Told my parents yesterday. Two weeks to pull my grades up, or I'm outta the class."

"Stoller," Joey said patiently, "he told me if I didn't straighten up, I'd get put on probation, too. But—"

Stoller ranted on, not even hearing. "And *these* two are doing extra credit for the hell of it." A soft crunch came from beneath the heel of his boot.

Joey reached for Stoller's foot, knowing Ira wouldn't hurt him.

Stoller grabbed Joey by the tunic, pulled him up, and punched him in the mouth. It happened with insane speed, but Joey had time to think: *He doesn't mean to be doing this. He doesn't know what he's doing, but later he'll be sorry.*

And then all thinking ceased for a minute as Joey concentrated on the pain in his lower jaw, and especially the inside of his lower lip, where the teeth had split open the tender flesh. When he came to himself, he realized he was sitting with his hand over his mouth, wearing the same stupid, dazed expression Carlos Siegel had worn minutes earlier.

"Ah, *hell,* Joey." Stoller sagged. "Now see what you made me do?"

Joey lowered his hand and said, "Leave the tape," but it came out burbly sounding because of the blood.

Ricia Greene stomped over to a stunned Stoller and snatched the tape out from under his boot, then went over to Joey. By the time she opened her mouth to speak, Stoller had vanished.

"How bad is it? Lose any teeth?"

Joey did a quick inspection with his tongue and

shook his head. "Cut the inside of my lip kinda deep."
He tasted iron and spat bloody saliva on the grass.

"Let's get you both to the school infirmary."

"No," Joey said emphatically, and rose quickly to
his feet. "It'll just upset my mom." He swayed dizzily.

Greene caught his arm. "You okay?"

"Yeah. Just got up too fast, that's all."

Carlos Siegel was back on his feet, standing beside
them. He was holding his nose with only one hand,
now; blood still dripped from one nostril. "He's right,
Ricia. It would really upset my dad . . . and besides, if
we go to the infirmary, we'd have to explain how we
got this way."

Ricia wheeled on him. "Well, someone *should*. You
want Ira Stoller to go around beating other people
up?"

"No. But if we report him now, when he's on
probation, he'll be out of the class for good," Carlos
said quietly. "He seemed to regret hitting Joey. And I
don't think my nose is broken." He fingered it gingerly. "I might be able to get the swelling down before my
dad gets home, so he wouldn't even have to know
about it."

Ricia retrieved the tapes and wiped the moisture
onto her tunic. "One looks like it's damaged—at
least, the casing's scratched."

"It doesn't matter," Carlos said, and Ricia gave him
a sharp look for that. "Joey, your bottom lip is
beginning to puff up."

Joey touched it and winced. "My mom's gonna *kill*
me."

"Maybe not. We've got a sonic stimulator at my
place. It'd take care of it and your mom'd never have
to know."

Ricia nodded. "Carlos's dad is a doctor."

"Yeah, and fortunately, he won't be home for hours.

But he's taught me how to use the stimulator. Why don't you come with us and get cleaned up? You've got blood down the front of your tunic," Carlos said, apparently unaware of the blood on his own.

Joey hesitated. Now that his senses had returned, he was once again on the verge of total, self-pitying despair at the thought of going home bloodied. Carlos's offer seemed like the only reasonable solution. He drew in a shaky breath. "Okay. Let's go."

Yet as the three of them left the schoolyard, the angry phrase echoed in his ears: *turtle lover.* And he had the odd feeling that he was somehow betraying himself, and Ira Stoller.

G'dath walked two blocks downtown and stepped onto the busy crosstown slidewalk rolling eastward toward Stuyvesant Preserve. He always caught the slidewalk at the corner of Fourteenth Street and the Avenue of the Federation, which New Yorkers called Sixth Avenue.

He paid little attention to his surroundings; his thoughts were still focused on Joseph Brickner, and the hatred he'd seen flashing in the young man's eyes. If there were only some way to break through the wall of misunderstanding he encountered from time to time in his students.

True, not all his students disliked Klingons; there were Siegel, Greene and Sherman, among others. And there were days when he was glad that his situation had forced him to take the teaching job, days when he felt it was far more meaningful work than his physics research.

This was not one of those days. Today he was looking forward to the upcoming trivision interview. He had not been entirely forthcoming with his students: the trivision article was not to focus on the class, but on its teacher. The point was to expose the discrimination G'dath faced as a Klingon living among humans.

And, for G'dath, to make widely known his qualifications as a physics researcher, and hope that part of the public response would include job offers. He then hoped that, through his research, he would contribute enough to earn the right to remain in the Federation after his temporary exchange visa had expired. The visa was completely unique, G'dath knew, and he was grateful for the chance to live even briefly among humans—something that no other Klingon had ever done, since even the Klingon Embassy staff studiously avoided unnecessary contract with humans.

More than anything, G'dath realized, he wished to remain on Earth permanently and conduct his research in a free society—without fear that his work would be misused. At the same time, he felt a sense of guilt—his students needed him. Some of them even appreciated him.

Or did they?

The slidewalk passed over the sunken Fifth Avenue Strip, the wide north-south slidewalk that ran from Central Park South to Washington Square. As he and his fellow passengers rolled past the Strip, G'dath noticed that he was being stared at by some and carefully ignored by others. Despite the crowding on the slidewalk, he had plenty of room. No one cared to stand near him.

All of this was nothing new. He was quite used to attracting attention wherever he went. *Perhaps they expect me to go berserk and begin tearing them apart limb by limb,* he thought. He did not see another of his kind anywhere on the slidewalk. He never did and, as always, it made him feel very much alone. He looked away and watched the buildings along Fourteenth Street roll by.

The slidewalk continued rolling east, leaving behind the commercial district, and entered a residential neighborhood. G'dath got off at Fourteenth Street and First Avenue, the southwestern limit of Stuyvesant Preserve. Some of his fellow passengers seemed relieved at his departure, and he wished for the millionth time that he could be less sensitive about such things.

If Tarzan and Jane were turtleheads . . .

G'dath walked along the pedway leading into the Preserve, an eye-catching collection of tall, well-designed apartment complexes set in the middle of pleasant, rolling parkland that lay hard by the restored banks of the thriving East River. Water from fountains played in the air as squirrels and sparrows skittered and flew. Young residents played in safe recreation areas while their elders relaxed on comfortable benches along winding walking paths that seemed more like nature trails than pedways.

Except for its great, old trees, the Preserve still looked new. In the mid-twentieth century, the slum housing that existed here was razed, and new housing was built—this time with consideration for the human spirit. In their turn, the twentieth-century buildings had been replaced in the middle of the twenty-first century. The grounds were well-maintained, and low-power shielding protected the outer walls of the apartment buildings from the elements. With proper maintenance, the Preserve might last another thousand years before reconstruction or a major renovation would be required.

Like its vile grandparent of the nineteenth century, Stuyvesant Preserve still played home to immigrants. However, those long-departed original residents could not have begun to imagine the distant places from which these latest immigrants had come . . . for some of them, like G'dath, were refugees from the stars.

G'dath strolled slowly through the grounds of the Preserve. The air was fresh and thick with the scent of green, growing things, and the happy sounds of children at excited play fell on his ears easily. Here, at least, was a place where he did not feel like a stranger. The Preserve played home to Andorians and Klingons, Australians and Ghanians, Andorians and Rigellians, Filipinos and Britons, Tellerite's and Argellians. No one seemed strange, because everyone was.

G'dath lived in a building near the center of the Preserve. Not ten meters from the front door of his building, he heard a slight rustle to his right. He quickly turned and saw a small movement in a thick crop of bushes some ten meters away. The area was largely hidden from view by a group of trees. He left the path and, walking onto the grass, went over to the bushes. He bent and peered into them, consciously adjusting his eyes to the darkness.

Two small bright spots of green looked back at him. *What is that?* G'dath wondered, adjusting his vision further. *It is an animal—but not a squirrel, that's for certain.* He sensed that something was wrong with it, whatever it was. *Hunger, that's it,* he realized. *That, and fear. Loneliness.* He understood the last.

As the pupils of his eyes dilated further and his retinas became more sensitive to the low light, G'dath made out a small nose and whiskers under the eyes. *It is a cat,* he suddenly realized. *No—it is a kitten, I believe they're called. A youngling cat. It is lost, perhaps, or willfully abandoned. Yes, abandoned. The kitten certainly does not look feral to me.*

The little cat and the big Klingon continued to study each other. *I wonder how long it has been here?*

G'dath wondered. *It appears to be thin but, as nearly as I can tell without examining it closely, it seems healthy.*

G'dath had no idea how old the kitten might be since he had no experience with the species. The much larger analog species on his home planet could not be domesticated. As a youngling on the family agricultural parcel, though, G'dath had had a pet targ, and his deep affection for the faithful beast lingered even now. He felt a similar pull toward this little one in front of him, although it was as unlike a targ as anything could be.

The attraction was apparently mutual. The kitten cautiously emerged from the bush and, after a moment, approached G'dath slowly. The Klingon blinked rapidly to help readjust his eyes for use in full daylight. Still squinting, he looked at the kitten. It was mostly gray, with white paws and bib.

The kitten looked suspiciously at G'dath with big green eyes, cocking its small head from one side to the other as it sniffed at him. The kitten's tail waved back and forth, sending semaphore signals in a body language known only to its fellow felines.

Instinctively, as he would approach a targlet that was a stranger to him, G'dath crouched slowly, extending his hand knuckles out and palm inward. The kitten tensed, as if ready to bolt. "Here, little one," the Klingon said softly. "No harm will come to you."

G'dath waited patiently and did not move. After a while the animal approached him. It sniffed tentatively at his outstretched hand and then rubbed its head against the Klingon's knuckles. G'dath passed his hand lightly over the kitten's head and scratched it between its ears. The kitten seemed to smile as its mouth stretched back and its eyes closed in pleasure.

G'dath stood. The kitten trotted closer to him and began walking back and forth in front of him like a sentry, stropping against his leg on each pass. *I appear to have been adopted,* G'dath thought. *However, the rules in the Preserve say I cannot have an animal in the apartment with me. There are no pets allowed. I am a law-abiding person. I suppose I could give the kitten over to the authorities.*

G'dath looked down at the kitten again. It was sitting on the ground, its head cocked slightly to one side, and it was gazing up at him with wide eyes.

It trusted him completely.

The Klingon shrugged his large shoulders. *It is time to begin breaking the rules,* he decided. He looked behind him, back toward the pedway, and saw no one. He extended his hearing and heard no one within range. *It is well,* he thought. *The fewer complications there are, the better for us both.*

"We are going home now, little one," G'dath told the kitten. He stooped and picked it up. The kitten remained calm. The Klingon hid the kitten under his jacket and casually resumed his walk toward his apartment building. He thought it possible that the doorkeeper might be able to detect the kitten if he simply held it in his arms . . . and it was probably wiser to conceal the little creature in any case. Despite his conviction that what he was doing was right, he was nervous about breaking a rule.

But the automated door and lift sentries failed to react to the kitten's presence, and G'dath reached the fifty-first floor and the door to his apartment without challenge. He spoke to the door using a specific and special phrase; it decided that G'dath was indeed the tenant of that apartment. A relay turned off the security shielding that kept the apartment from being entered by anyone else.

"Hello, there," came a soft voice behind him.

The Klingon wheeled, startled, but it was only Mr.

Olesky, the old human who had moved into the apartment across the hall a week or so before. G'dath had passed him in the hallway once or twice, and each time Mr. Olesky had greeted him pleasantly. That had surprised G'dath; simple courtesy was not something he encountered every day.

"Is something the matter?" Mr. Olesky asked, genuinely concerned. "Don't tell me you didn't hear me coming—not with that hearing of yours."

G'dath shook his head. "No, I did not hear you. I was . . . thinking." He held his jacket closed more tightly and hoped the kitten didn't make too noticeable a lump.

"Ah," Mr. Olesky said. "Thinking. I had an uncle who thought once. Wrong place, wrong time. Flitter landed right on him while he was doing it. Squashed him flat. Nobody in the family's done any thinking since."

"Truly?"

Olesky's thin lips curved into a crescent. "Joke. Say, are you cold?"

"Cold? Why, no."

"You're holding your jacket closed pretty tight, there."

"Oh. No, I am not cold. This is a—nervous mannerism of mine. It is somewhat analogous to a human, er, twitching."

"No kidding? Really? Well, you learn something new every day. Anyway, reason I'm here—package came for you this morning. I took it for you."

"A package?"

"Yeah. They needed a thumbprint on the delivery receipt, and the doorkeeper's short on thumbs. You expecting something from an outfit called Custom Electronics, over on Third?"

"Why, yes," G'dath said, growing excited. The chip

assembly, at long last! And with perfect timing. "Yes, I am."

"Here it is," Mr. Olesky said, handing a small box to G'dath. The Klingon reached for it, momentarily forgetting the kitten hidden underneath his jacket.

Mr. Olesky watched in fascination. "Hey, was that a squeak?"

"I did not hear anything," G'dath said as he slipped the package into a pocket. "Perhaps the building is settling."

Mr. Olesky nodded his head slowly. "Maybe so. Well, take it easy."

"Good-bye, Mr. Olesky. Thank you for taking receipt of the package for me."

"No huhu."

"Eh?"

"Don't mention it. See you around."

"Certainly. Thank you once more."

G'dath entered his apartment, closed and locked the door behind him with another command, and put the tapes on a table just inside the entrance. The kitten stuck its head out of G'dath's jacket and blinked.

G'dath took the baby cat and placed it carefully on the floor. "There you are, little one." The kitten stood still for a moment, looking around the room. Then it began walking here and there on its thin legs, sniffing in the direction of everything.

G'dath's apartment was small, but a large window gave it an atmosphere of airiness. The Klingon's taste in furniture came directly from his upbringing. He favored pieces of light design fashioned in walnut, with bright, textured fabrics for upholstery. He also had a rug of many stark colors, with red predominating.

Since G'dath was a devout person, there was a *vuv*

gho in a corner of the living room, its iconic center-piece oriented to the north in order to indicate the direction of the Birthplace—or, rather, where the Birthplace would be if this were his home planet and not Earth. The *vuv gho* was the very same one that, by tradition, had been placed by his sleeping mat during the night before his fourth birthday. Thus, the shrine would be the first thing a male youngling would see upon awakening. The *vuv gho* was one of the few items G'dath had been able to take with him when he'd left the Empire.

G'dath went to his computer console and seated himself. The kitten found a place next to his right boot, settled back on its haunches, and watched the Klingon's every move with great interest.

"Computer," G'dath said. And paused. As eager as he was to test the chip, he had assumed a new responsibility which could not be ignored. Quickly, he accessed public library files that explained the fundamentals of kitten care.

G'dath scanned the file and noted his most immediate needs. *A litter box?* he wondered. *What purpose could a box of trash serve—oh, I see. Ah, and there is specially manufactured food for them as well. There are toys available, too—and they have their own medical specialists. I shall need to make the acquaintance of one.*

After committing the essentials to memory, G'dath took a deep breath and consciously forced himself to relax. All his years of painstaking research now hinged on a simple test. As he spoke, he was aware of his quickening pulse. "Computer."

"Working."

"Load integrity routine, final revision."

"Found. Loaded. Ready."

"Stand by."

The door chime sounded.

G'dath leapt to his feet. Two possibilities occurred to him at once: first, that someone had learned about the cat, and second, that someone had learned about his invention. G'dath was not by nature paranoid, but he had heard how the Empire kept close watch on its former citizens. And then a realization struck him, one that made him smile grimly.

Calm yourself. Klingon agents do not ring doorbells.

Still, it could be someone come to evict the cat. He scooped up the unprotesting kitten and deposited it gently on the sleeping mat, then left, ordering the door to close behind him. G'dath put his eye to the small peeper plate set into the front door.

It was Mr. Olesky. G'dath ordered the front door to open. "Yes, Mr. Olesky?" he asked politely. "What may I do for you?"

"Oh, not a thing, not a thing," the old man said. "I just thought you might need this." G'dath looked down and saw that his neighbor was holding out a small freshpack of tuna.

"They like fish, especially tuna," Mr. Olesky said in a low voice, "and I had this on hand. I figured the poor little thing must be pretty hungry, and this'll give you a chance to run out and get some real cat food."

"Er, thank you," G'dath said. "Thank you very much. This is very thoughtful."

"No huhu. Just don't let anybody else in the building see the kitten; you know what'd happen. 'Bye, now." The old man returned to his own apartment.

G'dath remained at the open front door, overwhelmed by Mr. Olesky's thoughtfulness. Kindness always affected him that way, on those rare occasions when he encountered it. He allowed his front door to close after a moment.

The Klingon opened the bedroom door, and the

kitten came bounding out. It jumped on top of the table, landing squarely on the tapes placed there by G'dath, sending the squares spinning and flying. The Klingon picked up the kitten, which regarded him with bright eyes for a moment. It then yawned widely, and the Klingon smiled.

G'dath held the kitten a bit higher and looked more closely. "You are a male," he said, and the kitten squeaked agreement. "Some things in the galaxy do not change very much, do they? All right, Leaper, let us get you fed. A . . . a friend has brought you something good to eat. It will be a fine first meal in your new home."

He took the animal into the kitchen, opened the freshpack, and put the contents into a low dish. Leaving the kitten in the kitchen to enjoy his food, G'dath returned to his console, where the computer patiently awaited his next command.

G'dath retrieved the Custom Electronics package from his pocket and carefully opened it. Inside was precisely what he expected to find—a black plastic chip assembly, six centimeters across, with the merest fleck of gold set precisely in its center. That tiny bit of gold was the chip G'dath had spent several years designing and Custom Electronics had spent several months constructing. The Klingon had sacrificed much for this moment . . . but he knew that the culmination of his dream might now—literally—be within his grasp. Since G'dath was a religious man, he also felt it was beyond coincidence that the chip assembly had arrived today, the day before the WorldNews reporter was coming to interview him at the apartment about his life and work.

He plugged a small lead from the computer into a port on the chip assembly. "Run integrity routine," he ordered. The computer carried the schematics of the chip in nonvolatile memory and would spot any manufacturing defects in it. Given the complexity of the chip, the test would take several hours.

There was nothing to do but wait, and ponder his future. For if the chip functioned as G'dath knew it would, his discovery would revolutionize interstellar travel forever.

Chapter Four

KLOR STOPPED AT the entrance to Keth's quarters and pressed the buzzer, then paused as the door slid open. Keth sat in the dim, unlit room and stared at a holo on his desk of a handsome Klingon female, flanked by two strong sons. As Klor stepped inside, Keth thumbed a control and the holo evaporated.

Disgrace for a warrior, Klor reflected, was a hard thing; contemplating the effects of that disgrace on one's family was harder still. He stood at attention and shifted his weight, uncomfortable at seeing a once-honored warrior reduced to such. "Superior," he said quietly, "you wished to be notified when the subject G'dath received the chip assembly."

Keth's eyes were distant, as if they studied something very far away, but at Klor's words, they snapped into sudden, sharp focus. He leaned forward, arm across his desk. "And what has he done with it?"

"He has programmed it to conduct a self-test which will take some hours, Superior, and he has left the apartment."

Keth swore. They were capable of monitoring G'dath only at his work and dwelling.

"However," Klor added, eager to show his resourcefulness, "I have kept a constant monitor on his financial transactions. He seems to be shopping, at present, Superior. Only moments ago, he purchased several items appropriate to the care and feeding of a cat. I noted that he brought a specimen into his apartment earlier this afternoon."

Keth drew back in surprise and frowned. *"Panthera leo?* In an apartment?"

"No, Superior. I refer to *felis catus."*

Keth made a low noise of disgust. "Better ten tribbles in a household than one of those. I understand they do nothing but eat, sleep and shed fur. But . . ." Keth paused, and the light Klor had seen earlier in his commander's eyes glistened once more. "I understand cats can be used for experimental purposes. Experiments that might involve this mysterious chip assembly. This grows more peculiar by the moment. Have you completed the download of that design yet?"

"It just finished coming in," Klor answered. "Superior, the subject G'dath apparently designed the chip assembly himself. His name appears on the specifications."

"Interesting," Keth mused, and his eyes once again focused on a distant spot beyond Klor's shoulder. "So our theoretician is capable of doing more than dreaming dreams—he has some facility with the practical side of things as well. Very surprising." He looked back at Klor. "Is there any hint in his notes as to the purpose of the chip assembly?"

"None, Superior. The design notes with the file do not address the point, and the function of the completed chip assembly cannot be inferred by our computer. Also, it appears that a significant portion of the design is missing—perhaps due to an error in data storage."

Keth shrugged and leaned back in his chair. "No

matter. Perhaps we will learn more at the conclusion of this test. Call me if he constructs anything with the chip assembly."

Then he did something that Klor had never, in the dreary months of their service together, seen him do—he smiled, brilliantly, astonishingly.

And Klor returned the smile, understanding that his commander was in the throes of strategic inspiration—an inspiration that boded well for them both, but ill for the subject G'dath.

At fifteen seconds before fourteen hundred hours in San Francisco, Kirk entered Admiral Nogura's reception area and was greeted by one of his yeomen, a young Vulcan male. "Good afternoon, Admiral Kirk," the ensign said, rising quickly. "This way, please. The admiral will see you immediately."

The yeoman escorted Kirk across the waiting area to a heavy oak door marked PRIVATE in neat gold lettering and knocked softly just under the word, noting that it made a satisfying sound.

"Come," Nogura called. The door slid open, and Kirk walked in.

The head of Starfleet stood at his office bar, which was usually hidden behind a copy of a world map drawn in the sixteenth century by a cartographer with more imagination than fact at his disposal. Though there was a servitor, the admiral was pouring drinks by hand, from a flask that to Kirk's eye looked as ancient as Nogura himself. He glanced up and smiled as Kirk neared.

"I know it's early, but I thought that you might not mind celebrating a successful launch." Nogura handed him a generous snifterfull of dark amber liquid. "After the frustration we had this morning with the rain, I think we deserve a drink. Your favorite, if I'm not mistaken."

Kirk lowered his face over the snifter's crystal bowl and smiled at the familiar heady fragrance. "Saurian brandy. Sir, this isn't exactly cheap—or easy to get hold of."

"I know." Nogura's smile took on an air of good-humored mystery as he poured himself a glass. "That's why I'm having one myself. Have a seat, Jim. Over there." He nodded at the informal conference area in the corner nearest the window, which showed the same view of the Golden Gate that Kirk enjoyed, since the commanding admiral's office was located directly above his.

At Nogura's insistence, Kirk took the seat directly facing the view. Despite his genuine appreciation of the brandy, he felt on his guard; instinct—and some subtle hint in Nogura's tone when he'd requested the meeting—told him that the old admiral had not called him here for a congratulatory drink.

Nogura sat beside him. "That bridge is truly beautiful," he said fondly. "I've always loved it—there's nothing else quite like it anywhere. Did you know I was part American, Jim?" He lifted the snifter to his lips and sipped.

"No, sir, I didn't."

"I am. My three-times-great-grandfather was from this very city, as a matter of fact. He was born here in the twenty-twenties, according to the family records. My people had been in California for five generations by then.

"Great-great-great-grandfather was one of those who went back to Japan after the Greater Quake, when Tokyo opened its doors to American refugees of Japanese ancestry—that was before discrimination in immigration policy was banned, of course. I still have blood relatives here in the city, however, including more than a few great-great-great-grandnieces and -nephews."

Kirk shifted in his chair. After this morning's frustration, he was unwilling to patiently listen to small talk—and he was curious to know Nogura's hidden agenda. For the past few hours, he'd been trying to guess what it could be, without success. Kirk could only deduce two things: one, that it involved him, and two, that it was something he was not going to like. The brandy confirmed his second suspicion.

"With all due respect, sir," he said. "You didn't call me here just to celebrate the launch."

Nogura's gaze lowered to his snifter before he looked over at Kirk. "You know me too well, Jim. There *is* a problem." He paused, gathering his thoughts, then turned to face Kirk directly. "Did you see Timothea Rogers on the trivision this morning?"

"Yes."

"What did you think?"

Kirk hesitated, then decided against editing his first response. "She was awful."

"That is precisely the word I had in mind," said Nogura, nodding slowly. He sipped his drink, letting the silence grow.

"Jim," he continued after a moment, "when public relations in Starfleet was no more than a simple matter of mailing holos of starships to schoolchildren, Rogers did well. Now, though, the political situation is such that I need someone out there who doesn't appear on trivision as—as a cold fish. The political forces arrayed against us are making a good case for themselves. Starfleet doesn't do nearly so well."

"So you want me to do the job for you."

"Correct."

"I won't leave Operations," Kirk said quietly, but inwardly he felt the first stirrings of anger. He'd made it clear from the very beginning, from the day he agreed to give up the *Enterprise* the first time, that he would not be pushed into a bureaucratic post. Sure,

Operations required some degree of paper pushing, but it also allowed him to be near ships. Near the *Enterprise.*

Nogura eyed him with a birdlike tilt of his head. "Really? It seemed to me you could use a change."

"I had one eight months ago. I don't need another." He took a careful sip of his brandy, working to keep the anger from showing, yet sure all the while Nogura knew it was there.

"I see." The old admiral pondered this. "Have you spoken with Lori yet today?"

"No. Why?"

"No reason. Jim, I'm not asking you to drop your current job. You'll remain Chief of Operations. I'm just asking you to wear a second hat. Chief MacPherson can take over the day-to-day work on the refit of *Endeavor.* Your organization is in place, correct? Used to its job, morale high, skills sharp?"

"Yes, sir, but—"

"Hear me, Jim. No more rebuilding individual ships for you. I want you to go public for Starfleet and help me rebuild them *all.*" Nogura gestured expansively with his glass. "I want you to tell people about us. They'll listen to you. You are, after all, a hero."

"A hero? Admiral, excuse me, but where in hell did you get that idea?"

"You're a hero," Nogura said flatly. "Genuinely. Your mission was the stuff of epics. People became very excited about it. They're *still* excited about it." The admiral shrugged. "Regardless of whether you believe you're a hero or not, Jim, I need whatever it is you are. You know we have political problems. Rogers isn't helping to solve them; in fact, she's been responsible for causing some and making others worse."

"Agreed," Kirk said. "But I'm not the person for the job."

"You are." Nogura touched a button on the conference table, and a life-sized three-dimensional image formed in the opposite corner.

Jim blinked, surprised to find himself looking at Captain Kirk; the handsome, confident figure in the now-obsolete gold command shirt was talking, though there was no sound since Nogura had not activated it. "Why, that's me. What's this from, Admiral?"

"Your first formal post-mission media briefing, the day after you brought the *Enterprise* home. Remember that?"

Kirk grimaced. "Like the Christians remember the lions. I kept wanting to raise my shields and get the hell out of there."

"Indeed?" Nogura gestured at the hologram. "I know you were nearing your inner limits. In fact, when you went on your post-mission six-month furlough, I was afraid I wasn't going to get you back. The scars don't show, do they?"

Kirk continued to watch himself perform for the reporters. *Where was this thing held, anyway?* he wondered. *Here at the Admiralty, or at Spacedock? I just can't remember. Certainly not aboard ship.*

"Look at yourself, Jim," Nogura continued. "You're a natural with the press. You were still in command, answering all the questions and getting the reporters to like you—which they did. The coverage we received was very favorable, and that coverage turned out to be very important to us. The successful completion of your five-year mission was the primary topic of conversation at every Federation political dinner for weeks afterward.

"What I want you to do is make a number of public appearances on behalf of Starfleet. Explain to people what we do, and what we want to do in the years ahead. I want you to correct any misperception that we're a force for aggression. Tell people the truth: that we're the best chance for peace there is, because our mission is not to wage war, but to explore new worlds and open them to colonization or friendship."

Nogura fell silent; for a time, neither spoke as they watched the captain's image. And then Kirk said:

"I've seen enough."

Nogura pressed the button; the image vanished.

"There must be someone else, Admiral," Kirk said. "Someone who can do a better job than—"

"No," Nogura said emphatically. "I've thought this through. I need *you* to do it, Jim."

The steel in his tone reminded Kirk of an earlier conversation: the time the admiral had wanted Jim to accept a promotion to the admiralty. Jim had threatened to resign if the *Enterprise* was taken from him—he'd been that confident that Nogura would never call his bluff.

But the old man wasn't one to be outmaneuvered; he'd made up his mind.

God knows, Nogura had said, *I don't want you to resign if I can help it. But I can't stop you from leaving the service.*

And Nogura had made up his mind now.

Jim drew in a breath. "I'll do it. On one condition. That this new—assignment—is temporary, until you find someone permanent. I want to go back to refitting ships as soon as possible, Admiral."

Something in Nogura's features eased. "Of course, Jim. Of course. I thought that was understood. And . . . thank you. I know you hate this sort of thing, good as you are at it."

"I'll try not to let it show. When do I start?"

"Tomorrow morning," Nogura said. "I've arranged for you to be a guest on the 'WorldNews Saturday' interview program."

"You were that sure of me?" Kirk's lips twisted in a rueful little smile, but his tone was cool.

A temporary assignment, he reassured himself afterward, as he left the admiral's office. Only temporary, and then he would have—if not the *Enterprise,* other ships to refit. He had Nogura's word on it.

But he could not help wondering if that other Kirk—the younger, confident-looking one dressed in command gold—would have believed it for an instant.

Kirk had no role to play in the flight of the *Enterprise*'s command section, but he was vitally interested in its outcome. He arrived back in his office to find Riley standing in front of the trivision. WorldNews was showing archival footage of the *Enterprise* returning from her five-year mission, but Riley wasn't watching; his face was turned toward the window, and the view of the bridge.

"Cleared into a beautiful day, didn't it?" Kirk asked.

Riley turned with a start. "Admiral. Sorry, sir, I didn't hear you come in. I just thought you might want to see what the *Enterprise* was up to."

"Not the WorldNews feed. Put on our own closed-circuit feed instead, and let's have mission audio with it. I'd like to listen to the rendezvous traffic, but let's keep it down."

"Yes, sir." Riley selected the in-house feed with the trivision controls recessed into the surface of Kirk's desk. The commander then seated himself across the room as the admiral took his own chair.

Both men watched silently as remotely controlled trivision scanners mounted on Spacedock Four picked up the oncoming saucer. The scene was set against the brilliantly lighted Earth, its bright clouds modestly hiding the planetary geography behind a veil of vapor. The gentle and, to Kirk's ear, comforting chatter of mission audio occupied the auditory background. Kirk easily recognized Uhura's voice among all the others.

"God, this is a beautiful shot," Kirk said. "Window, go opaque."

The window behind Kirk turned completely black, shutting out all daylight. The trivision picture was solid and without interference. It seemed to Kirk as if he were hanging in space, sitting in a comfortable chair. He watched as the saucer slowly came toward him, rising. He felt as if he could reach out and touch it.

"Where's Spacedock Four now?" Kirk asked.

Riley rolled his eyes upward and did some figures in his head. "Near enough thirty-six degrees east, seven degrees south—right over central Tanzania, more or less."

Spacedock Four was not much more than a lattice of metal open to space. It was just wide and deep enough to service a cruiser-class starship. It rode a low orbit that skipped back and forth across the equator by as much as ten degrees of latitude. Its much bigger brother, the main Spacedock, bore no number and was an enormous enclosed facility in a much higher, geosynchronous orbit above the Atlantic Ocean.

As big as the main Spacedock was, it was always terribly crowded and busy. In contrast, the *Enterprise* could have Spacedock Four all to herself for as long as her renovation might take. There would be no pressure to get the *Enterprise* finished just because some other ship needed the dock space.

Captain Decker watched Spacedock Four grow in the main screen. The saucer was approaching it from below and to the rear. He could see the *Enterprise*'s engineering section floating serenely in the center of the lattice. The section was being held steady relative to the spacedock frame by a series of tractor-pressor beams set against its hull.

The last time Decker had been here, the new warp drivers had not yet been attached to the engine pylons. The engineering section had looked to him like a big white yam with three tuber sprouts sticking out of it at awkward angles. It had, truth to tell, been a rather disheartening sight. Now, with the drivers on, the engineering section looked less like a yam and more like part of a ship, although there were still large patches of the hull that hadn't yet been covered with trititanium plating.

Decker's job today was to put the last big piece of a very intricate puzzle into place, and to do it right the first time. The saucer would overtake Spacedock Four, pass it, and then back its way in so that it could be seated precisely on the main pylon by skilled gangs wielding portable tractor-pressor equipment. The complicated inbound maneuver was designed to avoid damage to the warp drivers, which rode aft of the neck and a bit higher than the saucer.

As the saucer passed Spacedock Four, one of the blank screens on Sulu's board suddenly came alive with a red, boxlike design. It blinked steadily, pulsing like a heartbeat; crosshairs in the center of the display wavered.

"Rendezvous cue on my board, Captain," Sulu reported. "Shall I begin alignment maneuvers?"

"Go ahead, Commander," Decker said.

"Navigation controls slaved to helm," DiFalco reported. "All yours, Sulu."

"Thanks, Suzanne," Sulu replied. He got busy, and the crosshairs in the rendezvous cue soon stopped wavering. The cue would guide Sulu into Spacedock Four, and it would allow him to position the saucer correctly above the neck of the main pylon in a close approximation of the precise mating position. Once all that had been done, Sulu would lock his board. The tractor-pressor gangs would then take over and pull the saucer down the rest of the way, using their push-and-pull beams to make the final, painstaking corrections that would seat the saucer correctly. If they bumped or missed, the damage to the saucer and the pylon could be considerable.

"Forward motion stopped," Sulu reported. "Orientation along x and y axes is right on the money. Minus sixteen meters on z axis, correcting." Sulu's fingers danced for a moment on her controls. The rendezvous cue then held steady and Sulu said, "We're lined up, Captain."

"Back her in, Mr. Sulu."

"Aye, sir. Closing with forward end of Spacedock Four, ten meters per second."

"Let's take a look."

"Rear view, Captain," Sulu answered. "Magnification one."

The yawning mouth of the spacedock appeared and grew steadily larger on the viewer as the saucer approached. Decker could see the worksuited teepee gangs at their posts here and there on the lattice of the spacedock, well out of the way of the saucer's path and ready to take over.

"Uhura, please get me the engineering section," Decker requested. "I want to talk to Mr. Scott." There was a brief pause, and then the chief engineer's familiar burr came over the bridge's speakers. "Aye, Cap'n? Scott here."

"We'll be in shortly, Scotty. Status on your end?"

Decker could almost see Scott shrug. "Nothing much to do now. We're all ready for the coupling. The tractor-pressor gangs are holdin' us as steady as the flow o' the river Clyde. All I can do is worry about how the gangs pull off the placement. Wish I was doin' it myself; we'll nae get a second chance there."

"We won't need more than one shot at it, Mr. Scott," said Decker. "I'm now having Uhura establish an open line between you and us."

"Aye, Captain. Scott out."

"Captain," Sulu said, "we're now entering Spacedock Four. Extrapolation shows us still within lateral tolerance for docking. I'm slowing us to eight meters per second."

"Very good," Decker said. He watched the viewer intently. The delicate-looking metalwork of the spacedock began rolling past them slowly. *Enterprise*'s engineering section floated in the center of the screen. Decker could see the tractor-pressor gangs tracking the saucer with their gunlike equipment, waiting for the word from their chief to take over.

"Five meters per second, Captain," Sulu said. "Range to docking, two hundred meters."

"Uhura, please get me the tractor chief," Decker said, and almost instantly there came a rough voice. "Welcome to Spacedock Four, Captain Decker. Head ganger here. Name's Billingsgate."

"Hello, Chief," Decker answered. "Ready to dance?"

"Just name the tune, Captain."

"Stand by, then. Mr. Sulu, distance to docking?"

"One hundred fifty-five meters."

"Bring us to a dead stop at fifty meters. Chief Billingsgate, you'll have us at your mercy in twenty seconds."

"Awaiting your word, Captain. Don't worry, we'll treat her kindly."

"You'd better, Billy," came Scotty's voice, "or I'll have your—"

"Quiet, all," ordered Decker. "Status, Mr. Sulu?"

"Speed steady at five meters per second, Captain. Distance now eighty meters."

There was a pause.

"Fifty meters, Captain," Sulu reported. "All stop."

"Take it, Billingsgate," Decker said.

There was a slight jar as the tractor-pressor gangs hit the saucer simultaneously at many points with their force beams. Then there came a sudden, loud *whap!* and a sharp, jarring shift to starboard.

"Dammit, crew six," came Billingsgate's voice, "you're two percent above nominal! Ease it down *now!* Crew three, boost two percent to correct, and cut to nominal at my signal." There was another *whap!* and a shift, this time to port.

"Cut!" the head ganger said. "That's got her, people. Great, great. Just super. Okay, she's steady and holding. Ease her on in, now. Crew one, start pushing as per program. Easy, *real* easy!"

"Helm, give us a front view, please," Decker said more calmly than he felt.

The scene changed to show the front end of the spacedock. Decker could see a gang of six handlers—undoubtedly crew number one—floating in the center of the spacedock around a large tractor-pressor assembly. The equipment, which had been quickly brought into position by its crew after the saucer had passed by, was being held steady by smaller beams aimed at it from the spacedock frame.

"Rear view again, please," Decker ordered.

"Rear view, sir," Sulu answered.

The scene shifted to show the forward ends of the *Enterprise*'s warp drivers filling the screen. They were huge—so much so that not very much of the spacedock could be seen beyond them.

Sulu consulted his board. "We're close now, Captain. Seconds only."

Billingsgate's voice came again. "Very good, people. Very good. Ease her on down, seven. Eight, watch that drop rate. One, stop pushing. Six, pull her even with the neck. All right, seven and eight, let her down now. Easy, easy."

There was a bump as gentle as the kiss of an Irish wind.

"Docked, Captain," Sulu reported.

"Mr. Scott!" Decker called. "Latch on!"

There was a quick series of heavy *thunks* from somewhere down below. Decker felt the vibration through his command chair.

"Latched, Captain," Scotty said. "I show all green here. I also show full environmental integrity at the dockin' interface."

"All green at this end, too, Captain," Sulu said.

"All of the saucer's environmental functions have been transferred to Engineering, Captain," DiFalco reported. "No appreciable delay in transfer. Saucer-resident functions are now on standby."

"Tractor-pressor gangs powering down," Billingsgate called. "You're being held in place by spacedock systems now, *Enterprise*. It's been a pleasure doing business with you."

"Same here," Decker said. "Thank you, Chief."

Just then, the bridge turbolift doors slid open and onto the bridge stepped Montgomery Scott. Decker swung his chair to face him. The chief engineer was smiling broadly.

"Just thought I'd be the first to welcome ye official-ly, Captain," he said brightly. "Besides, I had to check the functionin' o' the turbolift, now, did I not?"

"That you did, Mr. Scott," Decker said, rising, "and thank you for the welcome." He held out his hand, and Scotty shook it. It was only then that Decker relaxed, heaving a very audible sigh of relief—a sigh that was echoed by the others on the bridge, and one that was soon lost in laughter, cheering and no small amount of applause.

Kirk felt his gut begin to unclench. He watched closely as the trivision scanners showed the reunited *Enterprise* serenely maintaining station in the center of the spacedock. Everything seemed to be fine. *Nice, Will, very nice,* Kirk thought. *Couldn't have done better myself.*

He turned his attention back to the data display screen set into the surface of his desk. True to his word, Nogura had quickly supplied him with the details of what he would need to know for his appearance the next morning on the WorldNews interview show. The only thing Nogura had not supplied him with was the desire to do the show in the first place.

From what he could see, the Dart Project seemed to be going well. It was close to schedule and still under budget, although not by very much. Despite the rather high cost, Kirk felt that Nogura had been right about funding the project. It was certainly a worthy cause, and it would secure a great deal of friendly media coverage. He read on, the datascreen scrolling automatically as his eyes scanned the displayed text and graphics.

Kirk saw that a captain named Alice Friedman had been tapped as pilot of the dart. He noted that she had been asked by Nogura to appear on the show with Kirk but had begged off, claiming a very tight preflight schedule. Well, Kirk could understand and appreciate her problem—he'd been stuck behind the eight ball of a deadline once or twice himself.

He studied Friedman's photograph, and thought he saw a determined strength in her features.

"Riley?" Kirk called.

The office door opened, and Riley stuck his head in. "Right here, Admiral."

"I'm going to head home early. Anything pending?"

"No, sir, the board's clear. What time should I meet you at the studio?"

"The show starts at nine hundred hours, so an hour before that should do it."

"Got it. See you then. Good night, Admiral." The door closed.

Kirk ordered his datascreen to copy the Dart Project files to tape and then he dropped the squares into his briefcase. As he did so, it struck him that the briefcase was probably his most ridiculous possession. It was, in its way, a reminder of what Kirk had once been by helping to define what he was now. No other object could have symbolized his change of status so well. He had once sworn that he'd never condescend to own a briefcase. Well, he'd been wrong about that. He recalled the other Kirk he'd seen in Nogura's office, the Kirk who wore command gold. *I wish all those people who think I'm a hero could see me lugging this thing around. Since when do heroes carry briefcases home from work, Heihachiro?*

Chapter Five

In the Siegels' cheery yellow bathroom, Ricia watched as Carlos applied the sonic stimulator to Joey's throbbing lower lip. By the time they'd gotten to the apartment, Joey's lip was swollen tight and felt ten times its normal size. But a glance in the long mirrored wall above the counter revealed otherwise— the lip was only swollen to twice its size, and taking on a deep purplish-red hue. He looked like a wild man, all right. There were red-brown smudges of blood from the corner of his mouth to either cheek, and his auburn hair was a tousled mess. Not to mention the thumbnail-sized splotch of blood on the front of his tunic.

Joey closed his eyes and groaned.

"This shouldn't hurt." Carlos drew the stimulator away; it hummed softly in his hand.

"It's not that," Joey lisped, tasting blood. The sonic stimulator felt warm and sort of prickly, the pins-and-needles feeling of a limb waking up. "It's just—if my mom sees me like this—"

"She won't. Relax," Carlos said with quiet firmness, and carefully lowered the stimulator until it hovered a centimeter above Joey's lip. Carlos didn't look so great himself: There were streaks of dried blood on his nose and upper lip. The nose itself was swollen, and the normally dark olive skin surrounding it had turned purple-gray. Still, his black eyes were serene, the eyes of someone much older. Carlos didn't seem mad at Stoller. In fact, neither he nor Ricia had so much as mentioned Ira's name on the slidewalk ride to the apartment. Carlos was calm and steady as a Vulcan—only somehow warmer. *He'll be a doctor, like his dad,* Joey thought, watching the older boy's dexterity with the stimulator.

On Joey's other side, Ricia bent over, palms resting just above her knees, and inspected the lip more closely. "The swelling's starting to go down," she announced. Joey had never noticed before that she was nice-looking, with flawless creamy brown skin, and dark eyes framed by long lashes.

Joey probed the lip gingerly with his tongue. "It *is* starting to hurt less."

"Great." Carlos pressed a control, and the humming increased. "It won't take long now."

Ricia straightened. "So, Joey. What are you doing hanging around with someone like Stoller?"

Carlos's tone was mildly reproving. "Ricia, that's *his* business. Besides, we should be thanking him for helping us."

Her directness took Joey aback. "It's not that we're friends, really," he answered. It was getting easier to talk. "I just sit next to him, is all." Which was the truth. And after what had happened today, he was pretty sure he didn't like Stoller very much.

"Well, good, cause he's trouble." Ricia paused. "You said Dr. G'dath was going to put you on probation if you didn't improve—but it seems to me you must be pretty smart if they let you into the class at your age."

83

"You make thirteen sound like a disease," Carlos said, sotto voce, his eyes on his work.

Ricia lifted a coal-colored brow and gave him a look of disgust that was tempered by affection. "You know what I mean. *I'd* be pretty impressed with myself if I managed to get into the class two years early." She looked down at Joey. "The material's not too difficult for you, is it?"

Joey's whole face went warm, as if Carlos had passed over it with the stimulator, and he knew Ricia could see him blushing. Her question made him angry and defensive, and at first he was going to tell her to mind her own business, but her manner was so straightforward and concerned that he answered, "No."

Joey glanced down, and Carlos said, "Hey, hold your head up, okay?"

Joey raised his head and sighed, then said, without looking at Ricia: "It's not the material. I just . . . don't feel like doing any work." He glanced up at her, careful not to move his head. "It's summer, you know? I just got out of school. I should be on vacation."

"Hmph." Ricia folded her arms in front of her chest and leaned against the wall. "I suppose that's a reason." But her eyes had narrowed, and Joey knew she didn't believe it for a minute.

"And Dr. G'dath doesn't like me, anyway," he said heatedly.

"What makes you say that?" Ricia tilted her head and frowned, curious.

"'Cause he's a Klingon. Isn't that *enough?* Besides, the way he treats us . . . it makes me nervous, the way he makes us stand up and recite in class. Half the time I forget what I want to say. He tries to scare us—and you saw how he acted when I asked him to repeat a question."

"Hold still, Joey," Carlos ordered. "Almost done."

Joey held still.

Ricia rolled her eyes at the ceiling and sighed. "Brickner, you've got a brain. Why don't you use it? That's G'dath's *way*. He was raised as a Klingon. When I found out I was accepted into the class, I read up on their culture. Sure, G'dath has been living here for a year, but he's still going to be influenced by his Klingon upbringing. Everybody's thinking, whether they like it or not, is influenced by their culture. We all have certain unspoken cultural beliefs we're not even aware of most of the time—and G'dath's no different. Though he's more conscious of his than most."

"Ambassador Ricia," Carlos said softly, but Ricia ignored him.

"Don't you see," she continued, "he's not trying to scare us. He's trying to teach us not to be scared."

"Well, he sure has a weird way of doing it," Joey said.

"Not weird. Just Klingon. A lot of it's based on honor, personal pride—he won't make things easy for us, so we can learn more from the experience. Coddling a person is the ultimate insult. Challenging a person is the greatest compliment."

"He thinks he's doing us a favor by being so tough on us?"

"Don't sound so skeptical. But yes. Now that I know he notified your mom yesterday that you were on the verge of probation, I understand why he asked you the first question today. A Klingon student in the same situation would have been ready and waiting for that first question. He was giving you a chance to redeem your honor. And was probably surprised you didn't expect it."

"All done," Carlos announced, and Joey realized that the humming had stopped. He turned and studied his reflection in the mirror. The lip was back to normal size. He ran his tongue along the inside; there was only a tiny bump where the cut had been. It didn't hurt at all. He grinned up at Carlos. "Hey, great! Thanks!"

"No charge." Carlos smiled shyly. "After all, you came to our rescue. Oh, hey—" He glanced down at himself. "I better get these started in the recycler before Dad gets home." He pulled off his tunic, then waited till Joey—who was a little chagrined about undressing in Ricia's presence—handed over his. "This'll only take a minute."

"Okay," Ricia called after him as he hurried from the room, "but then *I* get to do your nose."

"Is his mom at work, too?" Joey asked. He stood up and pulled a hot, moist towel from the dispenser, then started wiping his dirty face.

"No." Ricia still leaned against the wall, her head turned in the direction Carlos had gone. "She died a couple of years ago."

"Oh," Joey said. For the first time in months, he suddenly felt like telling someone about Jase. "I kinda understand how he feels."

Ricia turned her head to look at him. "Did you lose a parent?"

Joey shook his head. "My kid brother. About six months ago."

"I'm sorry." For once, Ricia's tone was subdued. "I guess I've been lucky."

Joey flushed again. He didn't want pity, just wanted —for some reason he couldn't understand—for someone to know about Jase. They stood in awkward silence for a moment. The mention of his mother made Joey remember how she'd looked last night, when she'd told him about G'dath's message—near tears, and this time it was Joey who'd made her cry.

And that damn turtlehead.

Then he thought of Ira Stoller's joke. Maybe it would help lighten the mood.

He took a deep breath. "Hey, did you hear the one about Tarzan and Jane?"

Ricia blinked. "What?"

"If Tarzan and Jane were Klingons"—he didn't say turtlehead because she'd yelled at Stoller for saying it—"what would Cheetah be?"

Her expression hardened. "I don't want to hear this, Brickner."

Too late to stop now—and Joey honestly thought she'd laugh. "A gifted child," he said, and giggled.

But Ricia didn't laugh, didn't smile, just stared steadily at him, then said, very slowly: "If Tarzan and Jane were Klingons, what would Cheetah be?"

"I just told you."

"This is *my* joke, and the answer's different. Come on, Brickner. If Tarzan and Jane were Klingons, what would Cheetah be?"

"I give."

Ricia was still looking intently at him, still not smiling. "A Brickner."

"Hey," Joey said, "that's not funny."

"You're right. And neither is your version." Ricia sighed, and her posture relaxed. "Joey, don't you understand—the only reason anyone tries to insult an entire race is because they're afraid, or so insecure they need to degrade someone else in order to feel better, like they're worth something. Stoller calls G'dath a turtlehead because he's angry and has emotional problems, and picking on someone else draws attention away from his troubles. But you seem too smart for that."

"It was just a crummy joke." Joey threw the towel on the counter. "If I want a lecture, I'll go to class." He was oddly embarrassed, almost as embarrassed as

87

G'dath had made him feel today in class, and he was sorry he'd confided in Ricia about Jase.

"Look, don't get mad—"

He stomped out into the hallway and almost smacked into Carlos, who had put on his tunic and held out Joey's warm, clean one. Joey snatched it and tugged it over his head.

"Hey, Joey, you leaving already?"

"Yeah," Joey said shortly. "Thanks for everything."

Ricia had followed. Carlos frowned at her, his dark, heavy brows almost touching above his swollen nose. "Ricia? What did you say?"

"I really do have to go," Joey said. "My mom's gonna be getting home in an hour or so."

"Look, Joey," Ricia told him, "before you leave, I think you should know, G'dath's going to give you just one more chance to redeem yourself. If I were you, I'd be ready for it."

"I will." He headed for the exit as Ricia and Carlos followed.

"Good." She stepped in front of the door, barring his way. "Because the second challenge must be more difficult than the first. Knowing G'dath, my guess is he'll do it during the live trivision spot. Better get over those nerves."

"If you want to study with me and Ricia, just call. I'm in central listing," Carlos offered.

"Uh . . . thanks. I'll think about it." Joey pushed past Ricia and out the door.

The slidewalk home was pure agony.

He had forced himself not to react to Ricia's statement about the live trivision spot. He'd figured the WorldNews people would show G'dath lecturing or something—but it hadn't occurred to him that they'd show G'dath questioning students. And if what Ricia said was true, G'dath would call on him *first*.

Answering a question in front of the class was reason enough to be nervous.

Answering a question in front of the class for Dr. G'dath was reason to be doubly nervous.

Answering a question in front of the class for Dr. G'dath *on live trivision* was reason enough to die.

Cheer up, Brickner! You've got a whole weekend to write a paper—and *learn the assigned material backwards and forwards. And get over your nerves. Just think: your mom will probably be watching . . .*

By the time he made it home, Joey found himself wishing that Ira Stoller had simply killed him.

Kirk arrived home only to be surprised by the sound of Lori's footsteps back in the bedroom. It was unheard of for his wife to leave work early—almost as unheard as it was for him. He set his briefcase on the living room table and headed for the bedroom.

In the hallway, he hesitated. He wasn't superstitious, but he'd somehow known in his bones that today wouldn't be a good day. And he'd been right so far. There'd been the rain, then losing the *Enterprise* (of course, he'd known that would happen, so the premonition didn't count in this instance), then Nogura's insistence on the public relations job. And now he found himself not wanting to go back into the bedroom. He listened to the sound of Lori's movements, trying to gauge her mood: short, rapid steps, then a pause, then more quick steps.

Not good.

She hadn't been happy for months. He knew it, and did not know what to do. He suspected it had something to do with her missing out on the diplomatic post she had wanted so badly. Like him, she was enormously ambitious, and he knew Nogura's decision had crushed her. He also knew she'd been counting on him to help her get that post and he felt vaguely responsible for her disappointment.

Because she was so like him, he gave her what he would have wanted had their positions been reversed: room to nurse her wounds. He did not question her about it, gave her all the privacy she wanted.

She seemed to want a good deal of privacy these days.

Still, he'd waited patiently for her to recover. She was like him, after all, and that was what he would have done. Been furious at Nogura for a month or so, then set his sights on something new.

Only Lori hadn't gotten over it. Her silent unhappiness had grown to the point where he had given up. He would have welcomed a display of anger, of her old temper, anything but this distant, civil coldness. It had gone on long enough for him to realize that it had to do with more than just Nogura. It had to do with him, too.

Kirk stepped into the bedroom doorway. Lori glanced up, startled, silver and gold hair swinging, her lips parted slightly. On the bed sat two large suitcases, open and full of most of the contents of her closet.

On one level, he was surprised; on another, not at all.

"You're home early," she said, wide-eyed. For a second he thought if he took one step closer, she would bolt like a wild, frightened thing. And then she gathered herself and squared her shoulders as if steeling herself for a fight.

"Great minds think alike," Jim answered. It seemed a stupid thing to say, but then the situation was absurd. He stood and watched her pack. "Lori—"

"I'm leaving." Her eyes focused on the garment she was jamming into the overfull suitcase. "I guess that's pretty obvious. I've needed to do a little p.r. of my own, touring the new human settlements. I've been thinking about it for some time."

"Nogura told you."

She straightened and swiveled her head to look at him. "Told me what?"

"About the public relations job he gave me." Jim felt numb; ridiculous, to stand here making small talk. She couldn't be leaving. Not this suddenly, this casually.

The corner of her mouth quirked—in irritation, Jim thought—as she registered what he'd said. "Yes. Nogura told me. Seems we don't do much direct communicating these days." She returned to her packing and did not look at him. "I'll be gone for two, maybe three months."

A few months. Then she really wasn't leaving.

"I don't know if I'll be back."

His face hardened. He'd been patient with her—and she'd interpreted it as unfeeling distance. Maybe she was right; maybe he'd lost himself, been obsessed with the *Enterprise* refit, then launch. But he loved Lori, and he wasn't going to let her go easily.

"If I've failed you," he said calmly, "if I've done something to make you unhappy, I want to know. I love you, Lori. I don't want to lose you."

She turned her body and faced him; he saw pain flicker across her features. "We're not happy together, Jim. Neither of us. Maybe I'm just first to see it."

"I'm happy." But the words sounded false.

She shook her head. He crossed the room and moved to embrace her, but she kept shaking her head and caught his hands in hers. "No, you're not. And I'm not. Jim, we had a great affair. But we should never have married."

"I don't understand," he tried to say, but she raised a finger to his lips.

"Neither of us is where we should be. I *want* that

91

diplomatic post, and dammit, I'm going to figure out a way to get it, Nogura be damned. And you . . ." Her voice began to shake, and she drew in a breath to steady it.

"Nogura promised me the public relations assignment would be temporary," Jim said. "And then I can go back to what I want to do—refitting ships."

She gave a small, ironic smile. "You've been lying to yourself too long. That's not what you want to do, love. You want a starship . . ."

"I had one. And now she's Will Decker's."

". . . to command."

He released a sound of disbelief, not quite a laugh. "Lori, we both know that's impossible."

"The man I fell in love with didn't think so." She pulled away from him. "I should never have taken you away from the *Enterprise*, Jim, should never have overridden McCoy's recommendation and created the troubleshooter position.

"You had nothing to do with it," Jim said shortly. "The troubleshooter position at least gave me some exciting, worthwhile work to do. Nogura gave me no choice, remember? Accept a promotion to the admiralty, or resign. He made that clear enough."

She turned her head sharply and searched his face. "Have you ever thought, just once, what might have happened if you called Nogura's bluff?"

"I'd be a commercial pilot," Jim said. *"Then* I'd be in the wrong place."

"But have you ever actually done it, Jim? Have you ever called his bluff?"

Jim didn't answer. In a way, her question angered him. He did not believe in regretting past decisions, in bemoaning lost chances, or in worrying about what might have been. Yet there had been one or two nights when he'd awakened with Lori asleep beside him, and wondered . . .

Lori's voice dropped to a whisper. "I did. Today, for the very first time. And you know what? The old man *backed down.*" Then, more loudly: "He's been using us all along, Jim. Using *you*. Can't you see it?"

For a time, they were silent. Lori stuffed the last item into a suitcase, secured both, and switched on the antigravs.

"I can't change the past," Jim said finally. "I'm not sure I'd want to if I could. I'm more concerned with the present . . . and the future. Our future. Lori, is there anything I can do or say to convince you to stay?"

She shook her head, and he could see from her face that he'd already lost her. "No, love. I have to think things over for a while. If I stay, I'll just make both of us miserable." She squared her shoulders again, in the gesture that had become so familiar to him. "I'm heading for the transporter stage at the Admiralty. *Kongo* leaves orbit in six hours, and I might as well beam aboard and get settled. I've given the computer my itinerary and instructions on dealing with my mail and calls.

"Maybe I'll be back. We'll talk soon." She touched his cheek, and he pulled her to him. They embraced— more the sad, warm embrace of old friends than lovers—and Lori spoke softly into his ear.

"Just promise me one thing."

He tried to smile into her hair. "What's that?"

She drew back and looked up at him. When they first had met, her gaze had possessed an electric intensity that the past eight months had dimmed; he saw a spark of it now. "Get a ship again. It's what you want most, Jim. More than anything else. More than me."

He did not let himself react. She was hurting, he told himself, and had projected that hurt onto him. She could not deal with losing the chance for an ambassadorship, and so had decided that he could not deal with losing a ship. There was no point in arguing with her now.

Jim let her go. She picked up the suitcases and headed out quickly, so he could not see her face. He did not follow her out, but stood in the bedroom and listened to the sound of the apartment door as it closed behind her.

A little after twenty-one o'clock, G'dath returned to his apartment loaded down with packages. Leaper emerged from under the living room couch. Dancing around G'dath, he made clear his all-consuming interest in the bags and boxes the Klingon had brought home with him.

"I will give you your things in a while, Leaper," G'dath said. He put the packages down. "First, though, I need to see how the test of my chip assembly is proceeding."

The kitten ignored G'dath and continued to sniff and paw at the packages.

"Later, little one," the Klingon said patiently.

The kitten began to worry at the band around the biggest of the bundles.

G'dath sighed. "I hope you appreciate this, Leaper," G'dath said, and the kitten squeaked in response.

"All right, then," the Klingon said. "We will consider this interruption a test of my self-control." He picked up the big bundle, the one in which Leaper had been most interested.

Leaper paid absolutely no attention to him. He began poking at another package with his tiny paws.

"A moment, little cat," G'dath said. "We will take a look at the contents of all the packages."

G'dath began to unwrap the cat toys. He hoped they would make the animal feel even more at home. He had bought latex rodents, balls with bells inside them and other such things, all in accord with the tentative suggestions of the salesman at the pet supply store.

As it turned out, what G'dath bought didn't matter. When the Klingon came back from having stacked the cat food containers in the kitchen cupboard, he found Leaper ignoring the toys and playing gleefully with the wrappings.

With the cat fed, and amused, G'dath felt free to proceed with his own agenda. He entered the bedroom and saw that, as he had expected, the test of the chip assembly was still proceeding. He sighed with relief to see that, as yet, no errors were listed on the computer screen.

G'dath seated himself before the computer and watched as coding raced across the computer screen at a speed too fast for him to follow. If something was wrong with the chip, and if the flaw was in his design and not in the manufacture of it—well, it would be several more months before the Klingon could afford to try again—in fact, he might not get another chance before he had to return to the Empire.

An hour and ten minutes passed. Slowly.

"Test complete," the computer announced at last. "Results within design limits. Next?"

"End."

"Thank you," said the computer.

"Thank *you*," the Klingon replied, and his politeness to a machine was genuine.

G'dath rose and went over to the window, and looked outside. "Off," he said, and the bedroom lights dimmed and died.

It was an hour past sunset. From up here, nearly 250 meters high, G'dath could see many, many thousands of lights all over the city. He knew that each light represented several lives, and all of them were lives that G'dath would surely be affecting if his experiment tonight worked.

He looked up, adjusting his eyes. There were also many, many lights sharing the clear sky over the city with Earth's moon. Those lights were the stars, and some of them represented many billions of lives. G'dath knew he would be affecting those lives, too—if his experiment worked.

He would be affecting them all irrevocably, but would it be for the better? The Klingon fervently hoped so. The known galaxy was in enough trouble as it was, and he did not care to add to its problems.

G'dath went into the kitchen and returned to the living room with several pieces of fruit and a handful of sunflower seeds. His head bowed, he approached the *vuv gho* and placed the food in the shallow receptacle intended for it on the altar. "For success, if you will it," he said to his ancestors. He backed away reverently while murmuring a prayer. It was one that he had said daily during his childhood, and it comforted him now.

It was time to mount the chip assembly in the prototype. That almost trivial task was the last piece of the puzzle, the last stroke of the brush. It would constitute the last few moments of more than five long years of work.

G'dath retrieved the prototype from the padded box in which he'd kept it. The prototype was a transparent aluminum globe half a meter in diameter and stuffed with electronics. Transparent aluminum had been a fortunate choice. The globe was very strong, yet the aluminum was malleable enough to shape and work easily using only household tools. That do-it-yourself approach had saved G'dath the considerable cost of jobbing the work out.

The transparency of the globe allowed G'dath to see

its electronic innards. It may not have been completely necessary for the Klingon to see inside the globe,
but he liked the play of the interior lights against its
inside surface, and he believed in his heart that
aesthetics counted for something. He had come from
a place where they did not count for much at all, and
he had had quite enough of that.

There were three interdependent modules crowded
into the globe. One provided light shielding to protect
it, another served as a guidance system, and the third
housed the drive. The chip assembly he was about to
install would govern the drive and coordinate the
workings of the three modules with each other.

G'dath fit the assembly into place without difficulty.
The globe was now complete—the experiment could
proceed. Using the point of a stylus, he threw a small
switch just inside the access panel, and a number of
lights inside the globe began to glow softly.

The Klingon smiled in triumph. Whatever happened now didn't really matter very much to G'dath,
because his main theory had been proven. The lights
in the globe were glowing with power, but the globe
contained neither an energy source nor a receiver.

The power seemed to be coming from nowhere.

And that was the whole point.

G'dath stood there, holding the globe and admiring
it as Leaper, sensing the Klingon's pleasure, came up
and began stropping against his leg. After a while,
G'dath walked over to the window and Leaper trotted
after him.

G'dath looked at the sky again. The full moon had a
little more than an hour to go before it would reach its
zenith. He looked at the moon, studying it casually. It
was a remarkable moon, nearly unique in known
space for its huge size relative to its primary.

Like most aliens who had come to Earth, it had
taken him a while to learn to see the legendary man in

the moon. That wasn't very surprising, when even some humans saw not a man there, but the slender body of a woman or the crouched form of a rabbit. G'dath had long since come to see a face there, though, although he could not determine its sex. It had always looked to the Klingon as if the face were crying out, perhaps in pain, perhaps in dismay, perhaps even in wonder. Tonight, if all went well, his globe would pay that mysterious face a brief but significant visit.

G'dath slid his window open. The shielding allowed a bit of breeze to waft into the apartment. It smelled of the sea, of trees and of freshly cut grass. It also smelled of opportunity.

The Klingon set the globe on the windowsill. He was strangely unexcited. He already knew the principle behind the globe was correct. He'd known that ever since the internal lights had come on when he flipped the first relay. All that was left to do was to show how those principles might be applied on a more practical basis, and G'dath would satisfy himself on that score before he revealed the existence of his discovery to anyone. Then, perhaps, G'dath thought, he would be given the place that had heretofore been denied him in Federation society.

With no fanfare, G'dath again poked his stylus inside the access panel and tripped a series of relays. He now felt a gentle and welcome resistance when he moved the globe. It seemed to want to stay where it was.

"Inertial control, Leaper," G'dath told the cat. "See?" He moved the globe again, this time more quickly, and it resisted him more strongly than at first. Leaper blinked quizzically at the prototype.

The Klingon deactivated the globe's inertial dampeners. He then set the prototype on the windowsill and turned the dampeners back on.

"All right, little one," G'dath said. "You are my only witness, at least for now. You certainly came into my life on a most interesting day."

The kitten blinked again at the sound of G'dath's voice.

"So be it, then," G'dath said. He tripped another relay.

The globe began to rise slowly as the chip ordered it to expend the barest minimum of its motive force. It was a force that G'dath had not yet even named. It was something new and marvelous in the universe, and it had not been necessary for G'dath to name it to appreciate it.

The shielded globe slid easily through the shielding protecting the building, as one soap bubble might slide through another. It rose and then hovered hundreds of meters above the buildings of Stuyvesant Preserve, waiting for the next timed command to be issued by the chip. The blinking lights inside the prototype were still visible and he watched the globe carefully.

Suddenly there was a clap of thunder close to hand, and the globe vanished from sight. A panicked Leaper jumped up and ran at top speed into the bedroom to hide. The thunder hurt G'dath's ears, but he didn't mind very much. It was the sound of success. He'd seen no fiery flash of disaster, so the sound had not been caused by an explosion aboard the prototype. The globe had streaked away, as its programming ordered. The thunderclap had been caused by air rushing back into the vacuum—the tunnel in the sky—left behind by the prototype.

The globe was on its way. If all continued to go well, the globe would circle the moon, take a few readings to confirm its position, and be back hovering in front of his window in just under fifty-three minutes.

There was nothing to do but wait.

Suddenly there was another clap of thunder. The Klingon hurried to the window. It was indeed the globe, and it was descending slowly toward him.

G'dath was hugely disappointed. *True, it was a first flight,* he thought, *but I had hoped so much for a quick success.* Well, this will teach me a deserved lesson.

The globe re-entered G'dath's apartment and settled onto the windowsill. Whatever else might have gone wrong with the device, its inertial guidance system was functioning perfectly. The lights inside died as the prototype automatically turned itself off.

G'dath picked up the globe and inspected it. It looked fine. Its onboard shielding and inertial dampeners had completely protected it from the heat and shock of its rough departure and return.

G'dath opened the access panel and removed the chip assembly. Setting the globe back down, he went into the bedroom, connected the computer lead to the assembly port, and downloaded the trip log. He watched the screen carefully. There was a valid record of the globe's course, after all. G'dath felt slightly better, because the globe would have had to have gotten out of the atmosphere in order to be able to take the appropriate readings properly. He examined the data almost casually at first, and then much more closely.

The data were not at all what he expected.

The data were, in fact, impossible.

The Klingon checked everything carefully, over and over again, and finally became convinced that the data were indeed valid—and the implications of his experiment that night were far, far bigger than he could have imagined.

This would surely impress that reporter, if he dared tell her about it. He suddenly decided he would not—at least, not right away.

Leaper came back into the room, sniffing the air.

"Well, little one," the Klingon rumbled, pointing at the readouts on the computer screen, "what do you think about that?"

The kitten blinked at him.

"Very wise," G'dath replied. "I don't quite know what to say about it, either."

A cold chill ran over G'dath's brow. *What have I done?* he thought. Many races and beings would kill for what he had created and the incredible power he had discovered. Indeed, wars had been fought over far less important discoveries. His excitement over his success slowly became a dull sense of dread.

What have I wrought?

Chapter Six

KLOR WATCHED CURIOUSLY AS, on his console screen, the subject G'dath covered his hands with his face and bowed his head beneath the weight of an invisible burden.

Until a few moments before, the day had been dull and tiresome, as always. Keth had retired back to his tiny quarters and had not even come out for the evening meal. Klor, though he was desperate to go out and stretch his legs, had remained extra hours at his post so that he might learn the chip assembly's purpose. Normally, he would have ended his vigil and trusted the computer to keep a visual record of all that transpired during the dark hours; an alarm would wake him if the monitors detected weaponry or any type of espionage equipment in one of the subject's dwellings.

But tonight, he watched G'dath. And when G'dath began to construct a device with the assembly, Klor's pulse quickened. When the globe began to move under its own power, he was transfixed; when it disappeared in a clap of thunder, only to reappear an instant later, Klor rose to his feet. He knew he should have run to notify his commander, but he could not tear his gaze from the drama unfolding on the screen. Neither he nor the computer comprehended what had transpired in that brief span of time between thunderclaps, but G'dath's expression as he checked his equipment told Klor that it was something momentous.

And then, to Klor's surprise, G'dath buried his face in his hands.

So the dreamer's test has failed, Klor thought, with an odd sense of disappointment. Yet as G'dath lowered his hands, Klor saw his expression was one—not of disappointment, but of bewilderment, and something very much like awe.

He went to Keth's quarters and pressed the buzzer.

The door opened immediately. Keth was not asleep at this early hour, though of late, he had been given to retiring early. The commander sat at his window, staring out at the night sky. He swiveled in his chair as the door opened, his hands steepled in a gesture of reflection.

"The subject G'dath has created a device," Klor reported, and watched as his words ignited a spark in Keth's eyes. Without comment, Keth rose and followed him out to the console. Klor split the visual of the screen. Half of the picture continued to monitor G'dath, half replayed, at high speed, G'dath's construction and testing of his device. Keth leaned over, one hand on either side of the screen, and watched silently.

At last, Keth straightened. "We have been given a gift," he said softly. He turned toward Klor with sudden energy. "Send a message to our superiors: all data you extracted from G'dath's computer, as well as the visual you just showed me. Let us see if their computers are able to infer more than ours about this device."

"And then await their orders, Superior?" Klor asked.

"Perhaps," Keth replied, with a glint of humor and mystery in his eyes. "But before you act, consult me." He turned as if to leave, then hesitated. "You have served well, Klor. If things go well with our dreamer . . . I shall not forget."

Klor drew himself to his full height. "You honor me, Superior." He was uncertain what strategy Keth plotted, but he trusted his commander's shrewdness —and he dared, for the first time, to hope that there might be an end at last to this monotonous assignment.

Keth almost smiled, then turned on his heel and strode back to his quarters. For some time, Klor remained at his console, his energy renewed, and maintained his vigil. G'dath tested his device five times and five times got the same result. Afterward, he sat on his bed, the young cat curled asleep on his lap, and stared out his bedroom window at the moon. His expression was that of one who has beheld great beauty—and great hideousness—in a single glance.

Near dawn Saturday, Kevin Riley lay on his half-empty bed, still unable to sleep. The insomnia had been bad enough the past week, but after the curt message he'd received yesterday afternoon, he knew it was going to get a whole lot worse.

He should have gone to a doctor and gotten something to help him sleep, but the doctor would have asked him *why* he couldn't sleep, and then he would have had to talk about it and he wasn't in the mood to do that just yet. Besides, there was an odd masochistic satisfaction in lying here, reveling in self-pity. He did not *want* to fight it.

He had not wanted to fight it the first time Anab had left him, either—the day, almost exactly a year ago, that she'd told him she was shipping out on the *Starhawk*. But he'd found a way to deal with it, by losing himself in his work, by convincing himself her absence was only temporary.

They both knew she would be gone at least a year aboard the *Starhawk*, and he had talked her into extending their marriage contract so that it would expire at the same time as her assignment. She'd agreed, and he had been ecstatic. It meant she was coming back, and he centered his life around that moment. When her ship ventured too far out for contact between them, Riley was proud that he endured it stoically. Five months without a word from her, but it didn't matter. She was coming back.

Months later, when he discovered her vessel was in communication range, Riley controlled himself. He did not want her to feel pressured; he could be mature enough to wait for her to contact him. And she would call. After all, their extended contract was due to expire, and it was time to make arrangements again. Time for her to come home.

He waited as long as he could. The silence grew ominous; he began losing sleep. The very day their contract expired, he could bear no more, and called her. *Starhawk* was in communication range. It was so close, in fact, that there was no delay on the visual.

When Anab's face appeared on the viewscreen— her stunningly beautiful face—he drank in the sight of her, nectar to one dying of thirst. Her fine-boned creamy brown features, her dark hair close-cropped to reveal the long, dramatic sweep of neck and shoulder, her huge, heavy-lidded eyes . . .

Her eyes. He drew in a breath at the sight of them, and the coolness there. He looked into her eyes, and saw his worst fear realized. Before her lips moved, he heard what she was going to say.

I've decided not to renew our contract, Kevin.

Through some miracle of will, he gathered himself and faced her as coolly as she faced him, managed to hide the fact that he was shaken to the core. He did not, as he had a year ago, plead for her to stay.

A year ago, she had held out hope, had said she might return. Had said she loved him.

Her eyes held no love this time. She spoke for some time, explaining why she was leaving, he supposed, but he didn't hear the words.

All right, he'd said. *That's all I wanted to know.* And he'd cut off the channel.

Then, just yesterday, a terse message from her asking that he send along the rest of her things. He'd come home from the office and spent the evening packing them all. The last of her clothes in their closet—*his* closet, the framed lithographs on the walls. The ebony carving of a woman's head that so reminded him of her. The artwork was all hers, and without it, the apartment seemed bare, impersonal, anonymous.

Lying in bed, Riley closed his eyes and recalled the Anab of a year ago, the Anab with love and concern in her eyes. What was it she had said?

Get out of Starfleet. Find out what it is you really want to do with your life. Let someone who really wants it have your job. You're not doing Kirk any favors by working for him halfheartedly. And whatever you decide, do it for yourself, not because I or someone else thinks you should do it.

He wanted to work for Kirk, wanted to be the best officer he could be.

Yet at the moment, in his heart he knew he didn't give a damn about Kirk or Starfleet or anything else. Without Anab, none of it mattered. In a renewed burst of self-pity, he told himself that he was working for Kirk—and would continue working for Kirk— only because he didn't know what he really wanted.

Maybe he had stayed in Starfleet just to please her after all.

Riley drifted off into thoughts of her and finally dozed. Since it was Saturday, he hadn't set the alarm, but at some point he became fuzzily aware of bright sunlight streaming through the window, and croaked at the computer for the time.

0800.

He repeated it to himself, rolled lazily onto his side and dug his face into the pillow. He was verging on unconsciousness again when panic pierced him like a sword. His eyes snapped open.

0800. He was supposed to meet the admiral at 0800 at the WorldNews Bureau.

Riley bolted from the bed, concerned—not about whether he really wanted to remain in Starfleet, but whether Admiral Kirk would allow it.

Within twenty minutes, he had showered, dressed and found his way to the WorldNews reception lobby, where he was greeted by the show's producer—a petite, energetic redhead named Jenny Hogan—and led back to the waiting Admiral Kirk.

The green room, Jenny had called it, but as the door slid open, Riley had just time enough to note (with the detachment of a doomed soul) that the walls were taupe. And then his gaze met the admiral's. Kirk had been sitting at a table, eating a bacon and egg breakfast and calmly studying his datapad. His expression was perfectly composed—he did not even frown—but when Riley saw his eyes, he stopped in his tracks.

"Step inside, Mister Riley," Kirk said quietly. "I want that door closed."

It was the softness of his tone—softer than Riley'd ever heard it—that convinced Riley Kirk was not just irritated, but furious. And yet, Riley thought, some of the cold hardness in the admiral's eyes had nothing to do with Riley at all. And Riley knew that he had not been the only one to spend a sleepless night.

Of all the times to cross Kirk, he had to choose the worst.

"Yes, sir." Riley stepped forward three paces; the door slid shut. "Admiral, I apologize. I overslept, sir. I realize that—"

"You realize," Kirk said, in the same deadly quiet tone, "of course, that oversleeping is not an acceptable excuse? Mister Riley, you're twenty minutes late."

"Yes, sir." Riley felt warmth flood his cheeks and neck and knew he was flushing brilliantly; he was grateful for the beard that hid some of it. "I didn't mean to offer it as an excuse, sir. I realize—"

"You realize that I was depending on you to be here at 0800 to help me prepare for this interview?"

"Yes, sir."

"Then where is your datapad?"

Riley's bottom lip dropped as he released a gasp. In his desperate scramble to get to the WorldNews Bureau, he had entirely forgotten to bring his datapad, which held all his notes on the Dart Project and the refitted shuttle *Enterprise*. The blood which had rushed to his face seconds before now descended to the pit of his stomach. "My God." He closed his eyes. "Sir, I . . . I realize this is inexcusable. I . . ."

"Riley," Kirk said with a sigh, and Riley opened his eyes. The admiral's expression was, for an instant, no more, deeply weary. "I'm not interested in displays of remorse. I just need that information on the Dart Project, and I don't care how you get it. I want it *yesterday*. Is that clear?"

"Yes, sir. I'll get it right away, sir," Riley said, without any idea of how he would do so, and backed out the door.

* * *

After it closed again, Kirk sighed. The day before, he'd given up the two dearest things in his life, and he had no patience left for Riley. Whatever personal problems Kevin might face, they could not excuse twenty minutes' tardiness. Kirk had spent a restless night, yet he'd managed to arrive at the WorldNews Bureau at precisely 0800, ostensibly cheerful, mentally alert, and ready for the interview.

Perhaps he had misjudged his chief of staff all along; he wouldn't have expected this from someone of Riley's caliber. There had been an instant, when Riley first entered the room, that Kirk had been tempted to let him go. After all, he would shortly be as busy as he'd ever been, and needed someone at his side upon whom he could rely to handle details.

The door opened again and in walked a tall blond woman, proving a pleasant interruption to Kirk's train of thought. "Good morning, Admiral. I'm Nan Davis." She held out her hand.

Kirk recognized her instantly. "Of course. You used to do *Nan's Newsnight* on Centaurus. I watched your show pretty regularly whenever I was there."

She smiled. "A fan. Thank you."

They seated themselves at the table and Davis picked up a piece of toast. "May I?"

"Go ahead."

"Thanks." She took a bite. "I've been too busy to eat breakfast. You know, I wish I'd had the chance to interview you back when the *Enterprise* returned from her mission. There were some questions no one ever asked—questions I'd like to hear the answers to."

"Really?" Kirk poured himself another cup of coffee. "Well, today I'm all yours. Coffee?"

She shook her head. "I've had too much already. As for the interview, we'll hit the high points, don't worry. Are you all set?"

"All set," Kirk replied.

"Nervous?" She gave him a sly look.

Kirk grinned. "Never. But I *am* a little curious to know what kind of questions you have about the mission."

She smiled mysteriously. "You'll find out soon enough. Just remember the words of Oscar Wilde. 'In the olden days, we had the rack. Now we have the press.' Can I borrow your napkin?"

Kirk handed it to her. "Actually, I'm looking forward to this. The Dart Project deserves all the attention it can—"

"Whoops!" She glanced at her chrono. "I'm glad you want to talk about it, but save it for the air, please, I've really got to run. There are always millions of details to attend to before a show. See any crumbs?" she said, holding her face out for inspection.

"Clean as a whistle."

They both rose. "See you later," Kirk said.

"Count on it." Davis dashed out the door, which remained open as Riley returned. He stopped just inside the door and snapped to attention.

"I have the information you requested, Admiral."

Kirk realized that his anger had faded. Grudgingly, he said: "I won't ask how you managed it, Riley. Now have a cup of coffee. You look like you need one."

"Thank you, Admiral." Riley went to the table and poured a cup. "Have some yourself, sir?"

"No, thank you."

Riley hesitated in mid-pour. Without facing Kirk, he said, "It won't happen again, sir. Ever." There was a hint of a plea in his voice.

Kirk was silent for a moment. "Your word on that, Kevin?"

"Yes, sir."

"All right, then."

Riley's shoulders rose and sank three inches. "Thank you, Admiral."

"Don't mention it again. Ever."

Riley turned and handed Kirk the datapad. "My notes on the Dart Project, sir."

Kirk chose not to notice the WorldNews logo stamped prominently on the spine of the datapad. If Riley had "borrowed" it from someone's desk for a quick data transfer from his terminal over at the Admiralty, then so be it. Kirk appreciated the art of improvisation.

"Fine," Kirk said. "Let's go over this together; we still have some time. Sit down."

"Yes, sir."

Once they started, they worked well together . . . but of course, they went back a long way.

Fourteen-year-old Jimmy Kirk, traveling with his mother and older brother Sam, was beginning a scheduled one-week stopover on the remote colony world of Tarsus IV. The Kirks were waiting for a connecting flight to meet Jimmy's father. The family would be together for the first time in more than three years, and they were all looking forward to the reunion.

Before their flight arrived, however, the Kirks were caught in the turmoil that accompanied the rapid infestation of the colony's crops and stored food by what would later be named the Tarsean Blight. The disease ran through everything like fire through a tinder-dry forest. It rendered more than ninety percent of the food supply inedible.

Reports were made, and Tarsus IV suddenly found itself under a strict, Federation-imposed quarantine. Relief agencies quickly dispatched rations, but any aid to the already starving population would take several weeks to arrive at that remote location and even when it did, the blight would certainly attack any food supplies upon delivery and ruin nearly all of them. Stasis, irradiation and special packaging could hinder, but not prevent, the spread of the blight.

The colony still had its farm animals and a small amount of unaffected grain in storage, but there was far too little on hand to support everyone. Governor Kodos decided that, to save even half the population of the colony, the other half—some four thousand men, women and children—would have to be exterminated. Kodos was willing to gamble that the surviving half of the colony could live on short rations long enough either for sufficient aid to arrive or a counteragent for the blight to be found.

A secret lottery was conducted by Kodos and his most trusted associates. Colonists were chosen to die by the computer normally used to direct ground traffic in the capital city. Kodos then needed to find enough colonial police officials and reservists willing to follow his orders and enforce his plan. Here Kodos relied on instinct, and he selected well. The governor had to liquidate only four officials while finding the thirty or so that he needed to carry out the arrests and executions. Kodos regretted the necessity of those initial four deaths, but he had to maintain security and, he reflected, those deaths would spare four other lives. The books would balance.

Being offworlders, the Kirks and their fellow tourists played no part in the plans of Kodos. They were simply confined to their hotel rooms and put on short rations. They waited and, like everyone else on Tarsus IV, slowly starved.

About two weeks into the crisis Sam became ill. Jimmy, as hungry as the rest of them, decided to sneak out of the hotel and search for food. It did not occur to him that any remaining food would be under armed guard, or that it might be dangerous simply to travel the streets. He knew only that his mother was very hungry and his brother had become sick, and he wanted to help them. It was what his father would expect him to do.

Jimmy easily eluded the colony police stationed around the hotel and headed for the center of town. He kept a sharp eye out for cops and other potentially troublesome adults. Jimmy was fast and naturally athletic. Even weak from hunger, his energy reserves were considerable.

Jimmy found not even a scrap of food, although he searched high and low for hours. He traveled the city by sneaking along back streets and through alleys and, where necessary, over rooftops.

At one point, rummaging through heaps of trash in an alley, Jimmy was nearly spotted by a troop of colony police marching a line of people down the street on which the alley opened. Jimmy dove behind a pile of refuse and watched.

Everyone seemed to be heading toward the center of town. The people were being herded along like criminals, but they did not look like criminals to Jimmy. Some of the marchers were small children stumbling along in the wake of adults. And some of the adults were cradling infants or toddlers in their arms.

The police had not spotted him, but a young woman in the march had. Jimmy saw that she was holding a small, drowsing boy cradled in her arms. He watched as the woman muttered something to the man next to her. The man looked in Jimmy's direction, blinked and shrugged. The woman said something else to him and, after a moment, the man nodded slowly. Jimmy saw him lick his lips.

Suddenly the man howled and attacked the two colony police nearest him. Other police rushed toward the scene of the trouble. In all the confusion, the woman broke free and ran into the alley. The boy in her arms stirred but did not awaken.

113

"Son?" she said, running straight toward Jimmy. "Son, for the love of God, you've got to help us!"

Suddenly there were cries from the street. One of the police had spotted the woman running away.

Jimmy's eyes were wide. "The police. Behind you. They're coming."

"I know," she said, not taking the time to look. "Take my boy away. Please, son. Get him out of here. His name's Kevin. Kevin Riley. He's four." Her voice choked. "He's only four, for God's sake. Save him. Please!"

Jimmy had no idea what was going on, but he saw something bright and desperate in the woman's eyes, something that was not mere hunger, and it made him act instinctively. Jimmy reached out and took the small boy from her. He seemed to weigh hardly anything.

"Go!" she said, pointing down the alley, away from the street. "That way. Go quickly, and God help you!" The woman then turned away and bent to grab two heavy pieces of junked metal lying on the cracked concrete flooring of the alley.

Jimmy turned and ran, the woman's son cradled in his arms. *"Murderers!"* he heard the woman cry, and he knew that she must have thrown the metal objects hard at the police, because there came a heavy *smack* and a cry of pain.

Then Jimmy heard the whine of a phaser and a shrill cry from the woman . . . a cry that was cut off in the middle. A hint of greenish light glowed for a moment on the rough walls to either side of him.

He ran faster.

The police were after *him* now. They were shouting at him, ordering him to stop. Jimmy knew better. Rounding a bend in the alley, he found an open doorway and ducked inside.

The police ran on past.

Jimmy knew they would be back before long, but they would waste a little time looking for him. Thinking quickly, Jimmy decided to abandon the alley entirely and, instead, investigate the building he was in. It might afford a good hiding place.

The building was only three stories tall. Jimmy climbed the stairs as quickly and quietly as he could, puffing slightly. It was a residential building, with apartments clustered off the stairway, but Jimmy didn't hear any activity. He tried several doors as he passed them. All were locked.

As he reached the top floor, he heard his pursuers enter the building through the doorway below. Holding his breath, he froze.

Jimmy heard the men cursing a blue streak, but they didn't run upstairs to look for him. They left the building, and as their angry voices receded back up the alley, Jimmy began to breathe again.

An old-fashioned hinged door opened onto the roof. Jimmy ducked his head out and saw that the roof was surrounded by brickwork about a meter high—enough to block the view from nearby buildings. The only way he and the boy might be spotted was if someone flew overhead, but Jimmy decided that he could always duck back inside with the kid if he heard something coming.

His arms tired and aching, Jimmy put the kid down so that he sat with his back to the high wall. Throughout all the running around, the kid—Kevin—had barely stirred. *At least he's been quiet,* Jimmy thought gratefully.

Jimmy was sure that the building was empty, but nevertheless he moved across the roof silently. Cautiously, he peered over the rim of the brickwork.

And found that he was looking down at the town's

central square, but instead of the pleasant park that the Kirks saw when they'd first arrived on Tarsus IV, the square had been converted into a holding pen. Tall coils of barbed wire now fenced the square off from the rest of the city. Jimmy saw that there were thousands of people in the square and heard the dull roar of their conversations. Occasionally, he heard one of the police bark a command.

"Hello?" came a voice from behind Jimmy, and he whirled, but it was only the kid. He had gotten up and was wandering over, rubbing his eyes. "Where's my mommy?" he asked.

"She told me to take care of you. My name's Jimmy—er, Jim."

"I'm Kevin. I'm four. Where's my mommy and daddy? What are you looking at? Can I see?"

"It's not safe."

"Let me see."

"Oh, all right." Jimmy picked Kevin up so he could see over the wall, just in time to see a door open onto the long balcony that dominated the front of the biggest building on the square. A tall, bearded man emerged and studied the crowd below for a few moments. He thought the man's beard made him look like one of the Three Musketeers.

Jimmy and Kevin both watched as the man began to read from a piece of paper.

"The revolution is successful, but survival depends on drastic measures," he said in a clear, theatrical voice. "Your continued existence represents a threat to the well-being of society. Your lives mean slow death to the more valued members of the colony." He paused for a moment, and then continued in a lower tone. "Therefore, I have no alternative but to sentence you to death. Your execution is so ordered. Signed, Kodos, governor of Tarsus IV."

That was when the shouting and screaming began. The man with the beard calmly folded the piece of paper, put it away, and went back inside the big building. The door closed behind him as the police drew their phasers and leveled them on the crowd.

Thousands of people. Thousands.

Jimmy put Kevin down. "I want to see," the kid said.

"No," Jimmy said. He sat down next to the boy, his mouth dry. "No, you don't want to see this—and neither do I."

Then it came. Jimmy covered his ears against the loud, piercingly shrill whine of massed phaser fire. He looked up and saw an ugly green glow illuminating the bottoms of the low hanging clouds overhead.

"Make it stop!" the kid cried, putting his hands over his ears.

"I can't," Jimmy said. "Shhh."

He closed his eyes until everything was quiet.

When night at last fell and the last of the police had left the area, Jimmy picked up Kevin, left the roof and cautiously made his way back to the hotel, where his mother and brother were beside themselves with worry. Jimmy told his story to his family. The Kirks hid Kevin in their room and gave him a share of their own meager rations.

It was only three days later that a Federation relief team beamed down, released a genetically tailored counteragent to the blight into the atmosphere of Tarsus IV and, to its horror, discovered irrefutable evidence of the massacre in the square. The police officials who participated in the murders were arrested and tried. Kodos himself was never found—at least, not for many years.

Kevin Riley was placed with relatives who raised him in Ireland, on Earth. Jim Kirk did not see or hear of him again until many years later and many light-years away, when Captain James Kirk found Kevin Riley among his ship's complement. As Kirk soon discovered, Riley had only the haziest memory of the events of that terrible day and, in fact, he believed that it had been an adult who'd saved him.

Kirk never corrected him.

Chapter Seven

"GOOD DAY, EVERYONE," Nan Davis said as the studio lights brightened and the trivision scanners began whirring. "I'm Nan Davis, and this is WorldNews Saturday, coming to you live from San Francisco, California. Our first guest is Admiral James T. Kirk of Starfleet Command, and we'll be talking today about this summer's Apollo Tricentennial and Starfleet's role in the celebrations."

Kirk nodded at the nearest scanner. He had been interviewed by reporters before, but never inside a trivision studio, and had been curious to know how he would react. The effect was remarkably unintimidating. Other than a single tech who was monitoring the equipment to be sure nothing went wrong, only he and Nan Davis were on the set. With the exception of the scanners, there was nothing to indicate that he was addressing billions of listeners rather than one.

Davis swiveled in her chair to face him. Her manner was warm and personable, and Kirk liked her instantly, not just because he had seen her before on trivision, but at least partly because her manner reminded him of someone, though he hadn't figured out who. "Admiral, just why is Starfleet going to be celebrating Apollo Day a week from Tuesday?"

"Well," Kirk began, "I don't think anyone can disagree that the first manned lunar landing was important to history—as important as the first voyage of Columbus, in fact. It was the very first time that humans had set foot on another planet, and that's more than enough reason for Starfleet to participate in the celebration."

"But what do you say to those people who feel that there's no purpose in taking note of a nationalistic achievement these days, when nationalism doesn't mean very much anymore? You can't deny that the landing was the product of a nationalistic space race, can you?"

Kirk smiled. Davis was sharp. She wasn't going to let the interview turn into a commercial for Starfleet; she was going to ask some tough questions, and he admired her professionalism. Fortunately, this particular question was one he had anticipated. "I can't," he said. "Nor can I deny that the voyages of Columbus were for nationalistic purposes, either. Yet much of Earth still celebrates Columbus Day. It's a celebration of his achievements, not his motives.

"Similarly, the Apollo Tricentennial does not celebrate nationalism, but the bravery and daring of courageous explorers. For the same reason, we also observed the three hundredth anniversary of the launching of Sputnik by the old Soviet Union twelve years ago."

The prompt bug in Davis's ear buzzed briefly, and she turned to face the nearest scanner. "We're now going to show you archival video of that first lunar landing so long ago."

The viewers now showed faded, blurred pictures of two men in bulky pressure suits moving around the lunar surface. Their spidery spacecraft stood in the background.

"This video not been reprocessed for trivision," Davis continued. "You're seeing it just as the people of the world saw it three hundred years ago . . . except that they watched it live."

Kirk watched as the two astronauts skipped here and there between the lunar lander and the camera, never going very far in that first, careful exploration.

"Remember what year it was," Davis said softly as the world watched the ancient video. "Nineteen sixty-nine. Except for these two men you see here, and a third waiting in orbit for their return to the mother ship, there are no humans who are not on the planet Earth. None. The men of Apollo 11 are absolutely, utterly alone. If these two men run into trouble on the lunar surface, no rescue is possible. There are no well-stocked shelters waiting for them just beyond the next ridge. There are no rescue teams on constant standby over in Luna City.

"The only supplies these men have are whatever they brought with them in the small, fragile vehicle in which they landed. If that little spacecraft behind them fails to lift off—if its primitive, chemically powered engines fail to ignite for any of a hundred reasons—the astronauts can do little or nothing about making repairs. They will simply run out of air and die, as completely alone as anyone has ever been.

"Sometimes we speak of courage without really knowing what we mean by the word. Look at these men, and know that what you see here is beyond courage." Davis fell silent, letting her audience listen to the voices of the first humans to venture onto alien soil.

Kirk found himself moved by what Davis had said. Not only had the three men of Apollo 11 returned to

Earth safely, but six more flights had followed, and all personnel had returned safely from those missions as well—including a mission that aborted during flight. That perfect record, Kirk reflected, might just represent a bigger achievement than the manned landings on the moon. He knew what it was to bring a ship and crew home safely.

The archival video faded away, and Davis and Kirk were back on scanner. "Admiral," she asked, "just what is Starfleet doing to help celebrate the Tricentennial?"

"Well, soon after the Apollo program ended, there came the so-called space shuttle, which was the popular name for the first ground-to-orbit reusable spacecraft. Some shuttles were lost in accidents, others were junked, and most of the rest were allowed to deteriorate beyond the possibility of salvage. There's only one left. She is, in fact, the oldest existing true spacecraft in the world, and we're going to fly her for the Tricentennial."

"Tell us about it," Davis said.

"Certainly," Kirk said. "Starfleet has helped finance what we've been calling the Dart Project. The 'dart' is the space shuttle itself, the orbiter. The last surviving shuttle is one that was used only for unpowered glide tests nearly three centuries ago: the space shuttle *Enterprise.*"

"Nice name," Davis said.

Kirk smiled. "I think so. We've borrowed her from the Smithsonian Institution's Space Museum at Dulles Park, Virginia, where she's been undergoing a stem-to-stern retrofitting. She's getting impulse engines and everything else a modern sub-light spacecraft should have. Outside, she looks just the same as she did nearly three hundred years ago. But inside, she's being completely redone. We're going to take her on her first-ever powered flight—a flight for which she's nearly three hundred years overdue. Thanks to her new impulse engines, the space shuttle *Enterprise* will fly farther and faster than any other such craft ever did—directly from Earth to the moon on Apollo Day. Other antique spacecraft—ones maintained and flown by private collectors—will meet the shuttle on her way to the moon. Together, they'll all fly directly over the Apollo 11 landing site in the Sea of Tranquility in a great parade of spacecraft on the twentieth of July. It ought to be quite a show."

Davis turned to face the scanners. "You heard it here first," she said. "America's space shuttle will fly again on Apollo Day. We'll have more with our guest, Admiral James Kirk of Starfleet Command, right after this."

The lights dimmed. "Terrific!" she enthused. "Thanks, Admiral."

"Was it all right?" Kirk asked, sincerely curious.

"You're a natural," Davis assured him. "Starfleet made the right choice this time. When we come back from the commercials, we'll take some calls, if you're ready."

"I'm ready," Kirk said.

When the lights came back up, Davis smiled warmly at the scanners. "We're still talking with Starfleet Admiral James Kirk, and we're ready to take your calls at the code you see at the bottom of your picture. Remember—audio only, please." Her prompt bug buzzed again. "Our first call is from a little town called Gruetli, Tennessee. Go ahead, please."

"Hello?" came a male voice.

"Yes, go ahead," Davis said.

"Is this Captain Kirk?"

"Admiral Kirk is here, yes," said Davis. "What's your question, please?"

"I'd like to ask Captain Kirk if, you know, he misses the spaceship he used to be on? You know, the *Enterprise.* Thanks, Nan. I think you're just great, and I really love the show. Keep up the good work."

"Thanks, Tennessee." She swiveled toward Kirk. "Admiral?"

The same question Nogura had asked him yesterday; this time, Kirk was ready for it, and gave a direct answer . . . even if part of that answer was not entirely true. "No, I really don't miss my old ship. I've got a whole new set of responsibilities, and my job is a very exciting and rewarding one." Or had been, up to now. "My old ship, the *Enterprise,* has a new captain, and I'm absolutely certain he's the best man for the job. That's not to say that I don't still feel a great deal of affection for the *Enterprise.*"

"Our next caller is from Maryland," Davis said. "Go ahead, Hughesville. You're on the air."

"Hello," a woman said. "Is this the admiral?"

"Yes, it is," Kirk said. "Hello there."

"Hi, Admiral. I was wondering about something. You know, there have been an awful lot of books written about that five-year mission of yours. I was wondering what you thought about all the commotion."

Kirk grinned. "I've read some of the books you're talking about. A lot of what's in them is just idle speculation, and much of it is just plain wrong. No one's ever talked to me before writing one of those books, and I know for a fact that no one's ever talked with my former top officers, either—or has even tried to, I suspect."

"Admiral," Davis asked suddenly—he got the impression she was about to deviate from her prepared list of questions in order to satisfy her private curiosity—"why did you decide to leave your command and accept a job at the Admiralty? I understand that your Chief Medical Officer resigned in protest and your first officer resigned as well. Wasn't the *Enterprise* yours for as long as you wanted her?"

His poise never wavered, but the last of the grin faded. The question angered him. He didn't mind answering tough questions, so long as they pertained to Starfleet, but he hadn't expected to be interrogated about his personal life.

And he hadn't come here to be reminded of Bones and Spock. Davis seemed to sense the anger her question had awakened, but she held Kirk's gaze unflinchingly, waiting for her answer.

"Starfleet doesn't work like that, Ms. Davis. Starships aren't private possessions. You talked with Bob April here just yesterday morning . . ."

"The first captain of your *Enterprise,*" she mentioned for the benefit of her viewers.

". . . and let me say that if a man could hold onto a ship for as long as he wanted to, with no other considerations involved, then I wouldn't be here at all, because Bob April would still be sitting in the center seat aboard the *Enterprise.*"

"I guess that's true," Davis allowed. Her eyes were bright, intense—and Kirk suddenly realized who she reminded him of. He had seen that drive, that white-hot ambition, too many times before, in Lori's eyes. "But you still haven't addressed the issue of your officers."

"My first officer resigned and returned to his home planet for personal reasons, Ms. Davis, not to protest anything, as your question implied. And my Chief Medical Officer resigned to protest the fact that his recommendation was overridden, not to protest my promotion to the admiralty."

"I see," Davis said softly, and she drew in a breath

to ask another question—one Kirk could predict. *And what did your Chief Medical Officer's recommendation say, Admiral? And why was it overridden?*

He spoke before she had a chance to ask. "Let me add that I like my new job. I'm not responsible for one starship anymore. I'm in charge of more than forty, with more coming." *I know you're listening, Nogura— and I've just made it public record, in case you were about to forget your promise to me that this position was temporary.* "I certainly don't consider that a step down."

He heard the prompt bug buzz in her ear and knew that he'd been saved by another call. Davis gave him a look that said she would not forget the question. "And we have another caller, this one from Conyers, Georgia. Go ahead, please."

A gravelly voice with more than a hint of a familiar Southern drawl said, "Why don't you ask the admiral there to explain what a quarterdeck breed is?"

Bones, he had wanted to say, *I thought you were still offplanet,* and his first instinct had been to smile, until he registered the angry hurt in McCoy's voice—the same anger that he'd heard his first day at the Admiralty, when the doctor had taken it upon himself to come to Starfleet Headquarters and argue with Nogura in person about Jim's promotion. It had been over a year since he'd last seen McCoy, and he'd hoped that Bones had come to terms with losing the *Enterprise.* Although Kirk hadn't been too gentle with him about it, he'd been furious himself. What was it he had said?

Maybe you just wanted everything to stay as it was, all of us still on the Enterprise. *Well, grow up, Doctor. Things change.*

"Quarterdeck breed?" Davis's expression grew puzzled.

There was a faint hum as the caller dropped the circuit.

"An old nautical term." Kirk forced a smile. "And an old friend of mine playing a joke."

"Well," Davis said, looking slightly bewildered, "we seem to have lost the caller from Georgia. And at any rate, we have run out of time. Admiral, thank you very much." She swung her seat to face the scanners directly. "I've been talking with Admiral James T. Kirk of Starfleet Command about the resurrected space shuttle *Enterprise* and the plans to fly her to the moon on Apollo Day. Now, we'll be back with a first look at the top-rated competitors in next year's Winter Olympics, right after this."

The studio lights dimmed and died. "There, that's it," Davis said with satisfaction. The tech in the studio began stretching.

"Jenny?" Davis called to a red-haired woman who had just entered the studio. "Sign out a set of portable scanners for me, will you?"

"Sure."

"Isn't there more to do?" Kirk asked, puzzled. "What about the Olympics?"

"It's all prerecorded," Davis said, taking Kirk by the elbow and steering him toward the newsroom. "I'm through here for the day. I was wondering . . . I'm trying to convince my assignment editor to let me cover Apollo Day and it would really help my chances of getting the story if I were able to get a bit more background on it. Are you busy later on today if I wanted to make an appointment with you?"

"I'm free all day," Kirk said. "Beginning right now, as a matter of fact." The disturbing call from Georgia had already reminded him of Bones and Spock; he saw no point in returning home to the empty apartment and being reminded of Lori as well. And now that MacPherson was heading up the refit, there was no work to be done at the Admiralty.

"Ah," Davis said delicately. "I didn't want to intrude on your weekend. I know you and your wife probably don't have that much time to spend—"

"She's away on business," Kirk interrupted. So Davis had done a thorough job of researching him. She knew about McCoy and Spock, knew Kirk was married.

At least she hadn't found out—yet—about Lori leaving last night.

"I see." She tilted her head and studied him curiously. "Well, I'm afraid I can't do it just now. I'm on my way to New York to interview a Klingon."

"A Klingon?" Kirk half smiled. "What's a Klingon doing in New York?"

Davis's expression had become utterly serious. "A special program. He's an accomplished physicist who's teaching high school students because of misunderstanding and fear."

Kirk frowned. "That's not right."

Nan shook her head. "Of course not. And the fact that his students routinely rank in the top one percent of the North American pool after a year with him doesn't seem to matter at all."

"Are you sure?" Kirk asked. "There are supposed to be safeguards—"

"The safeguards that are in place sometimes don't work very well. People of ill-will can get around them fairly easily," Nan said. "Look, I'm sorry, but I have to run. My flitter leaves in less than an hour, and even at that I'm going to be late. Nice to have seen you again, Admiral. Could I meet you sometime later this afternoon?"

"Maybe I can save you some time, Ms. Davis. I think I'd like to meet your Klingon."

"You mean you want to come with me?"

"Yes, I would. You've gotten me interested in this. You know, I've never met a Klingon who wasn't of the warrior class. I think I'd like to. And who knows? Maybe I can do something to help him out."

Nan nodded. "Well, you're welcome to tag along, but we've got to hurry if we're going to catch that flitter. I wish I could get the brass to let me charter one, but—"

"Why don't we beam over to New York instead?" Kirk suggested. "I can have my aide call over to the Admiralty and reserve a transporter stage for us. Then you can be on time, do your interview, and we can have a late lunch afterward."

"Beam?" she asked. "Actually use a transporter? That would be fantastic!"

Kirk smiled. "Doing small favors for the media fits right in with my job description, Ms. Davis."

After Kirk and Nan Davis left, Riley went over to the newsroom to thank Jenny Hogan. She was standing with a group loitering at a newswriter's desk, laughing at a joke—such a tiny person, Riley thought. At the sight of Riley, she turned; the smile faded slightly, and a look of concern took its place.

"Kevin?" She excused herself from the group and came over to him. "Is everything all right now?" She wore a jumpsuit of forest green that brought out her sea green eyes and bright copper hair.

He smiled down at her, all self-pity momentarily forgotten. He had desperately needed a friend that morning, and Jenny Hogan had proven herself to be one. "It seems to be." He released a sigh of utter exhaustion. "I really think the admiral would have cut me loose if you hadn't—"

Someone called to Jenny with a question and she

took a moment to answer it, then turned back to Riley. "Excuse me. You were praising me, Kevin. Pray continue."

At the look of frank appreciation in her eyes, Riley blushed. He was, after all, a married—

Correction. As of yesterday, he was a bachelor again—with no desire to get encumbered so quickly. He liked Jenny . . . as a friend, no more. "Uh . . . sure," he stammered. "Look, if you hadn't lent me your datapad, I think I'd be out of a job right now. I owe you one, Jenny. In fact, I owe you several."

"So what was I supposed to do?" Jenny said, shrugging. "Let a fellow Irishman down? I'm a producer; I'm supposed to straighten out people's problems. Tell you what—if you really want to make it up to me—let's go out and get some lunch, just like the big people."

"It's not lunchtime yet," Riley said, a little nervously. "It's not even nine hundred thirty yet—I mean, it's not even half past nine."

"So let's go for a walk," Jenny said. "A long walk. It's a nice day. Then we'll go eat. Does your appreciation extend to the champagne brunch at the St. Francis?"

Riley's mouth opened; he closed it quickly. He could hardly be rude and refuse her, after what she had just done for him. And he liked being in her company—it certainly beat moping around the apartment alone for the rest of the day. Maybe all Jenny was looking for was a friend and he could certainly use one right about now.

"Sure," he said finally. "Sky's the limit."

But he could not shake a nagging sense of guilt.

Chapter Eight

THE DOOR TO THE APARTMENT slid open and there stood G'dath, big and thoroughly intimidating—until he smiled. "Good afternoon, Admiral, Ms. Davis. It is a pleasure to meet you both. Please come in." He stepped aside and allowed them to enter.

As they did, a gray blur flew out of the apartment, close to the floor, and headed down the hallway toward the lifttube. It startled Davis. "What was that?" she asked.

"That was Leaper," G'dath said. "My cat."

Kirk blinked. "Your cat?"

"Yes. A kitten, actually. Will you excuse me for a moment? Ms. Davis, you may put that case down anywhere you choose." G'dath hurried down the hall toward a small gray thing squatting about ten meters away. Kirk and Davis watched as G'dath reached down, picked up the kitten and spoke to it softly. The kitten wriggled and then settled itself comfortably over G'dath's shoulder.

"What's he saying?" Davis whispered.

Kirk grinned faintly. "I don't think I've ever heard Klingonese spoken so softly. I guess you could call it baby talk."

"The cat enjoys going out into the hallway," G'dath explained to them as he came back into the apartment and the door closed behind him. "I believe he thinks it is a part of our home that I do not let him enter, which makes him all the more anxious to explore it. But I do wish he would stay inside, for safety."

The kitten was looking at Davis with wide eyes. "He's beautiful," Davis said. She scratched Leaper's head in just the right spot between his ears, and the little cat closed his eyes in pleasure and began purring more loudly. "When did you get him?"

"Just yesterday, and it was he who acquired me." He told her the story.

"Now that's exactly the kind of thing I'd like to work into the interview, G'dath," Davis said. "It would help people understand you better, sympathize with you more."

The Klingon suddenly looked nervous. "I hope you do not include any mention of Leaper in your story. Having a pet is against the rules here."

"Far be it from me to cause you trouble with your landlord," Nan said. "All right. Where can I set up my equipment?"

"The living room, if you find it suitable." G'dath gestured with a huge, strong hand.

In a few minutes, Davis had the scanners set up, and they were ready to begin. "Admiral," she said, "I'm going to have you sit on that other chair back in the dining area, out of scanner range."

Kirk sat quietly as Davis and G'dath took two chairs in the living room.

"Thanks. All right, I'm going to tell the scanners where we are in the room, so they can find us and track us correctly." Davis snapped her fingers. "Over here," she called out. There was the faintest sound of gears moving as both cubes turned this way and that, their glassy square eyes locking onto Nan and G'dath.

Davis snapped her fingers and called to them again, but the cubes remained at rest. "That's it. All set. And we don't have to worry about making mistakes today, since we have the luxury of prerecording."

G'dath thought about it. "Which do you prefer—prerecording or working in real time?"

Davis didn't hesitate for a second. "I prerecord whenever I can. It saves wear and tear on my stomach lining."

"As when the *Enterprise*'s command section lifted off later than expected yesterday?" G'dath asked. "I imagine that must have caused some problems for you."

Her lips twisted wryly. "Sometimes things can get exciting."

"I thought the show went quite well, Ms. Davis," said G'dath. "I watched it at school with my students. The program was quite revelatory. We had a splendid discussion afterward."

"Thank you," Davis said. "Actually, your classroom work is one of the main subjects I want to cover. It will help people understand you better. What we want to do is give people an idea of what you're really like, as if they were the ones sitting across from you and talking to you. I want them to understand what's happened to you and how you feel about your situation and how it might be improved."

G'dath nodded. "As I told your producer, Ms. Davis," he said, "I have been on Earth for some years now, and yet I still do not quite understand how public opinion here is formed. If I can help to promote greater understanding between our peoples, however, I am more than willing to give it a try." He smiled again. "Shall we?"

"I was a physicist in the Empire, Ms. Davis," G'dath replied. "My specialty was the study of transluminal wavicles. I had been assigned to work at an institute on one of the border planets central to the dispute between the Federation and the Empire at the time of the crisis six years ago."

"A border planet? Seems rather out of the way."

"I believe my placement there was intentional." G'dath smiled. "To be blunt, I was considered something of a crackpot in that I was not given to practical research. Research in the Empire, particularly in physics, must show a practical result. I have always been more of a pure theoretician."

"How did you wind up on Earth?"

"When the idea of a trial exchange of scientific personnel was offered by Federation diplomats, I was sent because I was considered to be 'safe.' The Empire did not believe that I could provide the Federation with any useful classified information even if I chose to do so."

Davis nodded. "You said your specialty was in transluminal physics. Are you working in that field now?"

"No, Ms. Davis. I am not employed as a physicist of any sort. I cannot find a job in the field."

"And why is that?"

"I am told there are no openings."

"Do you think that's true?"

"I suspect it is not. I suspect that in spite of the spirit of openness that made my temporary visa on Earth possible, the people of the Federation do not trust me because I am a Klingon."

"What are you doing at the moment?"

"I am employed as what is colloquially referred to as a high school teacher," G'dath said. "I have been hired by the New York public school system to preside over and conduct an experimental class. It is good and worthy work. I like it and am grateful for it."

"But it isn't your real work?"

G'dath hesitated. "Without wishing to offend either my employers or my students," he said slowly, "I must say that teaching high school is not my real work. I would very much like to get back to my physics."

"What are your credentials as a physicist?"

G'dath began reciting his degrees, and after a moment Davis held up a hand. "I'm not quite following you," she said apologetically. "Are those the equivalent of doctorates? I think I've heard three go by so far."

"Two are the equivalent of doctorates," G'dath said. "The third degree is one level beyond that, and there is no equivalent within the realm of standard Federation education. I understand, however, that Vulcan institutions of higher learning bestow a degree somewhat similar in prestige."

"Oh," Davis said. "I suppose, if I supposed anything, that the Vulcans were the scholars of the known galaxy . . ."

". . . and the Klingons were the warriors?" G'dath finished for her.

"Yes."

G'dath nodded. "My race has that reputation. It is a stereotype and, like all such, it is vicious in essence." His expression turned stern. "I am no warrior. Most Klingons are not. My family are—were—peaceable farmers. My parents worked hard to get me admitted to the ranks of the scholars and to keep me there.

"It is true that I served in the Imperial Fleet when I was younger, because military service is compulsory even for those not of the warrior class. I was an assistant warp-drive engineer aboard a ship similar in size and capability to a Starfleet scout."

"Did you fight?" Nan asked him.

"Often," G'dath said. "We fought pirates operating on the fringes of the Empire. I was not technically a combatant, however. Only career officers are allowed the actual glory of battle—to determine strategy, actuate the weapons, and so forth."

"Was it glory, even for you?"

"Glory? There is nothing inglorious about protecting one's own kind from those who would just as soon kill or enslave them as not. We fought pirates and I am proud of my service with the Fleet."

"Did your ship ever have a confrontation with a Federation vessel?" Davis asked, and Kirk's ears picked up.

"No, it did not," G'dath said, his expression wry. "I think we would have been quite surprised to see a Federation vessel in that sector, since we were about as far from the common border as a ship could possibly be yet still remain within the Empire." He paused a moment, thinking. "We were also about as far from the center of the Empire as a ship could possibly be. It was lonely duty."

"What happened after you left the service?" Davis asked.

"I went back to school, as you might put it. I received my third advanced degree and went to work as a researcher."

"What did you find when you arrived on Earth?" Davis asked.

G'dath looked sad. "I found a common belief that I and my fellows were all untrustworthy and, without exception, savage. I found that I myself was considered likely to go mad at any given moment because the impulse to do so was 'in my blood,' as I believe someone once put it.

"It took me some time to secure my present teaching position. The New York school authorities met with virulent opposition when my hiring was first announced. To its credit, the school board stood fast on my behalf, relying on both the letter and spirit of the antidiscrimination laws. Since I have not gone mad and killed anyone, the controversy has died down, and I think the results I have gotten with my students have justified my employers' faith in me."

"You told me that you didn't think your present job was your real work," Davis said. "What have you been doing about trying to secure another position?"

"This very morning, Ms. Davis," G'dath said, "I dispatched my five hundred sixty-first application for an entry-level academic position in an institution of higher learning. I have long since given up seeking something more suited to my curriculum vitae. I have tried everywhere from Harvard, Oxford and the Sorbonne to community colleges in the American Midwest. I have, without exception, been told that there are no suitable openings for me. Ms. Davis, I do not wish to whine, and I do not seek pity, but I have two doctorates and a degree that is superior to a doctorate, and yet I am told repeatedly that I am not qualified for a beginning position that is generally staffed by someone still working toward a master's degree."

"What do you want?" Davis asked him. "What do you desire most of all? What do you want to tell the people of Earth?"

"I want to contribute," G'dath said simply. "I chose freely to live and work here among you. I can contribute a great deal to our common good. Why won't you let me?"

"Beautiful," Davis said. "I think I have enough. G'dath, there's something else I'd like to do. I need some shots of you walking around the neighborhood."

G'dath nodded. "Of course."

Kirk stood and stretched. "Interesting interview, Miss Davis," he said. "G'dath, I'd like to talk with you myself sometime soon about those pirates out on the Imperial fringe. We may have a few things in common. I pulled similar duty early in my career."

"Certainly, Admiral," G'dath said. "I will look forward to our talk. In turn, you might favor me with a discussion of your five-year mission. Your name was well known in the Empire, but I fear I did not receive an unembellished view of events."

Kirk grinned. "I'd be glad to."

Klor woke to the steel grip of a hand on his shoulder. Instinctively, he reached for the phaser on his belt . . .

And remembered it was no longer there. He no longer served at a warrior's proper post. He opened his eyes to see the monitor console under him, then glanced up over his shoulder.

Keth frowned down at him.

"Superior," he gasped, struggling to his feet. In his zeal to discover more about G'dath's mysterious invention, he had spent the night monitoring the subject's apartment (G'dath had finally gone to sleep a few hours before dawn), poring over G'dath's computer files, and replaying the incident with the disappearing globe. His superior was hatching a plot to restore his honor, Klor knew, and it made good political sense to remain in Keth's good graces.

Except that he must have dozed off after dawn—the light coming through the window indicated midmorning. He faced Keth apologetically. He was not required to stay awake the entire night, but to be caught sleeping at his post was unforgivable.

Yet in his excitement, Keth did not appear to notice.

"I have heard from our superiors," he said. It was Keth transformed speaking, no longer the downtrodden wretch of two days prior, but Keth, the commander. Head and body were held erect. His movements were confident, purposeful, and the spark in his eyes had been fanned into a blaze. "They are most intrigued by the design fragment. They require both the subject G'dath and either the complete schematic or the artifact itself as soon as possible." His thin lips stretched into a smile. "We are commended for bringing this matter to their attention."

Klor smiled; *we* are commended. "Shall I notify our superiors?" It was standard procedure.

Keth thought. "Not yet. Not yet. Let's see what our subject is up to."

Klor glanced at G'dath's screen and felt a thrill of panic. The subject was not in his bedroom, though Klor could see the youngling cat complaining at the closed door. The creature's small mouth opened and closed to reveal a flash of pink tongue and tiny, sharp teeth.

Keth dug his fingers deep into Klor's shoulder. "If the traitor has fled during the night . . ."

Klor fought back the fear and kept his head. He scanned the apartment quickly, and with dizzying relief found G'dath sitting in the living room, speaking to a human woman—a woman Klor found oddly familiar.

"Superior! This is the reporter from WorldNews! If he is speaking to her of his invention . . ."

Keth, his gaze fastened on the screen, leaned close behind Klor's shoulder. "Contact our superiors immediately and tell them—" He broke off and swore explosively. *"Z'breth!"*

Klor followed his commander's gaze to the screen . . . and saw that the reporter and G'dath had risen from their seats, and had been joined by a third party: a Starfleet admiral, one of the few that Klor recognized.

James T. Kirk. Klor sank into his chair.

Keth's narrow eyes had widened to show yellowed whites. "Kirk! Starfleet is involved! Do you know what this means?"

Klor watched as Keth's hope for political redemption headed for G'dath's apartment door. "Shall I send for support now, Superior?"

Keth's hand smoothed his chin as he answered with a reluctance that confused Klor. "I suppose we must. But inform them . . ." He paused, thinking. "Inform them—no phasers. Street weapons and hand to hand combat only."

"But, Superior—"

Keth glanced sharply at him. "No energy weapons are to be used, even to stun. The authorities would detect their use instantly. And I want no witnesses. Order the team to take G'dath into immediate custody. I want him alive."

"And the humans?"

"Capture the admiral alive, if possible. Kill the female."

Kirk, Nan Davis and G'dath stepped from the apartment building onto a sidewalk leading to a grassy, tree-lined park. The July sun was bright and hot, but the humidity was low, and a cool breeze came off the river. Kirk was grateful for a distraction, and G'dath and Nan Davis were certainly providing one. He hadn't expected to find himself strolling through New York in the company of a Klingon, but G'dath was a fascinating character. Kirk admired him for his persistence . . . and he admired Davis for wanting to bring the situation to public attention. The concern on her face as she listened to G'dath's story had been entirely unfeigned—there was nothing insincere about it.

As they stepped from the sidewalk onto soft grass, Davis set down her case, opened it, and handed Kirk one of the scanners. "Here, I'll put you to work. Just point the business end of this at G'dath and the cube will do the rest. I'll handle the other one." She motioned for him to move about two meters ahead of the Klingon. He did, and felt the cube hum in his hands.

Oblivious to the scanner, G'dath tilted his broad face toward the sun and briefly shut his eyes. "It is certainly pleasant enough for a walk. I am glad to get outside." He opened his eyes and sighed. "I fear I sometimes lose myself in my work, particularly on weekends."

Davis focused her cube on the Klingon, shooting from the right side while Jim shot from the left. "Work? What work is that, G'dath?"

It seemed to Kirk that a shadow passed over G'dath's face—a troubled emotion he could not read. It might have been fear, or reluctance, or indecision— or all three.

"My studies, I mean," G'dath answered quickly, averting his eyes. "I try to keep up with the latest developments in physics, but every day there is more and more to learn."

"Hold on," Davis said from behind the scanner. "You're starting to look glum all of a sudden. Could you smile or something?"

The Klingon drew back his lips to reveal two even, intimidating rows of large yellowish teeth.

"Not like that," Davis said, and though she successfully repressed her own smile, Kirk heard it in her voice. "Smile as if you *meant* it."

G'dath chuckled. "I'm not very good at smiling on command. The holo on my citizenship papers is proof of that."

"I've seen it," Davis said, "and you have a point. Just think of something pleasant. There, that's better. Makes you look more—"

"Human?" Kirk offered.

"Friendly."

G'dath's expression had brightened considerably. "It would be most difficult for me to look human. I will settle for looking friendly."

They kept walking and scanning until they reached a clearing, secluded by tall trees.

"Well," Davis said, "I don't think I need any nature shots—"

G'dath held up a hand and cocked his head. "Wait a moment. I hear something. It sounds very much like four people running toward us."

Kirk instinctively crouched as he heard footfalls behind him. As he turned, a fist holding a blackjack sliced through the air over his head. Kirk threw the scanner cube at his assailant and scampered backward just as G'dath disabled another with a sharp blow to the neck.

Kirk's attacker, a young, muscular human male with clean-shaven face and head and Gothic lettering tattooed across both cheeks, stumbled backwards as the scanner struck his shins and knocked him off his feet. While he struggled to regain his footing, another blur darted out from behind a tree—right toward Nan Davis.

"Nan!" Kirk cried. "Behind you!"

Davis turned just as a third man appeared behind her and swung the scanner she was holding, catching the thug in the stomach. Unprepared for the blow, the attacker—this one bearded and broken-nosed—dropped to his knees, the wind knocked out of him.

"Backs to each other!" Kirk ordered.

"What the hell is going on?" Davis demanded as the three of them fell into a defensive posture.

G'dath's attacker still lay unconscious, but Kirk's and Davis's had managed to get back on their feet and were joined by yet a fourth assailant. All were young, all scruffily dressed and dirty, and sporting brightly colored tattoos. And all, Kirk noticed with shame, were human. They began to form a wary circle about their victims.

"Occasionally there is hooliganism here," G'dath said quickly, as the men closed in. "Sometimes outsiders attack residents of the Preserve."

"That particularly ugly one there is wearing a Barclayite button," Davis said, pointing at her bearded attacker.

"Oh," Kirk said sourly. "Them." He could just make out now what the tattoo on the bald attacker's cheeks said: ALIENS GO HOME.

"Barclayites?" G'dath asked.

"They don't like nonhumans," Davis said. "They don't even like most humans. The movement started on Centaurus. I didn't know it had spread here." She cleared her throat as the attackers began to slowly circle and produced clubs and knives. "Uh, Admiral, not to spoil your fun, but can't you just call your friend Harry to beam the three of us the hell out of here? This *is* an emergency, after all."

"Oh," Kirk said, a note of disappointment in his voice. "Well, I suppose we could do that, all right." He began to reach under the flap of his jacket for his communicator, which was precisely when the three remaining thugs rushed them.

G'dath roared and, with one swipe of his mighty arm, two of the attackers went down. Kirk tackled the third. Davis picked up the scanner cube she had used against the first attacker and, standing over the two wrestling men, attempted to bash Kirk's foe over the head, but there was too much movement back and forth as the men fought.

There was suddenly a muffled "ulp" from behind her. Davis turned to see G'dath holding the revived first attacker by his collar. His feet dangled several inches off the ground. The man wriggled in the Klingon's powerful grip. "Let me go, you alien bastard!" the man cried.

"You are a loathsome little noise," G'dath said. "Ms. Davis, you should always watch your back most carefully in these situations. As for you, noisy one, go to sleep."

"Huh?" the man said.

"Enough," G'dath said, striking the man on the head and letting him fall to the ground. "Admiral, are you done?"

"One moment," Kirk said. He was sitting on the chest of his own opponent. "You going to behave now?" Kirk asked him.

"Go to hell, alien lover!" the man hissed. Wriggling a hand free, he produced a blade.

But before he could bring the blade to bear, Kirk brought his fist down on the thug's jaw. The man fell unconscious.

"Effective," G'dath said approvingly.

"You didn't do so badly yourself," Kirk said, rising. He tasted blood and wiped a thin smear of it from his lip. "I'm glad you're none the worse for wear, Ms. Davis."

"Well, thanks, Admiral. But your uniform's a little dirty."

"It'll brush off," Kirk said, grinning. "These new tearproof fabrics are a godsend. Time was when I would use up at least one uniform per month. How are your scanners?"

Davis bent to inspect them. "The one you were carrying is fine," she reported after a moment. "The case on mine is dented—can't imagine how *that* happened—but its memory is intact. They're still scanning, too. Not only didn't we lose anything from the interview or the walkabout, but I think we may even have some great shots of the fight. After tonight, you'll both be heroes."

"Astonishing," Keth mused as he watched the console, a finger placed pensively across his lips. "That was a highly trained assault team. There is more to our farmer than I thought." He glanced down at Klor, who saw satisfaction, not surprise, in his superior's gaze. Things had gone, Klor realized, exactly as Keth had hoped. Had planned.

"Superior," he asked, "are there any orders for the covert operations chief?" It was the question Keth expected; he therefore asked it. But he had already guessed that Keth would not answer in the affirmative.

"No. The team has been taken into custody by the local authorities, but their cover stories will hold against routine police interrogation." Keth smiled, again with astonishing brilliance. "Meanwhile"—he paused to give Klor a look of utter significance—"we must make our own plans."

Klor smiled himself. For at that moment, he knew beyond all doubt that they were going home.

Chapter Nine

AFTER NAN DAVIS and Admiral Kirk had left, G'dath released Leaper from his temporary prison in the bedroom, then sat in his living room and wondered if he had done wrong by not telling them about the globe. At the time, discretion had seemed the wisest course. He had not wanted to release the information until he understood its power—and its danger—fully.

He felt a small twinge of guilt over not telling Ms. Davis. She had been so kind to him, so attentive to what he had to say. And she had cheerfully consented to join in his conspiracy to keep Leaper's presence a secret. A most remarkable person: generous, intelligent, and quite lovely, for a human female. He did not often allow himself such thoughts. Because he was Klingon, no doubt Ms. Davis perceived him as singularly unattractive. No matter; he had long ago resigned himself to loneliness. But he felt he could trust her, and wanted her to have the story. It would help her career, just as he knew that today's interview would help his.

The attack had left them unharmed, but G'dath still felt shaken. Not physically, but emotionally. He found violence deeply disturbing . . . and this particular incident doubly so. Not because it epitomized the difficulties that he faced here on Earth . . . no, there was something deeper, some seed of worry that had taken root in his subconscious, that was slowly growing.

Without being aware of a conscious decision to do so, he rose abruptly to his feet and retrieved the globe from the closet. Its shining surface was unmarred and he could feel the hum of power through his fingertips. He opened the access panel and flipped the relay. The interior lights glowed. The globe still functioned perfectly, even after its repeated voyages of the previous night.

G'dath had been forced to believe the globe's star scans after its fifth trip. The data had been consistent with the globe's initial direction of travel. It was the distance traveled that proclaimed the revolution.

The globe drew power seemingly from nowhere, and that had been revolution enough, certainly. But the reservoir of power the globe tapped into had certain characteristics that could be studied, measured and put to work. That was what made it science and not magic.

When he had first begun investigating the subject many years before, G'dath thought that he might have reached into warp space without any need for the complicated technology and massive amounts of energy usually required. However, he soon satisfied himself that, whatever it was that he had tapped into, it was not warp space, but something beyond it. Whatever it might be, it was something that warp space—and, by implication, normal space itself—was contained within. There was no reason to believe that it stopped there, either. Wheels within wheels . . .

G'dath's findings were quickly leading him to a theory of cosmology that would make everything presently known about the universe obsolete. He would do for present-day physics what warp-space pioneer Zefrem Cochrane had done for the physics of Einstein—that is, obliterate it.

A worthy achievement for a high school teacher.

On the globe's first flight he had intended it to travel to the moon, circle, take some readings from the stars to confirm its position, and return. Instead, it had shot past the moon and continued on to a point in space just under a thousand lightyears away. It had then come back directly to his window. The globe had made the round trip in just under six-point-seven seconds.

G'dath had calculated the percentage of error involved in the globe leaving a particular point in space, traveling a thousand lightyears, and then returning to virtually the same spot, while allowing for the various motions Earth itself had made through space in the intervening time. His preliminary figures showed an accuracy in navigation to one part in sixty trillion—but he certainly had not designed the globe for that. Then again, he had not designed the globe to travel at nearly three hundred lightyears per second, either . . . but it had.

He had also calculated the energy expenditure required to transmit an object a thousand lightyears and back in not much more than several blinks of an eye. Expressed as heat, the energy should have been enough to vaporize the Earth-Moon system—but the energy was not heat. All of it had been realized as motion. Even if an insignificant fraction of that awesome energy had been turned into heat, at a minimum the globe would have exploded with the force of a huge matter-antimatter reactor, with all the consequences to New York that implied. G'dath shuddered. If he'd known of the potential risk to others, he would have never attempted the test. Instead, he would have given the globe to Federation authorities directly for testing far, far away from any inhabited area.

There were many unanswered questions about what had happened, not the least of which was just how the globe had caused no more than a relatively minor clap of thunder upon its departure and return. Its speed through the air must have been many times that of light for it to have made it to point X and back so quickly. The globe could scarcely have taken the time to dawdle at escape velocity during atmospheric travel.

The Klingon knew that he had a great deal more work to do before making any sort of announcement. He was disappointed that he could not go public immediately, but he had been waiting for quite a while for recognition—and this was much too important for anything but his best efforts. He knew it would be best for him to wait a little while longer. He would sort out the theoretical work, and then give the globe to the Federation for further—and *safer*—testing.

Besides, there were other implications of a technology this powerful.

He thought of Admiral Kirk, and of Ms. Davis's question: *Have you ever fought a Federation vessel?* He had been relieved to be able to answer in the negative —not because he feared what Davis or Kirk might think of him otherwise, but because he deplored the unnecessary expenditure of life. He had sincerely liked the admiral, and meeting Kirk reminded him of the fact that there were honorable warriors on both sides of a battle. A waste, to spill such noble blood.

Yet it had begun to occur to him that his invention could lead to conflict. Could *facilitate* conflict. An enemy with the globe could strike quickly, and disappear without incurring casualties.

G'dath noticed that Leaper was standing next to him. The little cat was looking up at him with bright, inquisitive eyes. The Klingon bent to stroke him.

"Leaper," he said, "do you understand what is meant by the term 'balance of power'?"

Leaper squeaked.

"No? Then permit me to explain. Postulate two rival political entities. Each is large and powerful. Each has its own sphere of influence. The friction between these two entities occasionally erupts into open hostility but, generally speaking, full-scale confrontation is prevented because each entity enjoys a rough equivalence with the other. Since neither enjoys a clear advantage, neither is willing to risk the peace that exists between them. Am I being clear?"

The kitten began to buzz.

"Excellent," said G'dath. "Well, then. The balance of power is easily preserved when each side possesses equivalent wealth, resources and technology. Now, if a serious imbalance exists between the entities in any of these three areas, friction increases, and the possibility of confrontation becomes much greater. Do you understand?"

Leaper blinked at him.

G'dath fell silent. He had intended the globe as a portable source of freely available energy. Instead, he had created something that had the potential of being the most terrible device yet invented—a device of unknown power that not only could be built cheaply, but was able to travel at nearly incalculable speed and with absolute accuracy.

He took the globe and gingerly set it in the closet. He did not shut the closet, but stood staring at his invention.

The attack today still bothered him. There was a warning contained in it somehow, something that his subconscious was trying to tell him.

A feeling of cold dread settled over him. Without the slightest doubt, he *knew* he was being watched. Had been watched. It was almost as if his surveillant had read his mind today. As he had walked with Nan Davis and the admiral in the park, he had been silently debating whether to tell her of his discovery. At one point, the words had been on his lips.

And then, the attack had come.

No. No, the assailants had all been humans. He was simply allowing his worried mind to create paranoid fantasies. He was not being watched. And yet . . .

In the Empire, he had taken for granted that Imperial operatives watched him.

Who was to say they were not watching him now? That they had taken note of his device—without quite understanding the implications of the data— and that the "Barclayites'" attack was meant to silence him?

But the attack had gone awry. Which meant that he had very little time before the next one.

G'dath stood, indecisive, in front of the closet for some time. Reason warred with fear, and in the end, fear won. Far safer to indulge paranoia with no harm to anyone, than to risk the alternative. He scooped up the kitten, who had been crying piteously at his feet, and said, with a cheerfulness that sounded forced to his own ears:

"Why are you crying, little one? Are you bored with having to stay inside all day? Perhaps I should take you outside for a little fresh air and sun—but only for a moment, and you must promise not to run away."

Sensing G'dath's inner turmoil, Leaper squirmed in his hands.

151

G'dath hesitated before shutting the closet door. If he really *were* being watched, taking the globe with him now would be the worst possible course of action. It would alert his observers to his suspicion, and he would probably be apprehended before he made it out of the building. But if they believed he was stepping outside only for a moment, he had a better chance of escape.

Not without misgivings, he left the globe. He had a plan for retrieving it that involved personal danger to no one. With any luck, it would be back in his possession within the hour—that is, if Nan Davis and Admiral Kirk were willing to help. He alone knew how to operate it, and he alone knew how to construct one. As a safeguard, he had stored only partial information as to its design in his computer. The missing information was in his memory.

And he intended to make himself quite unavailable to any interested parties. Making soothing noises at the little cat, G'dath walked calmly, resolutely out his apartment door.

In the St. Francis dining room, Kevin Riley stirred gratefully in his plush, comfortable chair and yawned. The subdued lighting and soft violin music made him want to lay his cheek against the table and fall blissfully asleep. Up to that moment, the momentum of his earlier panic had kept him awake—that, and the energy he'd absorbed from Jenny Hogan. She radiated it, and he was surprised he'd been able to keep up with her on the walk to the hotel.

Some of her radiance had dimmed and she was once again studying him with concern. He realized that he hadn't said a word since they'd sat down. Jenny had done all the talking. The waiter had deposited the food moments ago, but Riley hadn't yet summoned the strength to sample his eggs Florentine.

The silence grew until Kevin became nervous and decided to say something—but Jenny beat him to it.

"Kevin, where did you spend last night? You look like the last guy out of Iran before Khan Noonian Singh blew it up."

He poked at a poached egg with his fork and watched it quiver atop a bed of green, causing him to lose whatever appetite he had. Her question was nosy, no doubt about it, but she had such an ingenuous way of asking that he didn't resent it. Still, he was unsure: Had she asked out of idle curiosity—or was she trying to find out whether he was involved with someone? He decided to be as honest as possible with her, even if it meant talking about Anab. Even though he had just met Jenny, she had helped him, and there was something about her that made him instinctively trust her.

Kevin sighed again and set down his fork. "I just overslept, that's all. Insomnia. I've been having a terrible time with it lately."

"Oh." She took a mouthful of food and watched him with innocent wide green eyes. Like Riley, she was baby-faced. That and her small stature conspired to make her look at most twenty.

He could see from her expectant expression that he had failed to provide the information she sought. He tried again.

"I was alone, Jenny."

She looked down quickly at her plate with the faintest trace of embarrassment. "None of my business, of course," she said, but it was clear that he'd told her what she wanted to hear.

"I don't mind," he said lightly, and half grinned at the way she brightened immediately.

"So what's the matter? Your job? Jim Kirk doesn't strike me as an anxiety-producing monster." She gestured with her fork. "Especially considering how

153

he saved your life all those years ago. And to think that, after all that time, the two of you grew up to serve together in Starfleet."

Kevin squinted at her, certain that his confusion resulted from a lack of sleep. "I'm afraid I don't follow."

"Oops." Jenny bit her lip. "I'm sorry, I didn't mean to bring that up. Producers get into the habit of researching everyone's background. So when Kirk was scheduled for the show, I started digging into his history and noticed that it overlapped with yours back on Tarsus IV. Sorry. I didn't mean to mention it so . . . cavalierly. I know it must have been a horrible tragedy for you."

He forced himself not to tense at the mention of the place, and managed to answer her easily. "It happened a long time ago. I really don't remember much about it. I was too young. Kirk was on Tarsus, too—but I don't understand; what do you mean, 'what he did for me'? We didn't know each other at the time. We didn't meet until I was assigned to the *Enterprise.*"

She stared uncomprehendingly at him. "I found some old footage. Someone had done a human interest story on fourteen-year-old Jim—Jimmy—Kirk. According to the article, he rescued a child, four-year-old Kevin Thomas Riley, from being executed. The facts checked out. You're joking, right? Of course you knew . . ."

Kevin had not believed a word, had been certain that *his* leg was the one being yanked—unforgivably —until Jenny had hesitated when she said the name: *Jim—Jimmy.*

Something dark and forbidden stirred in his memory. Jimmy. Jim. *It's not safe . . .*

Riley raised a hand to his forehead. He had never quite understood why Kirk had been so interested in him, so keenly concerned about his career, so willing to give him a chance. The admiral had always claimed it was because Riley deserved it, possessed the ability to command.

But Riley's insecurity had never allowed him to believe it.

He closed his eyes and, for the first time in twenty-five years, summoned the face of the stranger who had saved his life. More than ever, he realized how deeply he must have disappointed the admiral this morning.

Jenny leaned forward, frowning with concern. "Kevin, are you all right?"

"Fine," Riley managed. "Just a little tired." He lowered the hand and smiled weakly. "Of course I knew about Kirk."

"So if it's not Kirk that's bothering you."

"It's not." Kevin paused, grateful to change the subject, but unsure how to begin. "It's me."

The interest and sympathy on her features was so sincere that his throat tightened. "Do you want to talk about it, Kevin?"

He took a breath and got hold of himself. "Jenny . . . I was married until just last week. I didn't want out. She did."

She paled and set down her fork. "Kevin, I'm so sorry. I shouldn't have pried—"

"You didn't. I volunteered. I guess, since I've started, I may as well tell you everything—if you want to hear."

She put an elbow on the table and drew closer. "I want to hear."

Riley focused at a spot in the far distance. "We'd signed for a year, and after six months, she took a one-year deep space assignment. I talked her into extending our contract to eighteen months, so when her assignment was up, our contract would be, too. I guess I was trying to force her to choose between re-enlisting and our marriage." He paused, amazed that he could speak about it this easily to someone, amazed that Jenny made it this easy—and a little shocked at himself for appreciating her company. He felt somehow disloyal. "It's not like I just lost her yesterday. I mean, we'd been apart for a whole year. I should've seen this coming. But . . . until last week, I guess I couldn't face it." His mouth twisted. "I called her the day our contract expired. I guess I should've taken the hint. And then, yesterday, she sent a message to my terminal, asking me to send her the rest of her things."

"Well." Jenny seemed overwhelmed. "So you woke up late this morning and had Jim Kirk ready to courtmartial you. Quite a day."

"I deserved it," Riley said sincerely. "But I *have* had better weeks."

His deadpan delivery made her giggle, and he found himself smiling. He took a bite of his food, and realized he was a little hungry, after all. "Enough angst. Thanks for listening, Jenny. I just wanted to explain because . . ." He hesitated.

"Because?" She had quit pretending to eat and leaned forward, intent on hearing what he had to say. He felt a surge of conflicting emotions. The look in Jenny's eyes was precisely the one he had hoped to see in Anab's. He felt deeply grateful, guilty, frightened, and attracted all at once.

Kevin dropped his gaze, afraid to meet hers. ". . . because," he said, his tone carefully neutral, "I'm grateful for a friend."

She smiled a little uncertainly, trying to puzzle out the implications of what he'd said. He decided to help her.

"A friend is about all I can handle right now, Jenny."

"Of course." Her smile broadened, but he heard the

156

trace of disappointment in her voice. "Who could blame you for that? Good friends are hard to come by."

The conversation went on to other things, and in spite of his exhaustion, Riley had an enjoyable time. Jenny recovered admirably and was quite a witty companion. At the end of it, they exchanged codes and Jenny told him to call her if he ever needed to talk to a friend.

He promised her he would. But of course, they both knew better.

Chapter Ten

ALTHOUGH SHE WAS still running on San Francisco time, in New York it was afternoon, and so Nan Davis settled down to lunch—though her body interpreted it as breakfast—with Jim Kirk. After the violent encounter in the park and the subsequent question-and-answer session with the local authorities, she felt a little shaky on her feet. The chance to sit down and finally get something to eat sounded like an ideal solution.

At the same time, she felt oddly exhilarated by the experience, as upsetting as it had been. It gave her a sense of camaraderie with Kirk. Formality seemed pretty ridiculous, after fighting beside him in a free-for-all—and they had begun using first names per unspoken mutual agreement.

She had been forewarned about the admiral's legendary charisma, and had been exposed to it before for a brief minute or so one time on Centaurus. Of course, that had been the public James T. Kirk . . . and she was beginning to think that the private Kirk was even more appealing.

Not that she intended to react to that charm, of

course. She'd done her research, knew that Kirk was married to a Vice Admiral Ciana—though she had been intrigued by the shadow that had fallen over his face earlier that morning when she had mentioned his wife.

As for Jim, he behaved as the total professional. The conversation did not meander onto personal topics, and they were in the middle of discussing the Dart Project when Nan's pager beeped.

She sighed sharply. It was probably Jenny, with an emergency at the studio. "Sorry, Jim. Would you think it terribly rude of me if I went ahead and took the call here?"

Jim gave a faint, gracious smile. "Not at all."

She removed the pager from her belt and flipped it open. "Nan Davis." She expected to hear Jenny's soprano pitch, and was unprepared for the booming bass that followed.

"Ms. Davis. I apologize for calling you on the pager. I would not have used the code you gave me were this not an emergency."

"Doctor G'dath!" She frowned and looked meaningfully across the table at Jim Kirk, who glanced up from his datapad with surprise, then frowned himself. "What sort of emergency? Don't tell me those horrible Barclayites came back?" For a moment she was honestly terrified that he had been seriously hurt. The earlier attack had made her ashamed of her own race, ashamed to be human. It seemed unfair that someone as brilliant, as talented, as kind-hearted as G'dath could be the target of such mindless hatred. She could hear the kitten yowling in the background, and street sounds. "Are you okay? Is that Leaper? Where are you?"

"Leaper is here with me, though he is rather annoyed at being restrained. I am unharmed—although this does have directly to do with the attack on us this afternoon. I am calling from a public communicator; I have left the apartment and am carrying the kitten with me. Ms. Davis . . . are you alone?"

"No. Jim—Admiral Kirk—is here with me. I'm in a restaurant, but there's no one listening to us."

"Admiral Kirk," G'dath said. "That is very fortunate. I need his help as well as yours. You see, this afternoon, when you interviewed me, I had originally intended to unveil an invention. However, its capabilities were so far beyond what I had expected that I decided to wait and gather more data."

"What kind of invention?" Nan asked.

"A . . . device. A globe that can travel through space for great distances under its own power. I do not know if this is a maximum, but the globe has maintained an average speed of just under three hundred and fifty lightyears per second."

Across the table, Jim Kirk gasped.

Nan's frown deepened. "What's that in warp speed?"

"The globe does not travel in warp space, so using those terms does not make sense. Suffice it to say that it travels many times faster than a Starship's top speed."

Jim Kirk moved his chair next to hers and gestured for the pager. She held it between them so that he could speak into the grid.

Jim's expression was one of growing skepticism. "Doctor G'dath, that's a pretty amazing claim. But why are you telling us this now? And what does this have to do with the Barclayites?"

"I have been thinking, Admiral; I have been working on this device for some time, but I was able to test the globe only this Friday. I find it rather . . . opportune that the attack occurred during the interview, before I was able to inform Ms. Davis about my invention."

Nan raised her eyebrows at Jim to mean *Do you think he's telling the truth? Or simply paranoid?*

Jim shook his head in a gesture that she interpreted as *Hard to say.*

G'dath seemed to sense their doubt. "Surely, Admiral, you have heard the rumor that Klingon citizens are watched."

"I've heard it, but I don't know if it's true. I suppose it's possible."

"My instinct tells me I have been watched, and that today's attack was the result."

Kirk's tone was faintly dry. "Why'd they wait until now?"

"Even *I* did not realize the capabilities of the globe until very early this morning, Admiral. I daresay it has taken my observers longer to do the same because of my . . . precautions. No complete schematic for the globe's design exists anywhere . . . except my memory." The Klingon paused. "Admiral Kirk, Ms. Davis, whether my instinct is correct or the result of paranoia, it is only logical to obey it. If I am wrong, the worst that will happen is that I will have made a fool of myself. If, however, I am right—"

"My former first officer was Vulcan, G'dath, and I think he would agree with your logic." There was a ghost of a smile in Kirk's tone, if not on his face.

"I get the impression I have just been complimented," G'dath said.

Nan leaned forward and spoke into the pager. "G'dath, what do you want us to do? Do you need a safe place to stay? My apartment is small, but you and Leaper are more than wel—"

"I appreciate the offer, Ms. Davis, but I cannot endanger you so. Admiral Kirk—"

"Yes, G'dath. You said you needed my help."

"The globe whereof I spoke. I have left it back at my apartment. I did not feel safe carrying it on the street, and I felt certain I would have been . . . intercepted had I tried to remove it from the apartment. It seems to me the safest course would be to simply beam it out of my apartment."

"True," Kirk said. "But why should Starfleet offer you the use of its transporter?"

"Because of what I offer Starfleet. The same type of logic applies: If I am lying about the globe's powers, then all you and Starfleet have lost is a few seconds' transporter time. But if I am telling the truth—"

"I get your point, G'dath. I'll get in touch with my transporter people. Give me your location and don't go anywhere. We'll retrieve you first, then the globe. If it can do what you say, I'm sure Starfleet will be willing to guarantee your protection."

"Thank you, Admiral. I suggest we make haste. I suspect that we may already be too late."

Keth had quickly neutralized the doorkeeper in the lobby—child's play for a trained operative—while Klor had dealt with the security block in the lift by shorting out the voice recognition system.

As the lift obediently carried them to the fifty-first floor, Klor glanced over at his commander. Earlier, when Klor had reported that the subject G'dath had left the apartment, Keth had flown into a murderous rage: G'dath was their means home! Klor was an imbecile to permit him to escape! So furious had Keth been that Klor dared not speak, even to protest weakly that G'dath would no doubt be returning soon, as he had not taken the globe with him.

And then Keth had issued a startling order: They

would go to the apartment themselves and seize the globe. Keth had not spoken since. Clearly, the threat of losing G'dath gnawed at him—so much so that Klor feared for his commander's sanity.

Now, on the lift, Keth's lips were drawn into a taut line, his brows into a bushy vee above grim, dangerous eyes, the eyes of one obsessed.

Earlier, the commander had promised Klor that he would win honor, would go home—but now Klor feared for his position, and was eager to atone for his mistake.

The lift stopped; the doors opened. Klor strode swiftly down the corridor until he found G'dath's number.

"Quickly." Keth pointed at the door. Crouching, Klor took a small instrument from the pouch on his belt and began to neutralize the security scanners embedded in the door frame. Fortunately, the designers of the system had not deemed it necessary to construct the device to withstand Klingon countermeasures.

A soft whoosh sounded as the door across the hall opened.

Klor glanced up over his shoulder and straightened. A human male—gray-haired, pale, feeble-looking—stepped from his doorway. To Klor's astonishment, the old man seemed totally unfrightened to find two Klingons in his building. In fact, he caught Klor's eye and smiled.

"I thought I heard someone out here," he said pleasantly, his voice reedy with age. "Are you friends of G'dath? I think he just went out a moment ago."

Keth and Klor stared, at a loss . . . and then Keth ordered: "Kill him."

Klor hesitated—not long enough for Keth to notice and give the commander further reason to doubt him, not long enough for the old man to notice and try to move out of harm's way—but long enough for Klor to feel regret. He had been taught reverence for his elders, and this gray-haired one certainly meant no harm—indeed, he trusted them, had *smiled* at them. Never before had a human smiled at Klor in friendship.

But Keth had given an order, and Klor knew that to disobey it now meant he would be labeled a traitor, and would not see home again.

He stepped forward and with an easy, rapid movement of his arm, caught the human on the side of the neck. Klor attempted, without being so obvious that Keth would notice, to deliver a blow that would disable without killing, but despite his effort, he heard the dull snap of bone.

It happened so quickly that the old one never cried out, never raised an arm in defense, but crumpled to the floor.

Klor scooped him up. The man was light, fragile in his arms. Keth reached out and took his burden from him.

"Complete your task, Klor. I will dispose of this."

"Yes, Superior." Strangely heavy of heart, Klor crouched down and returned to his work on the door. He listened as, behind him, Keth flung the old one back into his apartment. There was the heavy, ugly sound of the body striking the floor, then the hiss of the door sliding shut. Klor became aware of Keth's legs beside him.

"Hurry," the commander said. "The killing may not go unnoticed by the building security system."

An instant later, Klor cracked through the security field covering G'dath's door. It slid aside smoothly, and they entered.

The apartment was sparsely furnished; clearly,

G'dath had not succumbed to an Earther desire for comfort. Klor watched as Keth walked over to the *vuv gho* and contemptuously kicked it. A piece of fruit placed in the small offering receptacle bounced and rolled to the other end of the room.

"This way, Superior." Klor gestured toward the bedroom. Pulse racing, he dashed toward it and pressed the control that opened the closet.

The globe lay, shining and beautiful, on the floor of the closet. Klor reached for it, but Keth's arms restrained him. The commander bent down and hefted the device. From his surprised reaction, Klor saw that it weighed very little. He turned to Klor and bared his teeth in pleasure.

"This is the pebble that will crush the mountain of the enemy."

An hour later, G'dath sat in Admiral Kirk's office at Starfleet Headquarters and covered his face with his hands. Nan Davis sat nearby, stroking Leaper while the kitten buzzed drowsily. Kirk faced them both as he leaned against his desk, arms folded in front of his chest.

A scan of G'dath's apartment had revealed no globe. G'dath had insisted on beaming over to the apartment and searching himself, and Jim Kirk had insisted on coming with him. They'd found the apartment ransacked, and—as G'dath's instincts had told him—the globe missing.

That had not been the worst of it. As they were preparing to leave before the police arrived, G'dath had heard a commotion out in the hallway. He had peered out through the peephole of his door to see paramedics floating Mr. Olesky out of his apartment on a stretcher. A crowd of neighbors had gathered, and G'dath had overheard one of them say that the old man had been mysteriously beaten—and that the security in the building had been breached by experts. "Klingons," one of them had said. "Frances saw two of them hanging around the entryway on her way out this afternoon." Olesky, it seemed, was not expected to live.

A man who had only shown others kindness. G'dath groaned, only vaguely aware that Nan Davis had put a comforting hand on his arm.

His invention, less than a full day old . . . and already, there was blood on his hands. Had he possessed the globe at that moment, he would have destroyed it.

But now Starfleet knew of the device, and would pressure him to create another. He would do it—in the event a Klingon mind as adept as his own managed to fill in the missing pieces of the design, and discover how the globe functioned.

"Doctor G'dath," Jim Kirk said quietly.

G'dath raised his face and rested his chin against his steepled hands; Nan Davis gave his arm a reassuring pat and drew her hand away, and he tried to smile at her.

Whatever doubt the admiral had entertained about G'dath's veracity had been erased after the visit to the apartment. Kirk straightened and took a step away from his desk. "There's very little chance at this point of our operatives being able to retrieve the globe."

Nan Davis spoke up. "But the biggest danger is to G'dath himself." Her tone was indignant; G'dath looked at her, mildly surprised by her protectiveness.

Kirk nodded. "I agree—that is, if Doctor G'dath is absolutely certain they'll be unable to figure out the globe without him."

"Quite certain," G'dath sighed. "At least for the immediate present. However, it is possible that, given a few years, they might deduce the design. If they managed to capture me, I would of course tell them nothing—but I am not so arrogant as to think I could withstand the mind sifter. Even if I avoid capture now, according to the terms of my visa, I will have to return to the Empire in a year's time. I will certainly face interrogation then."

"We won't let that happen," Kirk said. "We'll keep you under tight security here in San Francisco for as long as you wish."

G'dath felt a sudden surge of worry. "My class. Ms. Davis was going to do a live segment from my classroom Monday morning. I cannot disappoint them . . ."

"Or my producers," Nan chimed in.

". . . by simply canceling. I would not want to cancel class, regardless. I have a responsibility to them. And I doubt a suitable substitute could be found on such short notice. But I cannot subject my students to any danger. One person is already near death because of me; I will risk no others."

Kirk raised an eyebrow. "I doubt you'd be attacked in front of a roomful of people, Doctor G'dath, especially in front of live trivision scanners. Most intelligence operatives prefer secrecy. You're in the greatest danger when you're alone. You'll have round-the-clock protection, of course, and to reassure you, we can provide additional security while you're teaching. We certainly don't want to endanger any lives, either."

"The security would be infallible?" G'dath asked.

"As infallible as security can be," Kirk said. "You have my word on it. I want you to know something else—I'm not going through regular channels on this. I'm having my own people arrange security for you as a personal favor. Going through channels is a tedious process—and frankly, it would take Starfleet a week to sort through your computer notes and decide if you were telling the truth about your globe's capabilities."

G'dath tilted his head, curious. "And why do you trust me, Admiral Kirk?"

He smiled with his eyes alone. "My instincts tell me I can. I'd appreciate it if you wouldn't disappoint them."

In the early hours of Sunday morning, Klor went once again to his superior's quarters. Klor had not slept since the subject G'dath had made his escape. He suspected that Keth had already informed the Empire of the fact—and Klor's role in it. Now Klor had nothing to do but wait to learn of his fate, which now rested in Keth's hands.

Depending on the commander's good graces, Klor might be demoted to an even less desirable position (though it was hard to imagine one existed), exiled, or perhaps even sent to prison camp. All depended on how Keth presented the error to Imperial officials.

But he had not spoken to his superior since. Keth remained closeted in his quarters, and Klor began to fear that the depression that had earlier consumed the commander had returned with a vengeance—and Klor could blame no one but himself. The chance that the two of them might somehow win honor and receive a more prestigious assignment for bringing G'dath's invention to the Empire's attention had escaped along with the subject. If there were only a way to redeem himself . . . but Klor had given up hope of doing so.

As the door to Keth's quarters slid open in response to the summons, Klor's hope of leniency evaporated. Keth was not asleep, rather, the commander sat in the darkness, his back to Klor, staring out at the predawn sky. Behind him, on the desk, the holo of his wife and sons glowed. Keth did not move or turn on the lights when Klor entered, but remained, shoulders slumped wearily in his chair, as if he had not slept in many days.

Klor stood in the doorway to allow the light from the hallway to enter and cleared his throat, but the commander remained as he was. "I am still unable to locate G'dath, Superior. However, you asked me to notify you if we received further orders. We are to assemble another assault team so that it is prepared to strike when the subject is found."

Still gazing at the fading stars, Keth spoke slowly, his tone so distracted Klor wondered if he had heard. "I am beginning to think I understand this dreamer, this son of farmers. I do not know where he has hidden now—but I know where he will be. Tomorrow."

"Where, Superior?" Klor asked, startled and yet hopeful that this was an example of Keth's legendary cunning.

Keth swiveled to face him, eyes glittering in the dimness, and smiled ironically. "I have not informed anyone of your error, Klor."

Klor's gaze dropped to the floor as he waited to learn of his fate. He did not permit himself self-pity or regret. As a warrior, he would accept Keth's decree without argument or plea. But he was unprepared for what Keth said next.

"Whether I do or not depends on you. How badly do you want to go home?"

Klor glanced up in confusion. "Forgive me, Superior. I do not understand."

"It's a simple question." Keth's tone was calm, but he studied Klor with frightening intensity. "How badly do you want to go home?"

Klor paused, trying to condense his feelings about the subject into a single sentence.

"To go home with honor," Keth said abruptly. "As a hero. How badly would you want that?"

He did not pause at that, but answered softly: "To go home—with honor—I would risk everything. My life."

Keth nodded, satisfied; his smile broadened. "Good. Very good. Perhaps I need not inform our superiors at all. My feeling is that the mistake was a most understandable one. Certainly we have all erred at some point in our career." He paused. "As far as I am concerned, our assault team is already assembled."

Klor tensed. If he understood his commander, Keth was suggesting that they two be the assault team; a bold and rather questionable move, to interpret orders so freely.

"I have a rather . . . unconventional plan. Do you trust me, Klor?"

"Without question, Superior." He answered immediately, and did not allow the hesitation he felt to be reflected in his manner or voice.

Keth seemed pleased. "What I propose is risky indeed. But as a warrior, I grow tired of living without risk." His tone changed abruptly. "Do you know how many seasons it has been since I have spoken with my wife? Since I have touched her . . ." He sighed and glanced at the family holo glowing on his desk. "Better to be dead than live with dishonor." He looked back up at Klor. "We can take no phasers, no weapons that can be detected, and we will rely on surprise and timing. If the plan goes awry, we will not even be able to depend on the Embassy for transport." He smiled briefly.

"We strike tomorrow morning, Klor. Can you be ready?"

"I will be ready, Superior," Klor said. There was

little choice; Keth had made the options clear. Join his plan for glory, or face further disgrace.

But in the subtle light, the gleam in Keth's eyes seemed not so much inspired as mad . . . or perhaps it was only a trick of the dimness and shadow. After all, Klor told himself, Keth's career as a commander was marked by brilliance . . . and true brilliance hovers on the edge of madness.

On Sunday afternoon, Nan got a call from her assignment editor: she was to cover the Apollo Day story. Nan was elated, and called Jenny to tell her to get in touch with Kirk's chief of staff on Monday— although Jenny seemed oddly reserved about the idea. And then she called Jim Kirk. They agreed to meet early Monday so Nan could get some footage of the Dart Project. It put her in a rush between assignments, but she had already prerecorded her introduction to the live segment in G'dath's classroom just in case. After all, the only live part of the segment was to be a portion of G'dath's lecture and a question-and-answer session with the students.

She asked about G'dath, and other than to say the Klingon was fine, Kirk offered no information on his whereabouts. Nan did not press. In some ways, G'dath and Kirk were very much alike: both men of the highest principle, both among the most talented in their respective professions—although G'dath's abilities had not been recognized by his peers. Yet. She hoped her piece on him would change that.

She had stopped worrying about whether G'dath had told the truth about the globe's capabilities. Like Jim Kirk, she trusted her instincts and believed him. Since the moment she'd first spoken with G'dath, she'd been deeply impressed by his sincerity, his genuineness, his warmth. If the Apollo Day story impressed the WorldNews brass enough that they promoted her to the New York Bureau, she hoped that she and G'dath could become good friends.

After the attack on Friday, he'd looked as though he could use one.

Early Monday morning, Kirk, Nan and Nan's technician, Eddie, shimmered into existence on the tarmac directly in front of the Dulles Park hangar leased by the Dart Project. A long time before, Dulles Park had been an airport. That had been back in the days when hurtling aircraft relied largely on the friction of wheel against pavement and brake against wheel to come to a halt. That haphazard way of doing business took no small amount of room. Eventually, though, aircraft had no longer needed runways to land, so Dulles had been closed, landscaped and reopened as one of the largest recreational parks in eastern North America.

But there was still one hangar doing business . . .

The first person they saw as they entered was Alice Friedman, the shuttle pilot. She was dressed in a painstakingly exact copy of a late twentieth-century NASA-issue jumpsuit. "Greetings, everyone," she called. "Welcome to the Dart Project." Hands were shaken all around. "You'll forgive us if we don't lay on much of a welcome for y'all," Alice said, "but time's pretty short and everybody's kinda busy. I'm only the pilot, so I have some time to spare." She smiled.

Kirk returned it. "It's a pleasure to meet you," he said.

"Yes, indeed," Nan said. "Thanks for having us, Captain Friedman."

"Likewise," grunted Eddie.

"Want to see our baby?" Alice asked them. "I think she's finally fit for company."

"Lead the way," Kirk said, and together the three of them entered the cool dimness of the hangar.

Kirk knew what he was going to see, but the sight nevertheless took his breath away.

It was Orbiter 101, the original space shuttle, appearing as fresh and new as she had when she had first been rolled out from a hangar at a U.S. Air Force plant in California. She had been named the *Enterprise* because one of the project managers for Rockwell International, the builder of the vehicle, had lost a brother stationed aboard the aircraft carrier of the same name during the recently concluded World War.

The *Enterprise* had pioneered a new era in the exploration of space. She had then been tossed aside callously, consigned to a museum storage building, and allowed to deteriorate over the decades . . . until someone had come along and cared for her as she deserved. Now she stood on her landing gear, proudly restored, the gleaming whiteness of her insulative tiling unscarred and unblemished by time or trauma.

She was gigantic. The space shuttle *Enterprise* was perhaps eight times the size of a shuttlecraft carried by a starship cruiser. The ship had been the queen of her era, short as that era had proven to be. The development of the impulse engine near the beginning of the twenty-first century had doomed the shuttle program. The shuttle could not even make re-entry under power; she depended instead on atmospheric braking and a limited ability to maneuver aerodynamically to land. Kirk remembered that she had been described as a flying brick. He decided again that her crew had indeed been people of great courage.

Her original markings had been restored, right down to the sans-serif black lettering that read UNITED STATES and ENTERPRISE. There was only one difference: The identifying American flags painted on her hull had been updated to the proper fifty-six stars, and they had been paired with the red and silver standard flag of the United Federation of Planets.

"Did we do good?" Friedman asked, smugly sure of the answer.

Kirk said nothing, but merely nodded slowly, drinking it in. Finally he said, "Let's go aboard."

"Right this way," Friedman said.

The four of them clambered up a temporary accessway that led to the access hatch and entered the ship. If the outside of the shuttle represented the faithful restoration of the work of twentieth-century artisans, its interior had done away with that original work ruthlessly. Everything inside the skin of the shuttle was on the cutting edge of twenty-third-century technology.

They entered the cockpit, and Kirk looked at the newly installed controls. They seemed about a thousand times simpler than the originals he'd seen pictured. "Now those look familiar," he said, pointing. "They look like something I'd see on a standard shuttlecraft."

"They're exactly that," Friedman said, nodding. "Using standard controls saved us a little time and expense. We didn't have to change things much to make 'em fit, so we used 'em."

"You're using standard impulse engines, too?" Nan asked.

"That's right," said Friedman. "We've installed a cluster of class-two impulse units right where the old engines used to be. Their thrust is directed through the old engine outlets."

"Those old outlets can take that kind of heat?" asked Kirk.

"Oh, sure," Friedman replied. "Compared to what those outlets were designed for, impulse thrust temperature is just a fairly warm breeze. They used to fill this sweetheart up with liquefied gases, and then they lit a match. Now that kind of business can get *hot.*"

"Why didn't you try to fly the whole launch assembly?" Nan asked. "You know, the tanks and boosters as well as the orbiter itself—the dart, as you call it?"

"We could have done that, I guess," Friedman said, "but the tank and SRBs—the solid rocket boosters— wouldn't contribute anything to the impulse configuration of the dart, so we forgot about 'em. We would have had to manufacture replicas in any case, because there aren't any tanks or boosters around anymore and doing that would have cost even more. So why bother?" Then she grinned. "Besides, she looks neater and cleaner this way, don't you think?"

"I do," Nan said. "When are you planning to take her up, Captain?"

"We're ready to go in just a few minutes," Friedman said. "It'll be her first checkout flight—a milk run up and down the coast at maybe five thousand meters. If everything goes okay, I'll take her all the way up and out tomorrow afternoon. That'll be a figure-eight around the moon. Call it six hours. That'll give us more than two days to nail down glitches before we head out for the parade of spacecraft."

"Do you expect any problems?" Nan asked.

"Nope. This is a sweetheart we've got here, I can tell you. She's been waiting a very long time for her day to come. She *wants* to fly." She patted the console.

"I agree," Kirk said, nodding. "She's ready."

"Well then, let's go." Friedman motioned them toward the hatch.

Nan hesitated. "I'm not sure I have enough time for a flight. I have a live segment in New York later this morning. Could we just set up the scanners inside and take a few pictures?"

"No problem. Tell you what—I'll even raise and lower her a few meters off the tarmac so you can get some shots of what it looks like from inside during take-off. Would that keep you on schedule?"

Nan grinned. "That would be perfect. Captain Friedman, you're wonderful!"

"I know. Hear it all the time. Besides, I figured you might want to see it for yourself instead of letting your technician have all the fun." Friedman returned the grin. "C'mon people, let's fly!"

Chapter Eleven

ABOUT FIFTEEN MINUTES before nine o'clock, Joey Brickner walked into the classroom feeling like a victim showing up willingly for his own execution. He'd spent the weekend studying and rewriting the paper, and had hardly slept for two nights. The school had sent a memo home about the trivision article on the class, so Joey's mom was all excited, and had told his dad and grandparents so they'd be sure not to miss it.

Great. So the whole world would watch as he made a fool of himself on worldwide 3V.

Carlos Siegel had called on Saturday afternoon to make the offer about studying with him and Ricia again. Joey had been polite—he liked Carlos—but Ricia had made him feel embarrassed about telling the Klingon joke, and he was sure now that she disliked him. Besides, by late Saturday, Joey wasn't feeling too charitable toward Klingons after his hours of study. The mention of G'dath's name would have been enough to make him start spewing anti-Klingon epithets. He was angrier than ever at the teacher, enough to wonder whether Stoller had been right. *Turtle-lover.*

As he entered, he saw Carlos and Ricia already at their desks. Carlos smiled, and Ricia grinned as if Joey had never left in a huff on Friday, as if he'd never made a fool of himself with the stupid Cheetah joke, and whispered: "Break a leg, Brickner."

Amazingly, Ira Stoller was early and in his too-small desk, his long legs and arms overflowing. Stoller was fidgeting nervously and looked pretty miserable himself that morning. Joey suspected the loss of bravado had something to do with the trivision scanners. Before he took his own seat in front of Stoller's, Joey paused in the aisle and looked steadily at Ira. Just *looked.*

It was enough. Stoller twitched nervously and whispered, with an apologetic little half-grin: "Hey, Brickner, Friday was an accident, okay? I didn't mean for it to happen. I just—I don't know, went a little crazy." He glanced nervously over at the trivision scanners to be sure they weren't yet recording.

Joey didn't smile, just looked at Ira for a while, and then said, in a low voice so the trivision people wouldn't hear: "Hitting people isn't going to solve things, Stoller. It's only going to make them worse. You just pick on people so you don't have to think of your own problems."

Stoller bowed his head a little and looked away as Joey slid into his seat. He had barely settled in when he heard Stoller's voice in his ear:

"So, did they tell anyone or what?"

Joey shook his head, and heard Stoller deflate behind him with a sigh. And then, an instant later:

"Hey, Brickner, want a match? My body temperature and a turtlehead's IQ."

Joey pretended not to hear. He faced the front of the room and waited along with the others, and *tried* not to think about the trivision scanners and what awaited him, but within a minute the inside of his mouth had gone cottony. After a weekend of studying and little sleep, his mind was an incoherent jumble of thoughts. He tried to mentally answer some of the questions he anticipated Dr. G'dath would ask, but kept losing his train of thought and forgetting the answer.

He would draw a blank when G'dath called on him. He *knew* he would. He tried unsuccessfully to swallow and folded his hands atop his desk, squeezing hard to still their trembling.

Still no Doctor G'dath—and he didn't see the reporter from WorldNews, Nan Davis, who was supposed to be here, either. There were only an older guy setting up the scanners and fussing with the lighting, and a very pretty red-haired woman who looked too young to be working with a trivision crew. The woman kept glancing at her chrono, then up at the door.

At five minutes before the hour, everyone started whispering impatiently. Doctor G'dath was *always* here by five till, usually by ten till, and of all days, today he would have been even earlier. Joey felt curiosity and the stirrings of hope. Maybe Doctor G'dath had gotten sick, or mugged, or someone had landed a flitter on him. Maybe there was justice in the universe after all, and class would be canceled.

But Joey's hopes were dashed when G'dath walked into the room at exactly one minute before nine.

An expectant hush fell over the classroom. The red-haired woman went over to the teacher and spoke quietly for a while. Doctor G'dath seemed restless and tense, and kept glancing over his shoulder at the door. Joey was stunned. Surely G'dath wasn't *nervous* because of the scanners, was he? He couldn't imagine the Klingon being afraid of anything.

The woman finished talking, and G'dath nodded

and said: "Very well." The woman went to sit in the back of the room, and G'dath went over to his desk. As usual, he didn't sit, but began his customary pacing back and forth.

The lecture would soon begin. *Please,* Joey begged the universe, *let me relax enough so I can follow what he's saying.*

G'dath began to speak. "Consider the development of nuclear weapons. Every sufficiently advanced culture faces the dilemma of what to do about them. We know of no spacefaring culture that does not at least know how to build such weapons. Whether they do or not is another matter—as is the decision about whether or not to use them."

He glanced briefly at the door, then directed his attention back to his students. "There are a limited number of scenarios, and examples of each are available for our inspection. Here on Earth, for example, a brief, one-sided nuclear war was fought to end the greatest conventional war ever known up to that time. A general nuclear war has in fact never been fought on this planet, although extensive preparations were taken to do precisely that—indeed, the nations of Earth, rich and poor alike, nearly spent themselves into bankruptcy paying for it.

"Who can provide us with a brief summary of the Klingon Empire's experience with nuclear war?" G'dath's gaze swept over the room.

To Joey, the question seemed to quiver in the air forever; his eye caught Ricia Greene's, and she gave him a nod that seemed to say: *Go ahead. You can do it.*

He remembered what he'd read—last night? the night before?—about the Klingon nuclear wars. Only he'd been so tired, he wasn't sure he remembered it right. There had been three . . . or was it four?

He glanced away from Ricia to see G'dath, looking right at him. G'dath was opening his mouth to call Joey's name.

Joey went numb. And then, he raised his hand.

The teacher's expression was one of utter satisfaction. "Yes, Mister Brickner?"

Joey rose. He would have to make the summary quick because he didn't think his wobbly knees would last very long. He wondered if their shaking showed up on the trivision scanners.

"There were three nuclear wars in the Klingon Empire," Joey began, feeling intense relief when G'dath nodded slightly in agreement. "The first occurred more than two centuries ago when K'tel the Terrible attempted to conquer—"

He broke off as the room filled with a loud whining hum. Two sparkling figures began to form at the front of the classroom—the woman from WorldNews and someone else? Joey wondered. But when the humming stopped, two Klingons stood at the front of the class, next to the teacher. One was as stocky and muscular as G'dath, though taller, and held a shining metallic globe about the size of a basketball under one arm. The other was shorter, slender, with a sharp chin and face, and slanting dark eyes; he brandished a large knife.

Joey and everyone else gaped at them, but Dr. G'dath didn't seem all that surprised—just a little sick. *It's a joke,* Joey thought, *some kind of crazy practical joke.* Behind him, Stoller giggled.

But the expression on the three Klingons' faces said it was no laughing matter. G'dath held up a hand. "Please," he said quietly, "do not hurt anyone here. I will come with you."

"I will decide the need to hurt," the Klingon with the knife said. Joey didn't like his eyes—there was something crazy/scary in them, like Stoller's eyes, only much worse. The Klingon turned and scanned the classroom.

Stoller giggled again as if certain it was all a bad joke, and said, half under his breath, "Give me a *break.*"

The Klingon raised the knife above his head; he was going to throw it at Stoller. Joey ducked.

G'dath stepped right in front of the Klingon and tried to take the knife. The Klingon brought it down into G'dath's arm, and the teacher released a low, quick cry of pain.

The red-haired woman and Ira Stoller screamed as the entire class released a great, collective gasp. Joey just stood and watched, unable to believe, as people jumped up from their seats.

"Stay," G'dath rumbled, in a voice so thunderous Joey imagined the windows rattled. He had separated from the crazy-eyed Klingon, who had lowered the knife. As the two of them stared intently at the other, sizing up the enemy, G'dath held his right arm just above the elbow. The sleeve of his blue-black tunic was darkening with a quickly spreading stain.

Everyone froze.

And then someone screamed. It was as if the last bell had sounded for the semester. Everyone began heading for the door. The Klingons shouted, but their voices were swallowed up by the noise. None of the students had seen the second Klingon put the globe on the desk and restrain G'dath. No one except for Joey, who stood by his desk as the others jostled past.

The tall Klingon had drawn a knife and now held it to G'dath's throat and pinned the teacher's arms behind his back. G'dath ignored the knife and strained to break free. His eyes were terrible—fiercer than any Klingon's Joey'd ever seen—and if Joey had been afraid of his teacher before, he was doubly terrified now.

The crazy Klingon singled out a victim in the panicked crowd and aimed his weapon.

"No!" G'dath roared. "No more blood on my hands—"

The Klingon threw before the first person made it out the door. The blade rose in a perfect arc and dropped into the middle of the crowd. A quick, strangled cry; the students drew back from the target, but Joey couldn't see who had been hurt.

"To your seats," the Klingon said. "Klor, fetch my weapon." He did not shout, did not even raise his voice. The room had grown utterly silent.

Hesitation. Slowly, reluctantly, people returned to their desks. Klor—the big Klingon—released G'dath and went toward the doorway, and at last Joey saw what had happened.

He wished immediately that he hadn't. Ricia Greene knelt, her large eyes now impossibly wide and shining with unshed tears; her face had gone gray. She bent over and pressed her hands hard, around either side of the knife handle that protruded from Carlos Siegel's back. Joey rose on tiptoe to try to see whether the boy was still alive, but Carlos's face was turned away, toward the door.

For a second, Joey couldn't get his breath, and his knees began to give way at last, but he leaned against the desk and forced himself to stand. He had to see; he had to know whether Carlos was still alive.

The Klingon crouched next to Ricia. She looked up at him, her eyes a little wild—but her voice was incredibly calm and soft.

Joey wondered what she thought of Klingons now.

Ricia glanced at the one who had thrown the knife. He was busy watching G'dath. She turned to the one called Klor. "He's going to bleed to death," she said. Her voice was very low. "You've got to help him. He may be human, but he's just a kid."

Klor looked away quickly, but in the brief instant he forced himself to meet Ricia's gaze. In that moment Joey saw that Klor did not like what was happening, but he had to follow the crazy Klingon's orders. Something startlingly like compassion flickered across his dark features, but when he looked away, his expression hardened quickly again.

"This does not help him," he said, nodded at the knife, and with a jerk, he pulled it from Carlos's back. Joey saw a flash of bloodied metal.

Ricia immediately covered the wound with both hands, pressing hard. As she did, an alarm sounded.

The crazy Klingon started and pressed his blade against G'dath's chest. *"What is that?"*

G'dath's expression was bitter, sickened. He had stopped holding his arm and let blood drip, ignored, from his fingers; his gaze was fixed on Carlos Siegel's still form. "The needless harm done to the boy has been detected by the sensor system," he said, his tone dulled. "The school computer almost certainly thinks there has been an accident. A medical team has been alerted and will arrive shortly. The police will also come."

"Warn them away."

"I cannot." When the Klingon threatened again with the knife, G'dath added wearily: "It is out of my hands. The system is automatic." He gestured with his good arm at the safety monitors in the corners. "It is possible that you are being watched by the police even now."

Joey felt a small stirring of relief. G'dath was telling the truth—and once the cops saw what was happening, they'd transport the Klingons straight to jail. But Crazy Eyes seemed to realize this. He grabbed Doctor

184

G'dath with the arm that held the knife and, with the other, pressed a control on his belt. The two were immediately enveloped inside a force field, and the Klingon adjusted the diameter of the field until it included G'dath's desk and the shining globe. Joey's small spark of hope was immediately extinguished. Impossible now for the police to beam them out of the building, or to attempt to stun them with phasers. Of course, the look of growing desperation on both Klingons' faces reminded him that now *they* couldn't use a transporter to escape, either.

"Klor!" the crazy one in charge commanded. "Do likewise!"

Klor bent down, slipped a hand under Ricia's arm, and with a smooth motion swung her onto her feet and away from Carlos. She tried to pull free, to no avail, and so turned to face her attacker, pommeling him with bloody hands. Her voice grew shrill. "No! Someone has to take care of Carlos—someone has to try to stop the bleeding."

Of all people, Ira Stoller cleared the rows of desks with a few bounds and put his hands over Carlos's wound. "It's all right, Ricia, it's all right." Ricia was writhing hysterically in Klor's grip, and Stoller spoke to her in a soothing, grown-up voice, a voice that didn't sound like Stoller's at all. "I'll stay here with him. I won't leave until someone gets here."

Ricia sagged in the Klingon's arms and said, in a high-pitched whisper that broke: "Thank you, Ira." Her face crumpled and she began to sob.

Klor moved back toward his commander and moved to press the control on his belt, but Joey could take no more. Moving entirely on emotion—because if he had thought, he wouldn't have moved at all—he rushed toward the Klingon. "Hey, leave her alone! Take me!"

Startled, Klor raised his knife and prepared to bring it down in Joey's chest. Ricia shrieked and covered her face with her bloodied hands.

"No more!" the commander barked. "Klor, do not kill. Take him. Hostages are to our advantage. Humans are sentimental in that regard."

The knife still in his hand, Klor grabbed Joey, threw him next to Ricia, then clamped his huge arm over both of them, hugging them to his chest.

The red-haired woman stood, her voice shaking with anger—and perhaps fear. She faced the commander, her lips white and trembling. "Are Klingons such cowards that they have to take children hostage? Why not take someone your own speed? Me, for instance."

The crazy commander actually grinned at her. "You look no more than a child yourself."

The woman frowned indignantly. "I'm twenty-eight years old."

"If you wish to join us," the Klingon said, with a smile that chilled Joey to the bone, "you shall. But these so-called children are old enough to hold rank in the Imperial Fleet." He nodded at Klor, who motioned to the woman to come forward. She did, apparently expecting an exchange to take place, but at the last minute, Klor held the woman at knife-point without releasing Joey and Ricia, and pressed a control on his belt. Joey heard a high-pitched whine and saw the blue shimmer of a force field leap up around them.

His face contorted by hate, Stoller looked up from his vigil beside Carlos. "I *knew* you turtleheads were strictly warp zero. If *I* were in your wimp army, I'd be a general already."

Joey caught his breath. Against his back he felt the trititanium-hard muscles of the Klingon's chest tense, and he knew if the force field hadn't been in place, Ira

Stoller would be dead. "Stoller," he begged, *"please shut up."*

"That is excellent advice under the circumstances, Mr. Stoller," Doctor G'dath said softly.

At a few minutes before nine, Kevin Riley sat at his desk at Starfleet Headquarters and stared vacantly at the messages left for Admiral Kirk. The admiral had gone with Nan Davis to inspect the Dart Project, and Riley was alone for the morning. The trivision screen was tuned to the muted in-house security feed of G'dath's classroom. Riley glanced up to reassure himself G'dath's class was proceeding smoothly— and to catch a glimpse of Jenny Hogan. G'dath had arrived without incident. Jenny went up to speak briefly to him, then took a seat in the back of the class. Riley found himself staring at the back of her head, at her shining copper-gold hair.

The brunch with Jenny on Saturday had been the brightest spot in Riley's weekend. He'd spent the rest of it huddled under a haze of self-pity—most of that time in a secluded booth at O'Reilly's Publick House. He'd drunk too much on the theory that it would help him sleep—and it had. For a few hours.

Certainly, he had enough reasons to be depressed: Anab and her terse message, his late arrival at WorldNews and resultant encounter with Kirk, his uncertainty over whether to remain in Starfleet. Anab's words echoed in his mind:

You're not doing Kirk any favors by working for him halfheartedly.

That was exactly what he'd been doing the past week or so. So consumed by self-pity, so unsettled about what he wanted now that she was gone from his life, that his job performance had slipped. His memory had abandoned him. In fact, he'd been forgetful all week and Saturday was just a particularly catastrophic example. Even before the WorldNews incident, Kirk must have noticed . . . and Riley felt ashamed to have failed the admiral's confidence in him. Especially after learning what the admiral—what fourteen-year-old Jimmy Kirk—had done for him on Tarsus IV. The realization had caused dim, long-buried memories of that terrible time to resurface.

Yet another reason to be depressed. Riley wanted to pull himself out from under his despair, as he had done the time Anab had shipped out, but this time he seemed to lack the strength.

Maybe what he needed was for Admiral Ciana to give him a good chewing out, the way she had when Riley, new on the job, had tried to resign.

Think about it, Riley. Think about all the trouble Kirk went to in order to get you that promotion. Believe me, it wasn't easy convincing Nogura. Kirk argued long and hard to get you. How will he look if you resign the first week?

But Ciana wasn't up to giving any advice these days, especially where it came to Kirk. Her aide had called Riley early this morning to ask if he'd heard: As of Friday afternoon, Ciana could no longer be reached at Kirk's address.

Which explained the hardness in Kirk's eyes on Saturday morning. Riley felt deeply ashamed: he had been so consumed by self-pity that he had been unable to pull himself together and face his responsibilities. Kirk had.

And Kirk seemed to believe Riley possessed the same abilities as he. Riley could not quite understand Kirk's faith in him: Kirk had saved his life, and Riley felt obliged to make that life count—but he did not know how.

He felt hollow, afraid. He'd acted out of fear all his life, and with good reason. He'd lost too much: his parents, Anab. The way things were going at the office, he'd soon lose Kirk's respect, and his job. If he let Jenny Hogan too close, she'd be another loss.

He knew he could easily be attracted to her, but he feared the risk, the responsibility. She'd called earlier that morning, her normally outgoing, cheery manner a bit subdued and cautious, to tell him that Nan Davis was going to be covering the Apollo Day story, and wanted Jenny and Kevin to work together to coordinate Davis's and Kirk's schedules.

Jenny was good enough to try to hide it, but Riley saw the trace of disappointment in her voice and eyes. She was attracted to him, and his little speech about friendship had hurt her, at least just a bit.

Watching her strained little smile on the viewscreen, he had thought dully: *Is this how Anab felt, when she talked to me?*

Riley gave his head a little shake, to clear away all thoughts of the two women, and concentrated once more on his computer screen, trying to sort the admiral's correspondence into some sort of priority, and to answer those messages which did not require Kirk's personal attention. For a few minutes, Riley worked steadily, forcing himself when his mind wandered to concentrate. Then, casually, he checked the trivision screen again—not to look at Jenny, he assured himself, but to be sure security for G'dath and his class was proceeding according to plan. Kirk had put him in charge of the Klingon's safety, and Riley did not want to disappoint the admiral again.

Riley glanced up at the trivision, then down at his work. Then back at the screen, this time bolting to his feet so quickly that his chair teetered behind him and crashed to the floor.

Riley never heard it. His eyes were focused on the silent drama on the screen. His brain was almost too stunned to interpret what it saw: Two Klingons had joined G'dath at the front of the classroom. One held the instructor—and a shining globe, what Riley realized was the stolen invention—inside a portable force field. The other, tall and burly, clutched two students in one arm.

Jenny Hogan leapt to her feet and challenged the Klingon as Riley watched, too stricken even to turn up the sound. He did not have to hear; Jenny was clearly offering to exchange herself for the two captive students. Riley felt a wave of admiration and pure horror.

Without taking his gaze from the screen, he slammed a hand against a toggle on his console. "Security Central! Nguyen, are you there? What the hell's *happened?*"

He had to call her name twice before Nguyen's breathless voice filtered over the audio channel.

"Lieutenant Commander, I can't talk long—I'm in contact with the security branch over in New York, and we're trying to figure something out."

"How'd they manage to get past the shields?" Riley demanded.

Five seconds passed before Nguyen replied—five seconds that told Riley he did not want to hear the answer.

"You didn't see what happened," Nguyen said dully, and took Riley's silence as affirmation.

Riley lifted his hand off the comm control and slowly drew back from his console. On the screen, the tall Klingon erected a force field around himself and his three hostages. Around Jenny. Students, realizing that the Klingons' weapons could not penetrate the field, began one by one to risk darting out the door to safety. As they went, Riley noticed at the edge of his screen that two still forms lay near the doorway. He couldn't see either figure clearly, but one of them was

190

being tended by a friend, and so probably alive. "How could this happen? How could they—"

"They beamed directly into the classroom, sir."

"Impossible! I ordered priority one security for the classroom. That room should be *shielded* from transporter beams, Lieutenant."

"No, sir." Nguyen grew suddenly firm. "You ordered standard security for the classroom. That does not call for shields, sir. I can bring the records up on the computer if you like."

"But I—" Riley said, and broke off, stopped by a growing sense of dread. He'd just returned from drinking when he'd gotten Kirk's message about G'dath, and his memories of his precise actions that night were blurry. He'd requested security for G'dath, been careful to check on the exact time of the class— and not forget the time difference. Certainly it had occurred to him that the classroom should be shielded.

Or had it?

"You said standard security, and I asked you to repeat, sir. Of course, it's not important . . ."

Not important. Riley watched as, on the screen, more students retreated out the door. What were the Klingons doing? Waiting for the police, no doubt—or for Starfleet to bargain with them.

Not important. Riley closed his eyes and felt, once again, the sick cold that had settled over him the first time he'd learned that a crew member under his command had been killed.

And he was responsible. He laid his hands, palms flat, against the desk and leaned heavily.

". . . what was ordered. What's important is that we have to figure out how to get everyone safely out of there."

"Yes, of course," Riley said numbly. "Lieutenant, is there any way we can beam them out?"

"The Klingons, you mean? Not with those force fields, sir." He heard another faint voice as someone at Security Central spoke to Nguyen. "Commander Riley, could you excuse me, sir? I've got to get with the New York people for a while. If you'd like to listen in and give us your input, we'd—"

"No," Riley interrupted. "Thank you, Lieutenant. I—I have some things here at this end I can do to help out. Keep me posted, though. Riley out."

He switched off the communication before Nguyen could respond. For a second, no more, he paused, still leaning on his desk, to make a decision.

When Shemry was a landing party member under his command, she had failed to respond to attempts at communication. Out of fear, he had taken too long to make a decision concerning her rescue, and Shemry had died. He was terrified again, but now he saw the choice: He could fail to take action out of fear—or he could take action despite it.

Desperation forced him to transcend himself. Jim Kirk had seen something in him, once—had told him he saw himself in Riley. Now, Riley hoped desperately that Kirk was right.

He pushed himself to a standing position and straightened as he remembered, hazily, the fourteen-year-old visage of Jimmy Kirk. Jimmy had not hesitated that horrible day and because of it, Kevin was alive today.

What would Jim Kirk do now?

He was no longer concerned about his future as Kirk's chief of staff—and at any rate, the mistake he had made now, a mistake that had put lives at risk, was far too grave for him to have any future in Starfleet.

Riley no longer cared. His career no longer mattered—but the lives he had put at risk mattered, and he would break whatever rules he had to to save those lives.

For what he knew would be his last act as a Starfleet officer, Riley headed out his office at top speed, bound for the Admiralty transporter stage—a plan already forming in his mind.

From inside the blue force field that enveloped him and his captor, G'dath watched, heartsick, as paramedics arrived and removed Carlos Siegel from the classroom. Carlos at least appeared to be still breathing.

Carlos, an innocent student, a brilliant boy, with such promise . . .

G'dath clenched the fist of his uninjured arm—he could not use his right one, but he no longer felt the wound that cut deep into the muscles of his upper arm—and closed his eyes lest his captor see the hatred there. For a moment, venomous words filled his mouth, but he remained silent. His two attackers had at least allowed the paramedics entry. Of course, they had little choice, being as much trapped inside their force fields as they were protected. They could do little more than threaten those inside the shield.

At least, G'dath noted with relief, the last student had escaped—except for the two held hostage. And Ira Stoller, who, to his teacher's amazement, remained at Carlos's side. He rose and followed the paramedics as they guided the stretcher toward the door.

Ricia Greene called out to him. "Ira."

G'dath peered through the shield at her with concern, but the Klingon called Klor had relaxed his grip, and did not restrain her, but stood behind his three hostages with his weapon at the ready. Something very like concern passed over Klor's features, and the sight gave G'dath hope. Perhaps later, if he managed to speak privately to the Klingon, to convince him of the situation's hopelessness . . .

At the sound of his name, Stoller paused in the doorway and turned.

Ricia's voice trembled. She'd stopped crying and composed herself, but her light brown cheeks still glistened with tears. "Joey's dad—someone's got to tell him . . ."

Stoller's face was white and drawn, but resolute. "Don't worry. I'll take care of it."

The paramedics left with their burdens, and Stoller followed.

"Farmer," Klor's commander said suddenly, in Klingonese. G'dath turned his head to study him. The commander's eyes were startlingly intense—not quite sane, G'dath decided, no doubt from the strain of waiting for the police to make the first move. Odd, to hear himself addressed in his native tongue after so many years, and for a stranger to know of his humble background. "The motive force in that device . . ." He nodded at the globe nearby on the desk, contained within the field that held them both. "A careful examination of your design specifications suggests it can be harnessed to power a vessel. How can we do so? Answer me quickly and truthfully, or the boy will die."

Klor, picking up on his superior's cue, hooked a powerful arm under Joseph Brickner's neck and held the tip of his blade to the pale, freckled skin there. Joseph's blue eyes became huge, but he held absolutely still and made no sound.

G'dath locked gazes with the commander, and for one of the few times in his life, considered initiating violence. Foolhardiness, of course. It would only lead to Joseph being harmed—another person injured, in

194

his account—and he dared not risk that. But the thought of reaching out to crush his captor's windpipe with his bare hands was alluring.

"Harm the boy and I will tell you nothing," G'dath said. "Release him and I will tell you whatever you wish to know."

Without taking his eyes from G'dath, the commander gave a single, curt nod, and Klor eased his grip on Joseph.

G'dath sighed. It was clear now what his attackers desired—to negotiate for an escape vessel—and the globe would provide fast, immediate transport to the Klingon Empire. To G'dath's torture and death.

To war.

Yet if he were caught lying now, Joseph might die. The commander seemed quite intelligent—and G'dath had no way of knowing how much he had deduced about the globe. Better to tell a little of the truth, and save Joseph's life—and hope that a means of escape provided itself before they all arrived in the Klingon Empire.

"The mechanism inside the globe generates an enveloping field," G'dath said. "Securing the globe against the chassis of the vessel would be sufficient to extend the field around the vehicle, if the flitter itself is not grounded. The flitter must be outside the atmosphere and in no more than a microgravitational environment, however, for the plan to work."

"You are telling me the truth? Swear it on the lives of the hostages."

Which meant if he was discovered to be lying, or had withheld information, they would die. "I swear on the lives of these hostages that I am tell—" G'dath began.

And broke off at the growing high-pitched hum that filled the room. He felt a rush of hope mixed with apprehension as a swarm of shimmering gold sparks coalesced into the figure of a man. The police, he expected, come to negotiate—but as the figure solidified, G'dath saw it wore a Starfleet officer's uniform.

The pale-skinned, bearded human stepped forward, his hands raised in a gesture of peaceable acquiescence. The Klingons tensed, knives at the ready—but they clearly were not willing to violate their force fields. Starfleet had beamed someone in, and could just as easily beam them *out*.

"Kevin!" Jenny Hogan cried.

The young officer ignored her—wisely, G'dath thought, for to show interest in her welfare was to give the attackers another weapon. "Who is in command here?"

"I am," G'dath's captor said.

The officer turned and addressed his words to the commander. "As you can see, I'm unarmed. My guess is you need transportation." He hesitated, looking for confirmation from the commander, who supplied it with a nod. "All right. I've negotiated with the police on behalf of Starfleet. A flitter with shuttle capabilities will land on the roof of this building within two minutes. Once the pilot leaves, it'll be empty. There's no tracer aboard, no tricks. You have my word as a Starfleet officer on that. Let these others go, and you can have me and the flitter. I'll take you wherever you say, or you can leave by yourselves—or you can kill me."

The commander smiled. "A tempting offer—Commander, is it not? I recognize the insignia."

"Lieutenant Commander Kevin Riley."

"Lieutenant Commander Riley, perhaps we can strike a bargain—if you agree to escort us to the flitter and guarantee our safety."

G'dath glanced sharply at the commander. He

sensed the Klingon was lying, and apparently Riley sensed it too, for he hesitated, and doubt flickered in his eyes.

"Fair enough," Riley said, apparently willing to play along. "Then let the hostages go now."

"That would be most unwise, to lower our shields before we are even safely in the flitter. We will discuss any release of prisoners once we are there."

"All right. But before we take off—"

"The release will occur before we take off. You have that on *my* word as an officer of the Imperial Fleet."

Lieutenant Commander Riley led them up to the roof, where the promised flitter waited. G'dath permitted himself to be herded into the vessel's interior —which seemed claustrophobically small with seven beings aboard; though equipped for spaceflight, the vessel was designed to accommodate no more than five. The commander led G'dath over to the vessel's console and instructed him to install the globe, which he began doing with reluctance. Fortunately, the injury to his right arm forced him to use only his left hand, which allowed him to be clumsy and take far more time than was actually required.

"All right," Riley said. "I've brought you here, and I'll keep my part of the bargain. I'll stay, but you have to let the other hostages go."

"I agreed to a release," the commander said, "but I did not agree to release everyone. We do not leave without the traitor and his device."

"I am no traitor," G'dath growled softly as he worked.

The commander pressed the cold metal tip of his blade against G'dath's adam's apple. "By rights, this invention belongs to the Empire."

"You gave your word—" Riley began hotly.

"Will you force us to kill another?" The commander's eyes blazed suddenly, with a fire that made G'dath's blood cold, and made Riley fall silent.

"You don't need the children or the woman," Riley said at last.

"Very well," the commander allowed. "Since you have behaved with honorable boldness by coming here unarmed, Lieutenant Commander Riley, I will keep my word." He lowered his knife from G'dath's throat—G'dath drew in a grateful breath—and nodded at his underling. "Klor, quickly. Release the girl and the woman."

There was a shrill pop as Klor's field dissolved. He shoved Jenny Hogan and Ricia toward the hatch without releasing Joseph, and before the Starfleet officer had a chance to move toward the freed women, Klor grabbed Riley by the arm, then pressed the control on his belt. Within three seconds, no more, Klor's force field was back in place, and Riley was now his prisoner.

"But the boy—" Riley protested angrily. "There is no honor in taking a child."

The commander was unmoved. "You are a Starfleet officer, and might be considered expendable by those seeking to capture us. No, Commander, I need the boy, to control both you—and his teacher."

G'dath studied Joseph's face. The boy's lips were gray, his eyes still wide with terror. *Unfair*, he wanted to shout at the commander. *You have already spilled the blood of an innocent old man and a boy—must you take Joseph, too?*

"Then *go*," Riley urged the women, who lingered uncertainly by the hatch.

Jenny Hogan put a hand on the hatch to steady herself, but before she stepped through, she stopped and stared at Riley with such reluctance that G'dath understood the two were more than acquaintances.

Behind her, Ricia Greene gave a nudge, and at last the two crawled out to safety.

G'dath felt a slight easing of his burden of guilt.

The commander had been wise to keep Joseph. And the more G'dath protested, the more his concern for Joseph would be used against him. G'dath remained silent and, for a moment, rested his hand against the vibrating globe to steady himself. Its interior blinked and sparkled with light—the device was truly quite beautiful. A deadly beauty that had already caused great harm to those he cared for.

How much more destruction would be caused before this day was through?

With a bitter heart, G'dath returned to his task.

Chapter Twelve

BALANCING THE number-two impulse units aboard the shuttle *Enterprise* was proving to be a touchy job. What with one delay and another, the shuttle had not yet risen even a centimeter off the floor of the hangar. Kirk waited with anticipation in one of the passenger seats in the cockpit. Next to him, Nan seemed to growing increasingly nervous—no doubt concerned about making it to New York on time—while behind them, the technician named Eddie had dozed off.

"I think that's got it now," said Alice Friedman, her face intent as she gazed at the control panel before her. "Control, what do you think?"

"Looks good," came the voice of the test director. "Let's try a little lift, Captain."

The roar of barely constrained impulse engines filtered through the cockpit insulation, and Kirk felt the sensation of movement.

"Yeah!" Friedman cried. "Awright! Control, I read us balanced to nine nines."

"We confirm that," Control said. "All right, Alice, goose her a little."

"Will do." Friedman flicked a row of switches on

the old-fashioned panel. "Coming to ten meters— we're there. Everything's in the green. Heck, we can fly this baby on up and out anytime, far as I'm concerned."

Control sounded more dubious. "Maybe so, Alice, but how about some thruster tests first?"

She sighed impatiently. "All right, all right."

Kirk's communicator beeped for attention. He frowned at the interruption.

"Kirk here."

He expected to hear Riley's voice—and instead heard that of Lieutenant Lisa Nguyen from Starfleet Security Central in San Francisco.

"Admiral, Lieutenant Nguyen. We've got an emergency here . . ."

Kirk knew who was involved before Nguyen even finished the sentence.

". . . it's G'dath, sir. A problem with the security. Two Klingon agents managed to get past our standard security measures and capture Dr. G'dath and a student, sir. I understand that they now have Riley as well."

"Riley? What was *he* doing there?"

"He took it upon himself to try and intervene." Nguyen then briefed him on the situation. At the end, Kirk merely nodded.

"Stand by to beam me over there. Kirk out." He closed the communicator and turned to the pilot. "Captain Friedman? I'm sorry, but I have to leave right now. Starfleet emergency."

"Can't argue with that, I guess," Friedman said, thumbing her radio switch. "I'm shutting down, Control," she called, even as she began hitting switches. "Admiral Kirk's got to leave directly." The shuttle settled easily on the hangar floor as the roar of its engines died away.

Nan glanced at him with concern. Once the noise level ebbed, she asked, "What is it, Jim? What's wrong?"

He told her, not yet able to decide how to react to the news himself. For Riley, he felt two warring emotions: anger at his chief of staff's failure to provide adequate security for G'dath . . . and an almost paternal concern for him. "G'dath and my chief of staff, among others, are being held hostage by a party of Klingons up in New York. They're aboard a Starfleet flitter now, heading for God knows where."

Nan gasped. "G'dath? Oh my God, what happened? Didn't he make it to class?"

"He made it. So did two Klingon agents."

"My God, Jenny—is she all right?"

"I'm sorry, Nan. That's all I know. Two Klingon agents, G'dath and other hostages are aboard a Starfleet flitter able to leave the atmosphere, and that could be extremely bad news. They might head anywhere within the Solar System, and there's no other Starfleet craft in any reasonable position to pursue." He paused as inspiration struck him, and turned toward Friedman. "Except this one. Captain . . ."

Friedman met his gaze. For the briefest instant, her expression was puzzled—and then it lit up with a broad, impish grin. "I guess you have a point, Admiral. She *is* a Starfleet vessel, isn't she? Give the word. I'm game if you are."

He rested a hand on Friedman's shoulder and gave her the kind of smile that had helped make Captain Kirk a legend in his own time.

Aboard the flitter, G'dath still crouched against the side of the console, supposedly installing the globe. He had finished moments before, but had not yet arrived at a strategy.

There was little time. The flitter was already airborne and mere seconds after the globe was activated they would arrive in the Klingon Empire, assuming the vessel's heading was correct.

Of course, G'dath could activate the globe's motive force for a few seconds longer than necessary, sending the tiny vessel beyond the Federation and Klingon Empires, close to the very edge of the galaxy. Doing so would prevent either Federation or Empire from possessing the globe.

Were he to do so, his Klingon captors would most certainly kill him—and worse, Joseph and Lieutenant Commander Riley.

The power source in the globe, if G'dath's theory was correct, could be short-circuited so that it quickly overloaded to dangerous levels. He could, if necessary, destroy the ship, and everyone aboard. It would be a quicker, cleaner death than the one that awaited them in the Klingon Empire—or at the galaxy's edge.

Yet the thought of Joseph held him back. For the boy's sake, he would wait a bit longer in hopes of rescue . . . though that hope was fast dwindling.

An abrupt dizziness swept him as he saw crawling black flecks dance in front of his eyes. G'dath closed his eyes and sagged weakly against the cold metal of the console wall, pressing with his good hand. The other, his right, was sticky and still dripped blood. He became distantly aware of Klingon voices, speaking his native tongue.

"We are getting away cleanly, Superior. Our altitude is now such that the last police craft has fallen back and away. There are no other craft within troublesome range."

"Excellent, Klor. Excellent."

And then he heard no more, felt no more, until strong arms, Klingon arms, reached under his own and lifted him. G'dath opened his eyes and found that he was lying across the back row of passengers' seats, with an open medikit beside him. Klor's dark face hovered over him as the tall, stocky Klingon began to apply a coagulant spray to G'dath's wound.

"This will stop the bleeding," Klor said quietly. His manner was not ungentle. Carefully, G'dath turned his head, trying to see if there was enough privacy to risk speaking openly—but he could see nothing except the backs of chairs. He squeezed his eyes shut and waited for the renewed wave of dizziness to pass.

When he opened them again, he caught Klor's gaze and, for the first time, noticed the Klingon's blue eyes—a deeper shade of blue than Joseph Brickner's. Perhaps they explained the sympathy he thought he saw on the Klingon's face.

"Your name is Klor," he gasped in Klingonese, careful to keep his voice low lest the commander overhear. Speaking was somewhat difficult, but he continued out of desperation. "I heard your commander address you by name. There are some things you must know about the device."

"Has it been installed successfully?"

"I do not know. Perhaps. But I must warn you of its dangers. You are taking this globe to the Empire because it will bring you and your commander honor, and glory, and because it will win more planets for the Empire. It will be used to vastly improve space travel—but it will also be used for harmful purposes. It has that capability as well.

"It will bring honor and glory to the Empire—but it could bring death, destruction. Do you understand what balance of power means, Klor?"

The young Klingon glanced away for an instant and nodded, his expression faintly sheepish. "I have observed your class for some time, G'dath," he said, in a low voice, "and so have become familiar with the concept."

Had he possessed the strength, G'dath would have

smiled at the realization that he was speaking to yet another of his students—one, who, until now, had remained anonymous. "If the balance of power between the Klingons and the Federation is disturbed, it could be disastrous."

"The Organians—" Klor began, and broke off. This time, G'dath did manage the weak beginnings of a smile. Klor had apparently been monitoring the classroom discussion concerning the Organians, and had remembered its outcome. The Organians could not necessarily be trusted to prevent another war.

"Even if the Organians prevent this conflict," G'dath whispered, "they have not prevented the Empire from engaging in other conflicts."

"But the Federation already possesses this design," Klor said stubbornly. He had finished applying coagulant spray, and began gently cleaning blood from G'dath's arm. "Therefore the Empire must as well, to maintain the balance."

"No. They do not possess the design. No one does." He saw the mistrust on Klor's face—but there was uncertainty there, as well. Instinctively, he felt that his younger captor trusted him. Out of desperation, he said: "Klor. I cannot permit my invention to be used for violence. Understand: I will destroy this ship first."

"You do not have the means to—" Klor began and broke off. His blue eyes widened as he comprehended G'dath's implication, then his dark brows rushed together. "You would not do that, Doctor G'dath."

"I will," G'dath replied softly. "And you must help me. Before either the Federation or the Empire misuses this device."

Klor finished cleaning G'dath's wound and straightened; his expression had hardened to stony unreadability. "I can listen to no more of this. I must report this to Keth immediately."

"Klor—are you of human ancestry?"

Klor averted his eyes and head quickly, thus giving G'dath his answer.

"I thought so. Then you, most of all, have an interest in this. For the sake of both your peoples."

Klor turned. "I will not hear this."

"Klor—" G'dath whispered.

But the young Klingon had gone, leaving G'dath to wonder whether informing him of the globe's capacity to self-destruct had been a deadly mistake.

Aboard the space shuttle *Enterprise,* Kirk stood over Alice Friedman's shoulder as Nan excitedly directed Eddie to scan certain shots. Kirk had ordered Nan and Eddie to leave the shuttle and both had steadfastly refused. *You'll have to physically remove us both,* Nan had told him—and if there had been time to do so, Kirk would have been greatly tempted.

He was both worried and furious about Riley. His chief of staff should have ordered priority, not standard, security measures. The classroom should have been shielded from beam-in attacks. Kirk was perplexed; this was not the work of the Riley he knew, the Riley he'd hired. That Riley would have ordered priority security, would not have allowed such a potentially tragic mistake to occur—though it sounded as though the Klingon agents might have been desperate enough to get past any security measures. They must have been insane to go barging into a public classroom, much less one with trivision scanners rolling. This did not sound like a covert action approved by the Klingon government.

For Riley to go dashing off without orders and come up with a scheme to swap himself for hostages—now *that* sounded like the Riley he knew, the one who reminded him more than a little of Captain James T. Kirk.

"We're going full-out, Admiral." Friedman glanced over her shoulder at him. "I'm not sure we can keep this up for too long."

"Can't we throw a tractor beam on them?" Kirk asked. "I'm afraid they're going to get away just as we're about to nail them."

"We can try." Friedman squinted down at her readouts and did a doubletake. "Hey, this is funny. I'm reading an unknown sort of power surge aboard the flitter."

"Can you identify it?"

"Never saw anything like it before. It's not from the engines, though. Even warp engines don't show a profile like that, much less impulse jobs. Oops— audio-only message coming in on the main ship-to-ship, Admiral. It's from our friends up ahead."

"This is Keth," came a deep, resonant voice. "You in the ghost ship. Break away. We hold three hostages. Desist, or they will die."

"What'll I do, Admiral?" Friedman asked. "You're running this show."

"How's that tractor beam coming?"

"Still charging," Friedman said. "I'm circuiting its power through the engines a few times to strengthen it. But the damn supercharging is slowing us down— you don't get something for nothing."

"Understood. I'll stall for a second. Can you let me talk to the flitter?"

"Sure." Friedman nodded at the comm grid on her console. "Just talk. Everybody in Starfleet will hear you. You're on the main channel."

Klor took his post at the flitter's helm while his commander swiveled in the adjacent seat to face the three hostages. G'dath still lay quietly across three seats in the last row, while the Starfleet officer and the boy sat in the row just behind Klor and Keth.

G'dath's words had shaken Klor deeply. He did not know if what G'dath hinted at was true—that the globe could be used to destroy the flitter. What way had they, then, of knowing whether the physicist had not programmed it to explode before they reached home?

And Klor wanted desperately to reach home.

Still, he could not bring himself to inform Keth of this new information. In the schoolroom, he had become convinced that Keth did not have a brilliant plan after all—that he had simply succumbed to madness and frustration, and burst into the classroom hoping, at best, to negotiate an escape with the police.

He no longer trusted his commander. In fact, he trusted his prisoner more. After months of watching the teacher day after day, Klor felt he had come to know G'dath very well. G'dath behaved honorably, even in private, and Klor had not yet seen the Klingon lie. What G'dath had said, about the device possibly starting a war—Klor believed it. And he understood now why G'dath's recent lectures had focused on the human/Klingon conflict, and the Organian Treaty.

Klor did not trust the Organians, either. And though he found the notion of battle glorious, he did not yearn for war, did not glory in the wasting of life. In space, killing seemed clean: The enemy died thousands of kellicams away. Killing one that faced you seemed far more difficult.

After observing his granddam's people, Klor's hatred of them had dulled. For he had come to realize that the Federation was not one huge, impersonal, evil entity, but billions upon billions of individuals.

Such as the old man in the apartment building who had smiled at Klor in friendship. The Earthers were weaker, perhaps, ofttimes lacking a warrior's courage . . . but not so different.

Klor's eyes flickered over the console screen. He

tensed as scanners revealed the blinking image of a rapidly approaching vessel. "Superior! Vessel closing in on our leeward bow. I am not familiar with the make, but it is considerably larger than our own."

Keth raised his head sharply and opened his mouth to speak, but Klor interrupted.

"Incoming communication, Superior, from the pursuing vessel."

Klor pressed the control, and a strong voice filled the ship's interior.

"Attention up ahead. This is Admiral James T. Kirk of the space shuttle *Enterprise*. Cut power and heave to for our approach. We are taking you in tow."

The flitter lurched suddenly, then began to strain; Klor consulted his screen. "The vessel has trapped us in a tractor beam!"

"No!" Keth thundered, jumping up. "I will not permit it!" He slammed a fist against the comm control. *"Enterprise,* this is Keth. You were warned. Because you have refused to break off pursuit, I will now kill one of the hostages." He jerked his head in Klor's direction, and switched to Klingonese. "Klor —the student."

Klor did not rise, but stared uncertainly into Keth's wild eyes. "But, Superior," he replied, softly, so that the scientist might not hear, "if the boy dies, how shall we control G'dath?"

Keth's eyes narrowed with rage. "You *dare* to question an order?"

Klor bowed his head. There was no point in denying it . . . and arguing with Keth now would prove futile.

With one fluid movement, Keth wheeled around, grabbed the gape-mouthed student by the front of the tunic, and jerked him to his feet.

G'dath had revived well enough to follow the Klingons' exchange and become worried again for

Joseph's sake—and to realize that the tractor beam offered the chance for a distraction. By the time Keth gave the order for Joseph's execution, G'dath had pushed himself to a sitting position. As Keth pulled Joseph from his chair, G'dath was already in motion, headed toward the console. He was bending over to trip a relay inside the globe when he saw the flash of silver. Keth had raised his knife, ready to strike, and there was a blur of gray and white as Riley threw himself in the way.

As the two grappled, G'dath jabbed a finger inside the glowing globe, and hoped for the best.

"Damn!" Kirk swore as he stood, one hand on Friedman's console, the other gripping the back of her chair, and stared down at the flashing display. He was only peripherally aware of Nan Davis and Eddie, who both had the good sense to stay out of the way.

Kirk could imagine what was happening on the flitter now: Riley—at least, the Riley he knew—was dying, or arguing with the Klingons to kill him instead of one of the other hostages. "Captain Friedman, are you sure we can't talk to—"

Friedman shook her head glumly, her plain, strong features reflecting the panel's blue glow. "No can do, Admiral. They've closed the channel. Interesting, though, they've lost their shields. Hard to say what caused it. Too bad we don't have any heavy-duty equipment on board—"

"A transporter," Kirk said quickly, mentally cursing the fact that he was not aboard the real *Enterprise*. "Any Starfleet vessels within transporter range of the flitter?"

But it was all taking too long. Riley was already dead by now.

Friedman peered at her board. "None at the moment, Ad—"

Kirk did not hear what followed. The next instant, he felt as if he'd been ripped from normal space and time and sent hurtling forward at enormous speed—though his mind and stomach had been left behind. Somehow, Friedman and the shuttle had come with him. The momentum forced the air from his lungs, pressed against his temples until he groaned with dizziness . . .

And then the shuttle's interior went black.

A few thousand kilometers away, in a spacedock in low Earth orbit, other ears were listening.

"Have you lost them, Lieutenant?" Captain Decker asked from his command chair.

"No, sir," Uhura responded. "No one's transmitting on ship-to-ship at this time. There's no traffic of any sort from those coordinates at all." Her tone was worried. "I'm tied in to the science officer's sensor board. What sensors we have operating show that the shuttle tractor beam was on for a brief period of time—less than half a second—and then failed, overwhelmed by a sudden flash of power from the flitter. The type and source of that power is unknown."

"Unknown?"

"Yes, Captain. Now everything's quiet."

"What's the course?"

Uhura blinked. "They're headed for the moon, sir. Both craft, I mean."

"ETA?"

"Practically there, sir."

"What?"

"I know, it's unbelievable, Captain. They're slowing now—enough to go into lunar orbit."

"Life signs?" asked Decker.

"Yes, sir—unchanged from before."

Decker nodded. "What about other craft?"

"I can't tell you much, Captain. I'm afraid our

sensor arrays aren't up to the job yet. There are some small space-capable craft in pursuit of the flitter, but they're far behind. The space shuttle is the only craft in position to do anything about the situation, as nearly as I can tell—except for one, sir."

Lt. Commander Sulu dressed in coveralls, was crouched on the floor of the bridge at the helmsman's position. He'd been working on helm circuitry, and several chip assemblies lay scattered at his feet. Quietly, he began replacing them inside the helm console.

"Are you finished with your circuitry work, Mr. Sulu?" Decker asked.

"Finished enough for now, sir."

"I see." Decker paused and thought for a moment. Then he said, "Uhura, where is Mr. Scott?"

"I'll find him for you, Captain."

Sulu seated himself at the helm position and ran the self-test routine. Lights glowed green, and he smiled.

"I take it you could do something if you had to," Decker observed.

"Aye, aye, sir," Sulu responded.

"Mr. Scott on two, Captain," Uhura said.

"Scotty?" Decker said into the air.

"Aye, Cap'n."

"Departure routine. How soon?"

"Eh, Cap'n?"

"I want us to make a short trip. Can do?"

"Cap'n—"

"Mr. Scott," Decker said, "I don't have time to listen to a dozen reasons why we're not able to do something we are damn well about to do anyway." His tone grew firm. "Miss Uhura, send a printout to the chief engineer summarizing the situation. Attach a transcript of the communications traffic you've been monitoring. Mr. Scott, you can read all that later. I ask you again: What is our status? Will we go when I say 'go'?"

"Oh, we'll go, Cap'n," Scotty replied. "Not far and not fast, but we'll go. We have impulse power, all right, but our top speed won't be much—maybe point-zero-five lightspeed, maybe less. I dinna expect to have to pull out o' spacedock for some time ta come yet. Most of our hull plating is attached, and the parts o' the ship we'd need the most have environmental integrity. O' course, much depends on how far ye want ta go."

"I want to go to the moon."

"We can do that," Scotty replied. "Fuel's at minimum, but it's enough, and our batteries are good. Environmental systems, aye; transporter, aye; sensors, maybe; weapons, nae; warp drive, nae."

"Helm, aye," said Sulu.

"Communications, aye," Uhura said. "Captain, Chief DiFalco is not aboard at this time. I could sit in as navigator—"

"No," Decker said. "I want you right where you are, Uhura. I'll punch our course myself. Get us a clearance from Starfleet Traffic. Mr. Scott?"

"Standing by, sir."

"One more question: When?"

"Just give the word, Cap'n," Scotty said. "Outside work crews are either back inside the ship or well clear."

"Fast work, Scotty."

"I passed the order the moment ye said ye wanted ta go, sir. I'll nae argue past the point o' sweet reasonableness."

"Noted. Lieutenant Uhura?"

"Yes, sir?"

"Resume the flight log."

"Yes, *sir!*" A moment later, she reported, "Starfleet Traffic wants to talk to you, Captain."

"Tell them I'm busy. Do we have clearance yet?"

"Uh, no, sir. That's what they want to talk about, sir."

A FLAG FULL OF STARS

"Put them on audio, Lieutenant."

"Aye, aye, Captain. Here they are."

"Enterprise, this is—"

"Traffic, this is Captain Decker. I am requesting clearance, emergency priority one, for twenty seconds from mark. Mark. Better keep everybody out of our way, Traffic. Decker out. Uhura, clear that frequency."

Decker went to the navigator's position and seated himself. He studied the board briefly. "Ten seconds. Uhura, tell the spacedock master to cut all tractor and pressor beams."

"Beams off, sir. We're free to move."

"I guess someone's listening. Mr. Sulu, thrusters at stationkeeping."

"Thrusters at stationkeeping, aye."

Decker punched in a course. He wondered briefly what Admiral Nogura might have to say when he found out about all this . . . but he knew that it would be better for all concerned if the old man found out what was going on only after the fact.

"For what it's worth, Captain," Uhura said, "we just received our departure clearance."

"Ahead dead slow, Mr. Sulu," he said, and he could not help grinning. "Take us out of here."

Kirk was the first one aboard the shuttle to come around. Still groggy, he peered out the front port. There was Earth, all right. A quick look at the terminator told him that not much time had gone by.

But Earth was so *small.* Kirk looked out one of the starboard ports and saw the moon. It was close.

Kirk looked at the instrument panel. They were in lunar orbit. *How the hell did this happen?* he wondered hazily. It must have had something to do with the shuttle being tied to the flitter . . . but how had a

214

flitter managed to drag along a multiton spacecraft in its wake?

The flitter had not moved relative to them. It was still hanging in space about fifty meters to port.

Blearily, Kirk studied the console. The shuttle's tractor beam had been completely drained. He set it on recharge, but it would take a while.

The others began to stir. "Are you two all right?" Kirk called, and there were slow murmurs of assent.

Friedman shook her head to clear it and winced. "Ouch." She rubbed her temple. "Shouldn't have done that. What happened?"

"We latched onto the flitter, all right," Kirk said. "There was some sort of power feedback, as near as I can tell. We've been out for a few minutes."

She looked out the window. "Those uglies are still out there. Lemme—" She looked down at her panel. "Whoops, never mind. No tractor beam. Damn. Wish I had me a big long rope. Hey, and another surprise out there. Incoming communication, Admiral."

"Put it on audio," Kirk said, trying to steel himself. No doubt the Klingons were about to announce that a hostage had been killed. But the voice that came over the subspace channel was a familiar one.

"This is Captain Willard Decker of the USS *Enterprise* hailing the space shuttle *Enterprise*. Do you wish us to assist?"

"Will!" Kirk grinned broadly. "As a matter of fact, we could use some of your technology right now. We've got three hostages on that flitter—one Klingon and two humans, including my chief of staff."

"So I heard."

"We need to get them out of there. Our scanners indicate their shields are inoperative. Can you get a transporter fix on them?"

"Affirmative, Admiral. At least, on those two humans. I don't know how we could differentiate one Klingon from another, though."

Kirk sighed. In the periphery of his vision, he saw the despair on Nan Davis's face. "Get the humans out, then we'll try to figure out some way to get G'dath."

"Will do, sir."

"Better hurry." Friedman looked up from her panel, her brow furrowed with worry. "I'm reading another power buildup starting aboard the flitter. Looks just like the one I saw before we wound up here."

Riley grabbed the seat of his chair and pulled himself up, then helped the boy to his feet. The kid was still wide-eyed with fear, but managed a shaky smile of thanks.

From the moment he'd beamed into the classroom, Riley had not allowed himself to think about anything except the situation, had not allowed himself to be afraid. It had helped to focus on the other two hostages rather than himself—and it had also helped to pretend that he wasn't Riley at all, but Admiral Kirk—and at the moment, Kirk would try to catch their captors off guard.

Riley scanned the ship's interior. The commander, the one who had given his name over the radio as Keth, had just recovered and had found his dagger. Riley knew that rushing him would probably prove fatal. Keth swayed, a bit unsteady on his feet, then abruptly whirled toward the pilot's seat and struck Klor full across the face.

Riley watched, shocked, as Keth spat a string of Klingon curses while Klor went sprawling onto the floor.

Riley spoke no Klingonese, but he knew that Klor did not appreciate what his commander had said. He

216

suspected it had to do with Klor's reluctance to immediately respond to the direct order to kill a hostage.

Klor rose to his feet and stood quietly, dangerously, and stared at Keth with undisguised hatred glittering in his eyes. Riley saw Klor's huge muscles tremble with restrained power, poised and ready to strike.

Keth would be no match. He was slender, a good head shorter, entirely overshadowed by Klor's bulk. Riley waited for what he knew would be a violent confrontation.

And then, slowly, Klor slid once again into the pilot's seat, but Riley saw the hatred that smoldered in his eyes.

Keth turned and stared hard at Riley and the boy, apparently trying to decide whether to go through with the execution.

Keth took a step forward, but stopped as a commanding voice emanated from beside the console.

Apparently too weak to stand, G'dath still sat beside the globe, where it attached to the side of the console, and steadied himself with his good hand. His voice was loud and firm, but Riley heard the strain in it.

"There is no need to kill, Keth. We are no longer held by the tractor beam. You will find that the shuttle's power has been drained."

"It is true, Superior," Klor said sullenly from his console. "The tractor beam has disappeared. However, the shuttle is recharging, and power will be restored within minutes."

The muscles in Keth's shoulders relaxed. "Then let us waste no more time. Dreamer"—he looked down at G'dath—"take us home."

Klor swiveled sharply in his chair, his expression one of something very close to alarm. For a moment,

Riley thought he was on the verge of saying something to his superior, but Klor merely looked hard at G'dath, and seemed to come to a decision. The Klingon returned his gaze to his control panel and said nothing.

"I cannot, for the moment. The globe must recharge," G'dath said. Keth raised his arm to strike, but the scientist never flinched, just wearily shook his head. "You may kill me if you wish, but it will not change the fact. It will take less than a minute and then we will be able to outrun our pursuers."

Klor spoke, a note of alarm in his tone. "Superior, the flitter's shields have suddenly failed." His huge hands danced busily over the controls in front of him.

"A power drain, caused by breaking free from the tractor?"

"No, Superior. Just a sudden failure. I can find no cause—"

He broke off and swiveled to stare at Riley. Keth turned and followed his gaze.

Riley felt blood rush to his cheeks. He had hoped that, by the time the shields failed as programmed, the hostages would have been rescued—or at the very least, pursued by a ship with transporter capability.

He hadn't counted on being rescued by a three-hundred-year-old space shuttle.

Klor faced his screen and emitted a low rumble of surprise. "A third vessel coming into range, Superior. A *starship*."

Riley smiled, but his relief was short-lived.

"Liar!" Keth spat. He clutched the knife just below chest level, and came toward Riley with it. "Honorless coward! Son of Earthers! You sabotaged the shields!"

Riley and the boy rose to their feet and would have backed away, but a row of seats blocked them. Riley tried to shove the boy behind him.

Keth's eyes were bright, maniacal, ringed with

shadow and set deep in his bronze face. He was a step away, ready to lunge forward and shove the blade into Riley's midsection.

Riley closed his eyes and heard, not the dull meaty thunk of the dagger thrust home, but the gently growing hum of a transporter beam.

Chapter Thirteen

JOEY SQUEEZED HIS EYES SHUT against the dizziness and reached out to try to steady himself against the back of a chair, but his hand touched nothing. The dizziness passed quickly, and he opened his eyes. A second ago, he had been aboard the flitter, standing next to Commander Riley and certain once again that this was *finally it*—the crazy Klingon guy would kill them all for sure.

And now he was standing in a big white room, watching as Commander Riley stepped down and crossed the room to where another Starfleet officer stood at a huge console. Joey looked down at his feet, which rested atop a slightly raised metal disk on some kind of platform. A slow trickle of wonder passed through him as he realized: a *transporter* platform.

"Welcome aboard, Commander Riley." The Starfleet officer—an older man with a mustache—grinned broadly. "Good to see you again, though I canna say much for the circumstances."

Welcome aboard. Then this was a starship. He had been rescued by a starship, and was safe. Joey took a step forward, but his legs went rubbery, and he sank to his knees.

"Good to see *you*, Mister Scott," Riley began, then turned to see Joey fall. He bounded up the stage, pulled Joey off the transporter stage and set him in a nearby chair, all the while speaking to Scott.

"There's another hostage aboard the flitter. I know you can't differentiate Klingons, Scotty, but he's the one closest to the power source."

The older man shook his head, but his eyes and hands were already on the controls. "A *Klingon?* What is the universe comin' to, Riley, when we start rescuin' Klingons."

"It's my teacher!" Joey cried, angry at the man's tone. He had finally come to his senses enough to realize that Doctor G'dath had not been rescued with them. He felt suddenly, awkwardly, near tears. Doctor G'dath was already hurt, and now that he and Commander Riley had escaped, that one Klingon was probably mad enough to kill him. "He's hurt, and he needs our help *now.*"

"Easy, lad," Scott said soothingly, as he adjusted a control on the console. "We'll help 'im, dinna you worry. I was only makin' a wee joke."

"Well, it wasn't *funny,*" Joey said.

Riley's eyes were focused on the transporter console. From his face, Joey could tell that whatever he saw wasn't good.

"Trouble?" he asked softly.

Scott's expression grew grim. He spoke quietly, as if he didn't want Joey to hear—which of course made Joey listen even more carefully. "That power source is raisin' the dickens with the transporter beam. We had a divvil of a time just gettin' the two of you aboard. And the interference is growin' worse by the second. I've locked onto 'im, but I'm not sure I can bring him aboard."

Stricken, Joey watched as an indistinct golden

221

shape formed on one of the transporter pads and began to shimmer.

Aboard the shuttle *Enterprise,* Decker's voice filtered through the grid on Friedman's companel. "Admiral Kirk? *Enterprise* here. We have retrieved two of the three hostages aboard the flitter."

Kirk half rose to his feet and leaned over the console. "And the third, Will?" Selfishly, he hoped it was not Riley—but felt no relief upon hearing Decker's answer.

"G'dath is still hostage. We're trying to beam him onto the *Enterprise,* but we're experiencing massive electronic interference, source and type unknown."

Kirk nodded. "Captain Friedman says there's another power buildup starting aboard the flitter. Will, we've got to stop that vessel at all costs. Can you get a tractor on it?"

"Negative," Decker replied glumly. "According to Scotty, something's draining our main batteries. We've diverted all power to transporter and life support."

Kirk paused and glanced over at Nan and Eddie. Collision shields might provide some protection for them, but he was angry at Nan, for insisting on coming, and most of all at himself, for not insisting that she leave. Of course, there'd been no time to get the two civilians off the shuttle, but the fact didn't lessen Kirk's concern. He swiveled toward Friedman. "Captain, I'm afraid we don't have many choices remaining. We're going to have to ram the flitter."

"Damn," Friedman replied, clearly more disappointed by the prospect of damage to her precious shuttle than by any danger to herself. "I was afraid you were going to say that, Admiral."

Kirk turned his head sharply at the touch of a warm hand on his shoulder. Nan stood behind him. Though her face was pale, her expression was utterly calm. "I figured something like this could happen when I insisted on staying, Jim." She tried to summon a weak smile.

Kirk did not smile back. "Then sit down and get ready. Use the collision shields and the portable life support stowed in the compartment under the seats."

Nan nodded and returned to her chair.

"Hey, wait a minute," Eddie said. "You mean we're gonna crash on *purpose?*"

"Quiet," Friedman said sharply. "Admiral, are you ready?"

Kirk nodded, settling into his own seat.

"Then let's do it. I got full impulse engines again. Still zippo on the tractor beam—and that surge aboard the flitter is building fast. Stand by."

"On my signal." Kirk waited for both Nan and Eddie to activate their collision shields. "One . . . two . . . three . . . now!"

The shuttle leaped forward . . . and came to a crashing halt well short of the flitter, as if it had struck a brick wall in space. Everything inside the craft went dark.

"Captain," Sulu said, "the space shuttle's in trouble. Her impulse drive is blow, and she's adrift. Damage to shuttle systems appears heavy."

"Status of those aboard?"

"Alive, sir. They still have hull integrity. Apparently the shuttle's light shielding protected the craft somewhat—but it's out of action."

"Enterprise, this is Kirk," came a voice.

"Go ahead, Admiral," Decker replied.

"Will, I'm afraid we're out of it. We hit what must have been some sort of protective field generated by the globe. Never even touched the flitter. Can you pursue yet?"

"Negative, Admiral. Scotty's doing his best, but we're adrift until we can get things sorted out. We're still trying to rescue the third hostage—at least as long as they remain within our transporter range."

"The flitter is fifty kilometers out, distance increasing rapidly," Flores called. "I see other craft attempting to give chase, but no one's in proper position. One hundred kilometers now."

"Dammit," Decker breathed. "They're going to get away."

G'dath had watched with almost unbearable gratitude as the forms of Joseph and Riley had earlier vanished to safety. As for his own life, he had no concern—and though he regretted the necessity of taking Klor's, he felt, after the look he and the younger Klingon had shared, that Klor understood and was prepared. Even if he had misinterpreted the message in Klor's eyes, the Klingon had not informed his commander of the globe's self-destructive capability, and for G'dath, that was enough.

If there were others like Klor, G'dath had great hope for the Empire.

"We are thirty-five standard units from the Federation craft, and distance is increasing rapidly," Klor reported from the helm.

"I will activate the globe when we are at fifty units," G'dath said. "I do not want even the relatively slight mass of the two Federation ships affecting our trajectory." Or being harmed in the explosion. "Any error at the beginning of our journey could mean disaster at its end."

As he spoke, he sensed someone observing him. He glanced up to see Klor watching from the pilot's chair. This time, there could be no doubt: Klor understood what G'dath intended, and met his gaze steadily.

Seconds passed. And then Klor's attention returned to his console.

"Z'breth," Keth whispered from where he stood in the aisle; he was apparently still dazed by the loss of his captives. And then he collected himself.

"Klor! Your personal shield! Activate it, and increase its diameter to include the prisoner." There was a small pop as Keth touched a control on his belt and activated his own shield.

"Fifty units," Klor said quietly, as if he had not heard.

G'dath slipped his finger inside the blinking globe and shut off a relay. The result would be an enormous build-up of power, resulting in an explosion. It would require no more than thirty seconds.

In a final gesture of disdain, Klor did not turn, did not respond to his superior's order, but sat and stared at the readout on the helm console. G'dath understood why: in his rage, Keth had cursed Klor's family and called him the son of Earthers, one of the worst possible insults—and one that was not far from the truth. For failing to obey the order to kill Joseph, Keth had promised Klor a court-martial . . . and utter disgrace upon his arrival home.

G'dath was glad a noble spirit like Klor's would be spared that dishonor.

"Klor!" Keth bellowed. When Klor again failed to respond, the commander strode over to the console himself and deactivated his shield, which dissolved with a small pop.

Suddenly dizzy, G'dath closed his eyes. Blood loss from the wound, he thought—but then he heard a hum, and realized the disoriented sensation was one he'd experienced but few times in his life, most recently this weekend: dematerialization.

He could not fathom how his would-be rescuers had managed to distinguish him from his captors.

225

The sensation passed. Perhaps the transporter had malfunctioned—or perhaps G'dath had merely imagined it. He felt a hand on his shoulder and looked up into Keth's piercing black eyes. Keth's other hand reached for the control on his belt.

At the same time, G'dath saw a huge hand on Keth's shoulder. Klor pulled his commander away before Keth had the opportunity to activate the shield.

The two Klingons grappled. The struggle did not last long; though Klor was clearly the stronger, Keth was faster. He wriggled free from Klor's grasp, withdrew his knife, and with a rapid, twisting motion, plunged it deep into Klor's chest.

Klor drew in a gasp and toppled backwards.

G'dath shut his eyes once more, aware even through his closed lids that the air around him was a-dance with light—the sparkling quiver of the transporter beam, and the blinding white, hot flash of an explosion. The universe erupted in a roar of light as the fabric of matter about him dissolved.

Brighter, brighter, painfully, unbearably bright until the light itself scorched his closed eyelids and made him cry out. When he could stand no more, he yielded to it, and embraced darkness.

Chapter Fourteen

WEDNESDAY MORNING, Apollo Day, was a school holi-day, and Ricia was smiling again as she stood in the hospital corridor and handed Joey a card to sign. She looked especially nice today, Joey thought, in a flow-ing turquoise tunic and tiny pearl earrings, her shiny blue-black hair tied with a neon purple ribbon. He knew she was dressed up more for Carlos than for Doctor G'dath, but Joey had promised himself he wouldn't be jealous of Carlos—at least, not for now. Carlos was out of intensive care, sitting up, talking and laughing, though he still looked pale and weak— mostly, Joey figured, from the shock of what had happened more than the wound. Carlos's father had been in the room when Ricia and Joey got there. A nice guy, but with pale coloring that contrasted sharp-ly with his son's, though he was quiet and a little shy, just like Carlos. Doctor Siegel had told Ricia that if she hadn't stopped the bleeding with her hands, Carlos might have died.

At that, Carlos had given Ricia a look, as if he'd finally figured out that she was a *girl,* for cripe's sake, and Joey had to look down at his feet and clear his throat while the two of them exchanged simpering glances and held hands. Sickening. Joey had to break things up by thrusting the get-well card in Carlos's face.

Of course, Joey couldn't complain, since Ricia had been awfully nice to him ever since Monday. It had been a very weird two days. Thank goodness Joey's mom had been at work and hadn't had a chance to look at the news until Joey was already safely aboard the *Enterprise*. That had been excitement enough. For the past two days, he'd been something of a celebrity and had talked to a dozen newscasters about his experience as a hostage. All of them wanted to talk about the horrible Klingons who'd terrorized these poor schoolchildren, and Joey kept having to point out to them that it was a *Klingon* who was abducted in the first place, and *that* Klingon had been injured trying to protect his students.

You'd think they could get it right.

He wanted to tell them how awful it had been, watching Doctor G'dath blink in and out on the transporter pad while the floor under Joey's feet lurched as the flitter exploded. Doctor G'dath had actually been in the flitter for the first millisecond or so of the explosion, and had sustained some pretty bad injuries. But none of the reporters seemed very interested in that aspect of the story—they just wanted to hear about the nasty Klingons with their big knives, about how Joey had been scared for his life. By Tuesday, Joey was so sick and tired of having lights and trivision scanners shoved in his face that he didn't ever think he'd be nervous about anything again.

"Here," Ricia said, dimpling. She handed him a stylus, then turned so Joey could hold the card steady against her back and sign. Stoller had done some pretty impressive work with the card—Joey hadn't known he was so talented with graphics. The card was as big as a letter-sized datapad, and the front said GET WELL, DOCTOR G'DATH in huge iridescent holo letters. English first, then Klingonese.

Joey signed the get-well card first, then found the special slip of parchment Stoller had carefully tucked inside. It looked neat, like an old-fashioned treaty, with fancy gothic lettering. He smiled when he read it, and when he put his signature on it, he thought of the Klingon named Klor. Maybe he should have hated Klor for what he had done, but it was hard after seeing the look of compassion on Klor's face. Being kidnapped by Klingons should have made him hate Klingons more—but instead, he could only remember how Doctor G'dath had thrown himself in the path of the knife intended for Ira Stoller—Stoller, who hated Klingons. Ricia had been right; G'dath's fearsome manner was just his way, the result of his culture. And Joey's fear of him was a product of Earth culture.

Maybe it was time to start transcending culture a little.

"All done," he told Ricia, offering her the card and his back. When she was finished, they entered G'dath's hospital room together. At the sight of the big Klingon, sitting alert on his bed, Joey smiled.

Propped up on his hospital bed, G'dath blinked at the swing-out terminal in front of him and tried to focus his eyes. The corneas had been seared away in the explosion, and his vision was just now clearing as he adjusted to the new ones. The skin synthetic had finally taken as well, though there had been problems at first, since the doctors had never formulated it for Klingon skin. The burns on his extremities and face no longer pained him, and within days, would be unnoticeable.

So many calls had come in over the past two days

229

that he had programmed the terminal not to buzz, but to take written messages, and they now filled screen after screen. Nan Davis's story of the classroom abduction followed by her interview with G'dath had turned him into an overnight celebrity. He had so many job offers from prestigious universities— Oxford, Beijing, Volgograd, Georgia Tech, to name a few—that he had quit scanning through them yesterday. He would sort through them all and make a decision later, but for now he wasn't up to talking to anyone.

He was grateful Carlos Siegel had survived, but Mr. Olesky's death had shaken him deeply. He still struggled to make sense of it. The globe had brought death more quickly than he'd ever anticipated, and he was glad it had been destroyed. He found it impossible to care about his discovery, or his work, or any of the job offers.

He'd already resolved to destroy all of his computer records. Through Federation channels, he had contacted the Organians and informed them of his invention and the subsequent events. They were willing to provide him with protection from the Empire, and to prevent knowledge of how to construct the globe from falling into either Federation or Klingon hands.

Ironically, he was forced to trust the Organians— there was no other choice.

He was thinking about his Organian treaty lecture of five days before when he saw two moving blurs pause outside his open door. He blinked, and the blurs resolved into Ricia Greene and Joseph Brickner.

G'dath composed his features into a more pleasant expression. "Ms. Greene. Mister Brickner. Please, come in."

The two entered and stood by G'dath's bed. Ricia seemed in an outgoing, expansive mood while Joseph was a little shy. But the boy was smiling, and G'dath was gratified to see—not hatred, but admiration, in his eyes. The sight of his students filled G'dath with a pang of guilt as he recalled the unread messages waiting on his terminal.

Ricia grabbed Joseph by the elbow and pulled him in. "How are you feeling, Doctor G'dath? Everyone at school's very concerned about you."

G'dath smiled faintly at the unlikely notion that *everyone* was concerned. "Indeed? That is most considerate of them. I am feeling quite well actually and by tomorrow I hope to return home."

"I'll bet you'll be back in class by next Monday. You watch," Ricia said cheerfully,

G'dath cleared his throat and briefly averted his eyes. Perhaps now was not the time to mention that he would not be returning Monday—or ever at all. "Ahem. Well, I'll certainly be fit enough for teaching duties by then."

Joseph took a step forward and awkwardly proffered something. "Here. This is for you, sir."

"Ah." G'dath took the card and made a show of appreciatively studying the front cover. "Thank you, Joseph."

"It's from the entire class."

"I see. And in English *and* Klingonese. This is most thoughtful of everyone." G'dath smiled up at both students, honestly touched by the gift. The phrase in Klingonese had been improperly translated. Rather than encouraging him to recuperate, it exhorted him to improve his performance. G'dath didn't mind the error, though. Somehow, the mistake made the gesture doubly endearing. "Did one of the students make this?"

Joseph nodded.

"Open it, sir," Ricia urged.

G'dath complied. A thick sheet of paper slipped out onto the bed as he did so. He paused before retrieving it to read the names signed inside, some of them with little messages: *Hurry up and get better!* and *We miss you* and *Come back soon!* Every student in the class had signed.

Guiltily, G'dath picked up the paper. On stiff parchment, the following had been printed in ornate lettering:

**WE, THE UNDERSIGNED, HEREBY PLEDGE
TO WORK TOWARD GREATER UNDERSTANDING
BETWEEN THE PEOPLES OF THE KLINGON EMPIRE
AND THE UNITED FEDERATION OF PLANETS**

The first signature—a sharp, erratic scrawl—belonged to Ira Stoller. G'dath read no further, but closed his eyes for a long moment.

After a time, he heard Ricia Greene say softly: "This is how we feel about things. We thought maybe if you knew, it would help you get well faster than just any old card."

G'dath opened his eyes to see his students shifting, awkward with the silence. He forced a wan smile. "Thank you, Ms. Greene. And you, Joseph. Please tell the others who have signed this—and the card—that it means a great deal to me."

A muffled squeak in the doorway made him turn his head. He frowned at the odd yet familiar sound and saw Nan Davis standing in the doorway. She was smiling energetically, but wore a long-sleeved jacket and hugged herself as if she were freezing.

"Oh, wow," Ricia said, her brown eyes round with surprise. "Nan Davis."

The reporter nodded at the two teenagers as she stepped into the room. "And you must be two of the students I didn't get to meet Monday. In fact, you're *the* Joey Brickner, aren't you? How does it feel to be so famous?"

"I don't think it's so hot," Joseph said, not at all fazed by Davis's presence. "I'll be glad when everyone's forgotten about it. About me, I mean."

Ricia gave Joseph a surreptitious tap on the shoulder. "I think we'd better be going now, Joey, and let Doctor G'dath talk to his guest. Take care, Doctor G'dath. We'll see you Monday."

Joseph nodded. "See you soon, sir."

G'dath took a long breath. "See you both Monday." When the students had left, he turned to Nan Davis. "Ms. Davis—"

"G'dath, please. After everything that's happened, I don't think we need to be so formal. Call me Nan. So tell me: Had any good job offers lately?"

G'dath sighed and angled his head toward the terminal. "As a matter of fact . . . probably close to fifty by now. I have given up taking calls, or even keeping track of the messages."

"That's wonderful! So you'll finally be able to do the important work you were meant to."

G'dath looked thoughtful for a moment. "Perhaps . . ." he began, and stopped, a little surprised at what he was about to say—and yet very sure of it at the same time. The piece of parchment with the students' signatures still rested on his lap and it crinkled softly as Leaper nestled against it. "Perhaps, Nan, I have already been doing the most important work of all." He gazed up at her. "And I do not refer to my research."

Nan's expression was quizzical at first, then grew thoughtful. "I see. I guess that means you'll be staying in New York permanently, now that you've been granted political asylum."

He nodded.

"You'll have a new neighbor, then. Thanks to your story, I've just been promoted to WorldNews' New York Bureau." She smiled brilliantly. "You wouldn't mind if I dropped by to visit Leaper once in a while?"

He returned the smile. "I wouldn't mind at all, Nan. Not at all."

Early Wednesday morning, Kevin Riley took a deep breath and stepped into Admiral Kirk's office doorway. "Admiral?"

Kirk sat at his desk and stared out the window as fog caressed the Golden Gate Bridge with ghostly fingers. At the sound of his title, he swiveled toward Riley.

The anxiety Riley felt must have shown on his face because after one glance, Kirk said: "Come in. Close the door if you like."

Riley stepped in and the door slid shut behind him. After Monday's experience, he thought he was past feeling much of anything—but the thought of what he was about to do was extraordinarily painful.

He had failed Kirk by fouling up G'dath's security. It was a matter of simple luck that only the two Klingons had been killed, and that G'dath and Carlos Siegel had all survived their injuries. Had things gone the other way, Riley's mistake would have cost three lives. And there was more than just the mistake with security. Riley had left his post without permission, had arranged for the flitter on his own authority.

Oddly, the experience had dissolved his self-pity and hurt over Anab, and his confusion about Jenny. In the face of death, everything became very simple, very clear. Anab had been right: Riley needed to figure out what he wanted. He knew now. And he was no longer so afraid of risk. After all, he'd risked his own life, and had managed to save a few in the process. The gamble with sabotaging the flitter's shields had paid off. He was glad he'd done it. He would gladly do it again.

He regretted only two things: one, that he would have to lose this job at the very moment he realized how much he wanted it, and two, that he had ultimately proved to be a disappointment to Kirk, the man who had saved his life. He had considered telling Kirk that he knew about Tarsus IV, but now was not the time. Riley did not want to revive any sympathy Kirk might feel for him because of the past.

But he would find some way later, to thank him.

Riley stepped in front of the admiral's desk and stood stiffly, not quite at attention. "I think you know why I'm here, sir," he said, and when Kirk did not argue, merely looked at him thoughtfully, hands folded atop his desk, Riley added: "I feel it would be best if I resigned my commission, sir. Unless you'd prefer to fire me."

Kirk released a windy sigh, rose, and walked over to his window. For a time, he studied the view, hands clasped behind his back. And then he looked over his shoulder at Riley. "Isn't this where we came in, Commander?"

Riley flushed at the admiral's reference to his first attempt to resign a year before. "Sir—this time is different. I tried to resign then because I wasn't sure I wanted this job."

"Are you sure now?" Kirk asked quickly.

"Yes, sir. I want this job. But I know I can't keep it." He paused, and said a bit more heatedly than he'd intended: "Admiral, three people almost *died* on my account because I made a thoughtless mistake. Because I was so overwhelmed by my own personal prob—" He broke off. "That's not important. The fact is, I messed up. That—that's all I wanted to say, sir. And that I'm sorry to leave your employ. It's been an honor."

"Kevin." The admiral turned and faced him.

Riley raised his eyebrows in astonishment. Kirk never addressed him by his first name.

"You're right. If you had ordered priority security measures instead of standard, this might not have happened. I probably should fire you." Kirk paused. "I've discussed this with Fleet Admiral Nogura, you know."

Riley repressed a nervous urge to shift his weight.

"Frankly, we couldn't figure out whether to court-martial you or commend you for heroism."

"Com*mend* me." Riley choked.

"Your actions saved the lives of the hostages. You were the one who suggested the flitter's shields be programmed to fail."

"Yes, sir, but—"

"And according to a trivision interview with Joey Brickner, you protected him at least once from being attacked by a Klingon."

"So we left it at this, Mister Riley. We will neither court-martial you *nor* commend you. As for your resigning—that's up to you."

Riley hesitated, sure that he was misunderstanding what the admiral was saying to him, that it was too good to be true. "You mean you're not firing me, sir?"

"For the moment, no."

"Then I'd like to stay on, Admiral, for a probationary period of two weeks." *During which time, I'll find a way to thank you for Tarsus IV . . .* "If my performance isn't absolutely stellar during that period, I'd appreciate it if you'd dismiss me."

"Done." Kirk smiled faintly. "Those *were* some pretty heroic actions, Mister Riley."

Riley relaxed enough to adopt a candid tone. "That wasn't really me, sir."

"Wasn't you?"

He grimaced sheepishly. "Well, sir, the whole time I was held hostage by the Klingons, I pretended to be you. I just kept asking myself what you would have done in the situation. You can see, it worked pretty well."

He had never in his life seen the admiral embarrassed—in fact, he would not have thought Kirk capable of the emotion—but now, to Riley's utter amazement, the admiral's cheeks turned a faint shade of pink.

"I'd appreciate if you'd keep that to yourself, Commander," Kirk said stiffly.

But as Riley left, he got the definite impression that the admiral was secretly pleased.

Kirk stood by the window and watched the door slide shut behind his chief of staff. He was glad Riley had chosen to stay. True, Riley had made a critical mistake concerning security—but Kirk had been proud of the quick, decisive action Kevin had taken to save the hostages. Kirk could not have done better himself, and when he and Nogura had discussed Riley's fate, the old admiral—who had never quite understood Kirk's faith in his chief of staff—had been impressed with Riley's heroics.

I suppose it takes one to know one, the old admiral had said.

Yet Kirk had been taken aback at Riley's words: *I pretended to be you.*

Kirk could not honestly say he was surprised. Riley's actions had reminded him more than a little of himself.

Scratch that: more than a little of the self he *used* to

be. Of the Kirk he'd seen a few days before in Nogura's office, the Kirk who'd worn command gold. Lori's voice spoke, unbidden, in his memory:

Get a ship again. It's what you want most, Jim. More than anything else. More than me.

Seeing Riley in action had made him remember that other Kirk again, had made him wonder if Lori could possibly be right.

Kirk sighed and returned to his desk, forcing himself to forget about Riley and Lori and the *Enterprise* until much later that afternoon.

Around 1700, he was still working at his desk when the companel buzzed. He answered it on the first signal, and sat back in surprise when Lori's features flashed onto the screen.

"Jim," she said. Her blond hair was casually tousled and she was out of uniform, draped in a peach sweater that suited her coloring perfectly. The tension was gone from her voice and eyes. She wore an awkward smile.

Jim smiled back, startled and pleased by the transformation, and more than a little hopeful at the warmth in her tone. "Lori. Where are you calling from?"

"Centaurus. I'm at the cabin. I had a few days' leave coming and figured I deserved a rest before starting the tour. I just picked up the WorldNews feed-out here and saw what happened to you and Riley and the Klingons. I just . . . I just wanted to see with my own eyes that you were all right."

Kirk spread his hands in a "here-I-am" gesture. "I'm all right." *But I'd be better if you were here.*

"Riley?"

"You know him. Came out of it without a scratch. Luck of the Irish." He paused. "You're looking a bit nonregulation these days. And beautiful."

Her smile turned shy. "Look, Jim, I've been thinking. Now that I've gotten away from the office . . ."

Away from Nogura, Jim heard.

". . . I've calmed down a little." Her expression grew serious. "I can think more clearly out here. I . . . I wondered if you could arrange a little time with me. The two of us could be alone here, without Nogura, without Starfleet, without any old baggage. Maybe we could figure out what we have with each other." She met his gaze directly, firmly—like the old Lori, and he reached out and touched the edge of the viewscreen in pure gratitude.

She saw it and smiled as if she understood.

"I'd like that," Kirk said. Lori had always known what she wanted. Perhaps if he spent some time with her, talked with her, he would begin to find himself again, catch a glimpse of the Kirk he had seen in Nogura's office—the one he'd seen in Riley, the one who knew what *he* wanted. "Just let me make a few arrangements. I'll call you with my ETA."

"I'm glad. I won't keep you, love. I know you're getting ready for the parade of spacecraft over there. Take care."

"Take care."

Her image wavered and was gone.

Kirk thumbed the intercom control. "Mister Riley."

"Yes, Admiral?"

"Book me transportation to Centaurus—as soon as possible."

"Yes, sir, Admiral."

Kirk swiveled in his seat and ordered the trivision unit to tune into the WorldNews feed of the parade of spacecraft. The parade was nearing the moon, and would overfly Tranquility Base in less than an hour. The picture shifted here and there to show some of the

239

scores of ancient and modern spacecraft participating in the historic flight.

Suddenly, there she was, and Kirk's breath caught. Whatever scars the shuttle had suffered a few days before did not show—she looked magnificent, her hull a glaring white against the infinitely deep blackness of space. She was at last in the place she was meant to be, and Kirk trusted that the civilian VIPs aboard were having the time of their lives.

Nice job, Scotty, Kirk thought. Another miracle from the miracle worker. The shuttle's blown impulse engines had been replaced hastily by a complaining—yet, Kirk suspected—gleeful Montgomery Scott after the shuttle had been towed to Spacedock Four at Kirk's order. Scotty had ripped the impulse units out of one of the shuttlecraft already aboard the starship *Enterprise* and had stuffed them into the aft section of the space shuttle. Since the jury rigging had been done by Montgomery Scott, it worked just fine. To guarantee it, Scotty was aboard the shuttle even now, babying the engines along. The units fit like a size-eleven foot in a size-nine shoe, but the shuttle flew. It also seemed right and proper that the younger *Enterprise* had contributed something of itself to the older.

Kirk watched the shuttle cut through the hard vacuum of space, and thought of the resolute courage of the men and women who had flown aboard her, and other craft just like her, so many years ago. That kind of courage had not died out. Kirk knew it could be found wherever one cared to look—in the soul of a peaceable Klingon or even that of an errant chief of staff.

On the shuttle's hull, the U.S. flag rested beside the UFP banner. The stars on the old flag made Kirk think of G'dath and his people. Perhaps someday—with the help of G'dath and others like him—their home stars would be represented by the silver and scarlet banner of the United Federation of Planets.

He stood up and, still watching the shuttle, saluted. Then he ordered the trivision off, gathered his things, and left with a light heart, knowing he would soon be where Lori was.

THE
STAR TREK
PHENOMENON

___	STRANGERS FROM THE SKY	65913/$4.50
___	THE TEARS OF THE SINGERS	69654/$4.50
___	TIME FOR YESTERDAY	70094/$4.50
___	THE TRELLISANE CONFRONTATION	70095/$4.50
___	TRIANGLE	66251/$3.95
___	UHURA'S SONG	65227/$3.95
___	VULCAN ACADEMY MURDERS	72367/$4.50
___	VULCAN'S GLORY	74291/$4.95
___	WEB OF THE ROMULANS	70093/$4.50
___	WOUNDED SKY	66735/$3.95
___	YESTERDAY'S SON	72449/$4.50

• • • • • • • • • • • • • • • • • • • •

___	STAR TREK– THE MOTION PICTURE	72300/$4.50
___	STAR TREK II– THE WRATH OF KHAN	74149/$4.95
___	STAR TREK III–THE SEARCH FOR SPOCK	67198/$3.95
___	STAR TREK IV– THE VOYAGE HOME	70283/$4.50
___	STAR TREK V– THE FINAL FRONTIER	68008/$4.50
___	STAR TREK: THE KLINGON DICTIONARY	66648/$4.95
___	STAR TREK COMPENDIUM REVISED 68440/$10.95	
___	MR. SCOTT'S GUIDE TO THE ENTERPRISE 70498/$12.95	
___	THE STAR TREK INTERVIEW BOOK 61794/$7.95	

POCKET
BOOKS

Simon & Schuster Mail Order Dept. STP
200 Old Tappan Rd., Old Tappan, N.J. 07675

Please send me the books I have checked above. I am enclosing $_____ (please add 75¢ to cover postage and handling for each order. Please add appropriate local sales tax). Send check or money order—no cash or C.O.D.'s please. Allow up to six weeks for delivery. For purchases over $10.00 you may use VISA: card number, expiration date and customer signature must be included.

Name _____

Address _____

City _____ State/Zip _____

VISA Card No. _____ Exp. Date _____

Signature _____ 118-33

THE

STAR TREK

PHENOMENON

____ ABODE OF LIFE
70596/$4.50

____ BATTLESTATIONS!
70183/$4.50

____ BLACK FIRE
70548/$4.50

____ BLOODTHIRST
70876/$4.50

____ CORONA
70798/$4.50

____ CHAIN OF ATTACK
66658/$3.95

____ THE COVENANT OF
THE CROWN
70078/$4.50

____ CRISIS ON CENTAURUS
70799/$4.50

____ CRY OF THE ONLIES
740789/$4.95

____ DEEP DOMAIN
70549/$4.50

____ DEMONS
70877/$4.50

____ DOCTOR'S ORDERS
66189/$4.50

____ DOUBLE, DOUBLE
66130/$3.95

____ DREADNOUGHT
72567/$4.50

____ DREAMS OF THE RAVEN
70281/$4.50

____ DWELLERS IN THE
CRUCIBLE
74147/$4.95

____ ENEMY UNSEEN
68403/$4.50

____ ENTERPRISE
73032/$4.95

____ ENTROPY EFFECT
72416/$4.50

____ FINAL FRONTIER
69655/$4.95

____ THE FINAL NEXUS
74148/$4.95

____ THE FINAL REFLECTION
70764/$4.50

____ A FLAG FULL OF STARS
64398/$4.95

____ HOME IS THE HUNTER
66662/$4.50

____ HOW MUCH FOR JUST
THE PLANET?
72214/$4.50

____ IDIC EPIDEMIC
70768/$4.50

____ ISHMAEL
73587/$4.50

____ KILLING TIME
70597/$4.50

____ KLINGON GAMBIT
70767/$4.50

____ THE KOBAYASHI MARU
65817/$4.50

____ LOST YEARS
70795/$4.95

____ MEMORY PRIME
70550/$4.50

____ MINDSHADOW
70420/$4.50

____ MUTINY ON
THE ENTERPRISE
70800/$4.50

____ MY ENEMY, MY ALLY
70421/$4.50

____ PAWNS AND SYMBOLS
66497/$3.95

____ PROMETHEUS DESIGN
72366/$4.50

____ ROMULAN WAY
70169/$4.50

____ RULES OF ENGAGEMENT
66129/$4.50

____ SHADOW LORD
73746/$4.95

____ SPOCK'S WORLD
66773/$4.95

more on next page...

STAR TREK®

THE NEXT GENERATION

☐ STAR TREK: THE NEXT GENERATION:
ENCOUNTER FARPOINT .... 74388/$4.95

☐ STAR TREK: THE NEXT GENERATION:
#1 GHOST SHIP .... 73515/$4.50

☐ STAR TREK: THE NEXT GENERATION:
#2 THE PEACEKEEPERS .... 73563/$4.50

☐ STAR TREK: THE NEXT GENERATION:
#3 THE CHILDREN OF HAMLIN .... 73555/$4.50

☐ STAR TREK: THE NEXT GENERATION:
#4 SURVIVORS .... 74290/$4.95

☐ STAR TREK: THE NEXT GENERATION:
#5 STRIKE ZONE .... 73516/$4.50

☐ STAR TREK: THE NEXT GENERATION:
#6 POWER HUNGRY .... 67714/$3.95

☐ STAR TREK: THE NEXT GENERATION:
#7 MASKS .... 70878/$4.50

☐ STAR TREK: THE NEXT GENERATION:
#8 THE CAPTAIN'S HONOR .... 68487/$3.95

☐ STAR TREK: THE NEXT GENERATION:
#9 A CALL TO DARKNESS .... 68708/$3.95

☐ STAR TREK: THE NEXT GENERATION:
#10 A ROCK AND A HARD PLACE .... 69364/$3.95

☐ STAR TREK: THE NEXT GENERATION:
METAMORPHOSIS .... 68402/$4.95

☐ STAR TREK: THE NEXT GENERATION:
#11 GULLIVER'S FUGITIVES .... 70130/$4.50

☐ STAR TREK: THE NEXT GENERATION:
#12 DOOMSDAY WORLD .... 70237/$4.50

☐ STAR TREK: THE NEXT GENERATION:
#13 THE EYES OF THE BEHOLDERS .... 70010/$4.50

☐ STAR TREK: THE NEXT GENERATION:
#14 EXILES .... 70560/$4.50

☐ STAR TREK: THE NEXT GENERATION:
#15 SPARTACUS .... 70836/$4.50

☐ STAR TREK: THE NEXT GENERATION:
#16 CONTAMINATION .... 70561/$4.95

Copyright ©1988 Paramount Pictures Corporation. All Rights Reserved.
Star Trek is a Registered Trademark of Paramount Pictures Corporation.

POCKET
BOOKS

Simon & Schuster Mail Order Dept. NGS
200 Old Tappan Rd., Old Tappan, N.J. 07675
Please send me the books I have checked above. I am enclosing $_____ (please add 75¢ to cover
postage and handling for each order. Please add appropriate local sales tax). Send check or money
order–no cash or C.O.D.'s please. Allow up to six weeks for delivery. For purchases over $10.00 you may
use VISA: card number, expiration date and customer signature must be included.

Name _____

Address _____

City _____ State/Zip _____

VISA Card No. _____ Exp. Date _____

Signature _____ 100-15

Follow the adventures of the Starship *Enterprise* by beaming aboard Paramount Pictures' Official *STAR TREK* Fan Club. When you join, you receive a one year subscription to the full-color Official *STAR TREK* Fan Club Magazine filled with exclusive interviews, articles, and photos on both the original *STAR TREK* and *STAR TREK: THE NEXT GENERATION*. Plus special columns on *STAR TREK* collecting, novels and special events as well as a convention listing and readers' comments. Members also receive with each issue our special merchandise insert filled with all the latest *STAR TREK* memorabilia.

Join now and receive an exclusive membership kit including an 8 x 10 full-color photo, embroidered jacket patch, membership card and more!

Don't miss out on another issue of The Official *STAR TREK* Fan Club Magazine. Join now! It's the logical thing to do.

Membership for one year — $9.95-US, $12.00-Canada, $21.95-Foreign for one year (US dollars only!)

Send check, money order or MasterCard/Visa order to:

STAR TREK: THE OFFICIAL FAN CLUB
P.O. Box 111000
Aurora, Colorado 80011 USA

©1989 Paramount Pictures. All Rights Reserved. *STAR TREK* is a Registered Trademark of Paramount Pictures.